What Are You Like?

What Are You Like?

Anne Enright

Atlantic Monthly Press
New York

W

Copyright © 2000 by Anne Enright

Originally published in Great Britain in 2000 by Jonathan Cape,
Random House, London

Published simultaneously in Canada
Printed in the United States of America

FIRST AMERICAN EDITION

Library of Congress Cataloging-in-Publication Data
Enright, Anne, 1962–
    What are you like? / Anne Enright.
        p. cm.
    ISBN 0-87113-816-6
    1. Women—Ireland—Dublin—Fiction. 2. Dublin (Ireland)—
Fiction. I. Title.

PR6055.N73 W47 2000
823'.914—dc21
                                            00-038619

Atlantic Monthly Press
841 Broadway
New York, NY 10003

00 01 02 03   10 9 8 7 6 5 4 3 2 1

W

for my parents

Has the rain a father . . .
What womb brings forth the ice?
Job:38

1

Crossing the Line

Dublin, 1965

She was small for a monster, with the slightly hurt look that monsters have and babies share, the same need to understand. The gravity of that look, pulling everything into her, was enough to make you hum and walk around the room. She saw everything, ate it with her eyes, she made women's breasts ache and men rattle their keys. Naked, she brought tears to your eyes. You felt this baby was all skin, holding the soft little parcel of her insides: her fresh little kidneys, the squiggle of her guts, her quail's bones. You could eat her, that's all, her bladder like a sweet little onion and her softly sprouting brain. You could bend down and kiss her on the tummy: she was all so neatly packed, like the gift she was. So perfect, they said, you could almost take her home with you. And they handed her on from arm to arm, with the dip that people make when they give away a baby – letting her body go and guiding her head, as though it might not be attached. Nothing worse than being left holding the baby, they seemed to say, except being left with the baby's head.

She smiled.

'Wind,' they said, patted her back and laid her on the sofa. Her father sat in a chair by her side. This is what I have to show, he seemed to say, while his hands hung limp. No wonder they moved in a pack: the kitchen soon stuffed with aunts, uncles silent in the hall, looking for a football to tip, or a rug with an uneven pile.

In fact her father was thinking of the ceiling, when he leaned his head back, and of the wallpaper, when he faced the wall. When he looked at the baby, he thought of the

3

baby; and when he looked at the fireplace, he thought about coal.

He thought, once, about how he had made her – the map on the sheet when he was done. She was another country, that was all. She was something else again. She was a bad joke, but you laughed all the same. So he did laugh, and they took it as a sign.

'Goodbye now, Berts.' And, when they were gone, he picked the baby up and walked around the room.

Why do men have nipples? and what would happen if he dropped her on the floor? What would happen if he cracked her on the mantelpiece, or swung her by an arm against the wall? All her little sacs would burst and leak. He could feel the soft snap of her bones.

Berts looked out of the window at the street, the bundle pushing and straining in his arms. He tried to think, but his eyes got stuck in the net curtains like a film of tears in front of the glass. The curtains were white. He loved her by choice. He made the choice to love her. That was important. That was all. She turned her face to his chest and sucked his heart until it bruised.

It was hard to say how Berts' wife had used her day in the new house they had bought; moving from room to room, crossing from carpet to lino, pausing on the wooden saddle across the door. The nights he knew about, but something about daylight made her uncertain. It was winter. It was hard for him to imagine her there.

'What do you do all day?' he said.

'This and that.'

She spent a lot of the time in the bath, she said, and Berts suddenly knew she was pregnant. He remembered the night he looked at his map on the sheet and saw a whole country congealing in the cold, the way she lay there in the dark, thinking. The way, in the days to follow, she had pushed the furniture back so the chairs rubbed their necks against the wall.

So that is what you do, he thought – and we did it. The whole world around him seemed to bulge and push. But when he looked at his wife he thought, perhaps, that she herself did not yet know.

She was quiet. She cooked the wrong things. She lay down and pressed her cheek to the floor, her eye skimming the carpet all the way to the skirting board. At first he thought it was the baby making her mad but, as she bloomed, she shrank and the brightness in her eye became too hard. The real signs were those to do with size. She put the cup into the milk, you could say, and not the other way around, she put the bag into the clothes and not the clothes into the bag, she poured water on the floor and squeezed it back into the bucket.

Most of the time it did not matter. Women have their own rules. Why not turn the world inside out – bake a chicken in stuffing, wrap a sheet around the washing machine? They went to his in-laws for the Christmas and she treated her own mother like a child. He took this as a good sign, a tender sign, but her father would not let her into the milking parlour after she tried to feed their own milk to the cows and, after that, manure. Or she spilt milk on grass, or she wanted to swim in the rain. Back home, she switched on the shower when she was in the bath, lit candles in the daytime, ate steak and bit her hand. She pulled him to her every night, as though to make children where there was already a child, as though to unmake the child and let it swim away.

'Like killing a dead thing,' she said once when he was done, and he thought he had murdered it. 'Making a pregnant woman pregnant.' It was the first time she had mentioned the baby and he was very moved.

There was a kind of pleasure to it that he had not seen in her before, never mind the crockery in the hot press, the cutlery in bed. The house filled up with unread books, and she sang to the radio as she cleaned. Something seemed to lift as she moved with the melody and he thought that music might mend her, once and for all. But now – when the world was the right way out again, when she stopped drinking out of the hot tap and could pass a mirror without turning it to the wall – now she was happy, or unhappy, or both, without cause. The sound of distant bells made her tongue swell, she said. The sound of a tap dripping smelt of roses.

All the time he watched her middle, wondering what would come out of her, because one day she would be sane again, though who, in their right minds, would be able to describe the child?

They sat in the kitchen eating their tea and they talked about storage space.

'Jam at the back,' she said. 'Salt on the top shelf. That's what's important.'

The dinner was all wrong. It was the wrong day for fish and the ketchup was in the sugar bowl. He found himself shouting at her while she stroked the pattern of little triangles on the table top and ran her thumb along its metal rim. She tried to tell him what it was that frightened her – it was a word, she said, but she couldn't remember which one.

That night Berts pushed into her blindly, delicately. It was a kind of mental probing, and what he found there frightened him. His wife said nothing, but all sorts of 'words' came into his head.

They sat in the doctor's waiting room and watched a blonde child ripping up the magazines. His wife stared at the ribbons on the little girl's collar, the dog-shaped brooch pinned to her dress, the snot running down to her mouth, and her tiny, fat, violent hands. She leaned forward and Berts wondered should he intervene. It occurred to him that, apart from Mass, he had not seen his wife outside the house since they were married. And here she was, stretching out her hand, searching for a word.

'Dotey,' she said, at last. 'Hello, Dotey.' And he thought how strange women are. How love conquers them.

The doctor nodded to him, as he sent her off alone into the consulting room.

The secret places of your wife, said the nod.

The secret places of my wife, said his. Dr Meagher would make the child inside her feel ashamed of itself, just at the touch of his hand. Still, when Berts got the call from the receptionist, he was afraid to turn the knob on the door.

'Well?' he said.

Whatever was wrong, Meagher didn't seem bothered by it, by the fun fair of his wife, with all her different rides. He prescribed rest — because rest was the thing, he said, and pills are not for the pregnant. Her system, he said, would settle down. It was a question of hormones — a little wild perhaps, in the head, but the healthiest thing for a body, in the long run. A sort of spring clean.

She was upset, Berts could see that. She was worse when she was upset. He lifted his wife's coat and tried to put her into it, but she kept circling it, until they both began to spin around. Then she stopped. She caught the coat and pulled the sleeves inside out so that the lining showed.

'Now,' she said. And slipped her arms through.

Meagher watched as they turned to leave. He watched her pause at the window and then, with an effort, move to the door. She turned to him and said,

'Hello.'

Meagher lifted his pen. He set it back down again.

'Just one more thing,' he said.

Berts always told himself he would do the same again, if he had to, because he couldn't bear the thought that they had not been free. And what made you more free than the ability to die, if needs be? The baby would live and that is what babies are for. She would die, because people do. It was the timing that made him feel giddy.

Other people had their secret. He hardly knew what it was — a place with no proper map and no way home. Perhaps he did mention it. He was sure he mentioned it. He was sure he said the word to her and that she looked at him

7

like it was the one word she could not, would not recognise.

'England?' as if he had just said 'Aubergine'.

She was the cleverest woman he had ever kissed. Berts looked at his wife, who could not tell a contradiction any more; everything for her was all confused and all the same. Jam at the back, salt on the top shelf — those were the decisions she made, all the rest was candles in daylight, and swimming in the rain. All the rest was growth.

At the end of the fifth month they took her in and Berts found that he missed her around the house. The carpets seemed emptied of pattern, the cushions made no sense. It was a week before he could bring himself to wash a dish and when he did, it was with surgical precision, putting on the rubber gloves, lifting each plate out of the water like a newborn thing. There was a smell in the house and he started to clean from one corner to the next, leaving nothing out. When he reached the bedroom he stopped, looked over the threshold, and closed the door. From that day, he went for his dinner from one sister to another and slept on the sofa downstairs, dreaming of upholstered breasts, waking with his head hanging over the edge and his face to the floor.

On the day they said she died he went into the bedroom again. He stripped off the sheets and smelt along the mattress. He lay down on the floor and, with the length of his arm, swept her shoes from under the bed. He tested the heater and sniffed the sockets. Then he opened the wardrobe door. There was a paper bag on the shelf where she kept her vests and her vests were gone. He wondered where they were, as he looked at the mess of turnips inside the bag, slimy and stinking — did people take vests, when you were giving away clothes? He lifted the bag off the shelf and slid the door shut. That wardrobe had meant so much in the early days of their marriage, fitted and white. She had probably cooked the vests. In any case the smell was gone now, as he carried the bag downstairs and out the back door.

The baby didn't seem to mind. The baby was the thing. She fed earnestly and slept like the dead. She filled her nappy with a look of bereaved surprise, but otherwise she cried or was delighted – by him, by the tassels on the lampshade, by the flex of the kettle, by the way water poured and then was gone. But mostly, it has to be said, she was delighted with herself.

The first words she spoke were 'Ma Ma'. It was enough to break your heart, said the aunts, but Berts understood.

'Maria,' he said. 'Maria.' What could be more monstrous than her birth? Only this: that the first word to bubble in her throat was her own name – twice.

The sisters were terrific, but it wore Berts down to hear the hidden banging of brothers-in-law when he knocked at their doors. Still, she had a gaggle of mothers and it seemed to suit her; each day a different house to be carried through, a different floor to crawl on: Teresa's blue Tintawn, Lucy's lozenges of red on a grey ground, with little black curves, Joan's brown lino in Inchicore, with a hole sprouting hessian by the cooker. Thursday was all russet leaves that you could never pick up, scattered across Mrs Hanratty's floor, but Friday was the best day of all. His sister Bernie had no children. She had Axminster flowers spreading pink and green and grey and the baby moved from one to the next, sitting on their open petals like a careful frog.

They were all fine women in their way but they were worn out, that was the thing of it, and Lucy was foolish and Mrs Hanratty was being too kind. Besides, he spent all his time in the old car he had to buy to ferry her around. A vindictive Lancia, as bad as his wife. The electrics were not the best. Press the indicator switch and the wipers came on, the whole lot fused in the rain.

He knew, as he stood at the side of the road with his head under the bonnet, that he would have to marry again. The thought overwhelmed him. He still did not understand. There wasn't a part of his wife that had wanted to die. There wasn't a single cell of her that had wanted to die. You would think, they said, that she would let go, turn her face to the wall. But she did not. She looked at them and looked at them and looked and looked.

Berts kept to his own side of the bed at night with the baby in a cot across the room. I need to go away, he thought, imagining a journey where he travelled the coast all the way round and back to the house again. It would be important, he thought, to keep to the very rim of the land, his journey shorter when the tide came in, the sea hungering for him, then slipping away, over and over, from Wicklow Head to Valencia to Malin Head. The trip was so fresh and real in his mind it exhausted him. Night after night he scrambled over rocks and took paths along cliffs and down to the sand, seaweed cracking and slipping under the sole of his shoe. He took an imaginary piece of red wool and wove it around an imaginary map, curling into coves and wriggling around headlands, then stretching it out along a ruler for miles per inch. It was amazingly long. He worried about piers. Should he travel the length of them, going up the near side and coming back by the far?

He would start from his house and walk to Dublin Bay, then set his face north or south. The choice was important. There was a difference between walking with the sea on your right-hand side and the sea on your left. He switched until he became dizzy and decided on the left – because his wife had slept on that side, because death was on the left.

Left meant south. He would travel from Bray to Wexford then, a straight flat coast. A right turn for Cork; he would twist his way around the headlands of Kerry, then loop his way around Loop Head, after he had jumped the River Shannon.

When does the coast become a river bank? At the change of water, from fresh to sea salt. It was a shining line of salt, then, that he was tracing around the country, he saw it

glittering and lacy in his mind. He would walk up one bank
of the river, cross at the first bridge and walk back along the
other bank, while yesterday's path pulled away from him on
the far side. Then the headlands of Galway and Mayo,
which made you hungry just to look at them. Donegal
would be the worst of it and, after Donegal, the North
proper, where he would slip past policemen with guns and
keep his mouth shut. Round the curly head of Ireland,
down to the docks of Belfast and the sweep of the Mournes,
after which it was a quick slither south and home.

He saw himself standing again on the spot he had started
from, looking at the Pigeon House and Dublin Bay before
turning inland. The house would be the same when he got
back, but it would be better the second time around, or at
least different. His wife would be dead, but he would be
alive, with a circle inscribed around that life. She would
leave him alone.

But perhaps it didn't stop at Dublin Bay. Shouldn't he
walk back on the other side of the street, so the circle would
close at his own front door? Or would it close inside the
house? Should he wind his way around the walls until he
got to the exact place he started out from – this bed, and his
side of this bed? Would he cross, last of all, the space left by
his wife?

Or would he cross it first, as he set out? But, as he rolled
over the hollow she had left in the mattress, he might catch
the edge of her absence like an elastic band on his foot, he
might drag it with him around the entire country, until his
wife's death had filled the map, emptied the map.

There was no doubt about it, he would have to start from
his own side. He would have to cross her last, or even not
cross her at all, but, by skirting the bed at the end of his trip,
leave her outside the circle, on the side of the sea. But
would that mean he would have to head north instead of
south when he reached the coast? End up walking
widdershins around the country, like some sort of eejit?

Night after night, he set out in his mind, from one side of

the bed or the other, edging around the inside walls of the house, with the room to his right or the room to his left. But he got mixed up going from the bedroom to the bathroom, or he crossed the line coming down the stairs. Out in the streets, he clung to one side of the road and it led him, around corners and up alleys, all the way to Phibsboro. He took his courage and crossed at traffic lights. Then he stood on the far side of the road turning this way and that, sick and dizzy, until, back in his bed, he started to cry.

Years later, he realised how simple it was. He should have put his faith in the constancy of the left-hand side. Left would always be left. She was on the left, the sea would be on the left, that was all.

It was a relief to bring a woman into the house after the year was passed, though it was still hard to say when Berts' wife had actually died. The sisters turned out on a Tuesday morning to a cold church scattered with old women and muttered their way through the memorial Mass. The baby cried and smiled. It was done.

Evelyn was a nice girl. Berts knew she would grow to hate him and he welcomed it as his due, but she surprised him with love and he thought again how strange women are. He had Maria to look after so there were no dances, or trips to the cinema – just a baby to pull at her, the grime in the sink and the yearning in his pants. He bought a record player and a record and they waltzed in the front room while Maria watched them from the sofa, her mouth set like Churchill's at the Yalta conference. Berts' hand sweated into the arch of Evelyn's back until the artificial silk of her blouse grew limp and started to cling. Their talk stopped and the record stopped but still they circled around, while on the sofa Maria began to think and then to shit, her eyes intent, mournful, forgetful of the room. And as their turning slowed to a sway and the carpet seemed too thick to let their feet take another shuffle Maria started to fill her nappy, her face fixed on some distant, unknowable thing. By the time

Berts leaned in to kiss Evelyn, Maria's bottom was in the air like the green velour was pushing it out of her, and the kiss that they had waited for, tasting of sweat and lipstick, the surprising coolness of Evelyn's tongue and the bitterness of Berts' Sweet Afton, was not finished until Maria swung her backside over the edge of the sofa and let it fall, splat, on to the floor.

'Who would have thought', said Evelyn, 'that so much could come out of them,' as she hung the towelling down by the side of the toilet bowl, and flushed.

Evelyn was neat, and soft about the eyes, but her mouth was too wet and her smile settled pouches of fat around her chin. She would not age well. Berts watched as she speared the new nappy with a safety pin, so firm you could hear the crunch of the cotton threads. The chain around her neck hung down over Maria's watchful eyes.

But the child fixed on her. She amazed Evelyn with her hunger, took her first steps towards her. She tried out sounds, like small moves into the future, and one of them was 'Ebbelyn'. That settled it. On the night they came back from the honeymoon Berts picked the child up from Bernie's, brought her back home and put her in her new room. The noise of her crying made his lovemaking so fierce that his new wife said, 'You've put me into next week,' and she stood naked before him before going downstairs to heat the milk.

They were a family.

Berts could not sort through the different kinds of pain he felt: perhaps it was the grief that comes to the man who wins. When Maria looked at him he turned his pockets inside out and,

'Look,' he said. 'All gone.' But he knew it was a lie. He began to shore up small losses that would count against him. He slurped his tea like an animal and turned his back in the bed but Evelyn did not seem to mind. Perhaps she wasn't very bright. All day long she played with the child, infatuated, kind. One day he saw her go to unbutton her blouse.

That was it, then. He made love to her every night and kept a secret chart, he wore his underwear loose and took cool baths. This child understood too much, had always understood too much. He did not like to see her touch his wife.

But Evelyn was so happy pregnant, he thought he had won again and the same need to spoil it came over him. She was mad for paintshops, colour swatches, books full of wallpaper and he indulged her for a while, teasing her along. He picked his moment, though. When it came to carpets, he stalled.

'They're not three years old,' he said, making her fight for it.

'I want my own carpet,' she said, finally, as he knew she would say, now that she had her own child.

And Berts said, 'My wife chose this carpet. You know that. My dead wife.'

Maria watched them. She was sitting on the carpet in question, which was brown in patches and beige in others with black spidery bits scattered here and there. She sat with her backside spread firmly over the floor, her hand poised on its way to her mouth, a stray button between finger and thumb, while they said things that could not be unsaid about her dead mother and her living father and the child he had conceived to supplant her. And when Evelyn was crying and Berts had walked away she put the button into her mouth and swallowed it.

'Would you murder me as quick?' cried Evelyn from the kitchen.

It was then that Berts told her about his wife on the bed, the child filling her stomach and the tumour filling her brain. How they wheeled her down to the operating theatre, her pelvis surging and her face blank. How they took out the child and turned off the machines, and waited. And later, when he touched her corpse, as he was obliged to do, he felt the size and carelessness of the stitches under the cloth and he knew that she had bled to death, and that it had taken her all day.

What kind of child comes out of a dead woman? A child with no brain? A child with two heads? Or no child at all? Just the smell of one maybe, or its wriggling, in the shape of a box. Evelyn looked at Maria, sitting on the carpet, all flesh and smiles and spit. She was small for a monster. She was not enough.

'She was born innocent,' said Evelyn. 'Like the rest of us.'

But Berts was looking at her now with a silence so hard she could feel it tighten around the back of her neck.

After that they said no more about it, but changed the wallpaper and left the carpets and decided to love each other if they could.

2

A Bed of Roses

New York, 1985

When Maria was twenty years old, she fell in love.

She met him in a café, high up in Spanish Harlem. He slid open a plate glass window and stepped outside and Maria, who was just drinking a cup of coffee, looked at him and said, 'Oh shit.'

It was one of those places with art on the walls and ceramic mugs that set your teeth on edge. They were on the top floor, looking towards the park – all you could see were the backs and staggered roofs of the brownstones on the next street down. Someone had pitched a two-man tent on top of one of them, and three windows had a fluffy blue sky painted directly on to the glass. Deeper south was the pop-up book of the Manhattan skyline, a distant surprise.

Maria was taking it easy, eating a sandwich. She was wearing brown shoes with black trousers, but otherwise, everything was just fine.

She saw his loose-knuckled hands as he worked the lock, and the fresh skin of his neck. She saw his profile as he twisted through the opening, his curly black hair. He looked like a guy from another life, a different magazine. She tucked her feet, in their wrong shoes, back under her chair.

The window gave on to a tar-paper ledge, too big for a balcony, too small for a roof garden. There were a few potted plants out there – nothing else. Maria looked for a twenty-dollar bill blown into a corner. She looked for a stalled cat, or a bird trapped by its reflection in the window pane.

Maybe he just liked the weather. He was out in the bare skyline now; he was part of the picture. He put his hands back to steady himself. Three fingertips bulged white against the glass, and

'Oh shit,' said Maria to herself as he pushed away towards the rail.

He turned, as though he had heard, and looked at the place where she was sitting.

Maria drew breath. There was nothing between them but the reflection on the glass. She thought of the view shining back at him; her face a dim reminder among the buildings and clouds. She saw his eyes privately meet themselves, before he turned back to the yellowing sky.

When he slid the glass back again she could feel how different the room seemed to him without the reflecting sheen – how open and dark and real. As he passed her table she said,

'Thought you were going to fly away,' and he laughed, as he tried to focus on her in the dim light.

When he saw her properly, he stopped and said, 'What accent is that?'

'Irish.'

'That's what I thought.'

'Well, you were right,' she said.

He stood there.

'You?'

'I'm from all over,' he said, in a London sort of voice.

'Ah. I should have known.'

Their flirtation was already weary and sweet. They might as well talk as strangers; like each other the way strangers do, suddenly, entirely. Never mind all the rest.

'Nice little town,' she said. 'Allover.'

'For a while.'

He smiled. Maria lifted her coffee and took a sip and could not swallow it.

That night she pressed her forehead against the dark windowpane. When she went back to the café three days later he was there, as she knew he would be. When he sat down at her table, Maria realised that she would take him home. Sometime. Soon. Never mind all the rest.

He stayed for a week.

Maria used to say that first ride lasted three days, but they both knew that if he left, on Monday morning or Tuesday afternoon, he would never come back again.

They lay by her window with the sound of radios coming up from the street, listening to the warm air fights. Couples who had to exhaust each other before they could put the key in the door. Couples who put the key in the door, and turned back to fight one last time. From the distance the sound of shots or a cab backfiring and Anton jolting beside her in the bed.

'Uhh, got me.'

That was the thing about Cowboys and Indians, he said. It wasn't about shooting people: it was about dying. Huge dying. He stood up on the bed and clutched his chest. He staggered back and staggered forward again, then pitched down beside her.

'You, you . . . you got me,' and looked at her and fluttered his eyelids shut, and let his head slump back.

He had a long waist and short legs; as though the top of him had surged ahead, leaving the rest behind. She loved the way his jeans bagged between his belt and the arch of his backside. She loved the vanity of his shirt, which brought out the colour of his eyes. His eyes were nearly green when he wore the shirt, and grey in bed.

Anton.

He rolled over and played the theme from *The Virginian* along her thigh.

He told her how his grandfather used to play the piano along the edge of the kitchen table, starting slow, then speeding up until he was thundering through some silent sonata, grunting whatever notes he could catch. When he

21

got a bit wrong he would stop and throw his hands up in the air. Then he would smile.

The next morning she went back to work. She pictured him in daylight, walking her single room, getting paler. She pictured him naked among her things.

She was surprised to see him when he opened the door. This small handsome man. This charmer.

'I missed you.' His eyes were bright and creased at the edges, everything they saw was slightly funny. She cooked a meal and was afraid of him. She did not know what tone of voice to use. They ate politely and when she was clearing the dishes he caught her and pushed his face into her stomach, while his hands pulled at the backs of her thighs. Maria put the plate down.

On Saturday, she brought him to a party at her friend Cassie's and they came back white-faced with hate. They stood in the street and argued about Cassie and her Buddhism, and her boyfriend with the big teeth. They argued about Tibet in general. When they finally got back in, the room looked as though it had been robbed.

Anton leant against the wall and watched her as she undressed. He told her about a Japanese girl he had slept with once. He said Japanese women were all muscle, didn't care who they fucked. Maria went to the ice-box and took out a jug of cold water for the night, imagining the scant torso, the unreadable knot of anatomy between her thighs.

There wasn't enough room to ignore each other in the bed. Maria finally got up and sat in the armchair. He was watching her in the dark, through half-shut eyes. When he closed them, she walked over and slid her hands under the sheet, not kissing him until after they came.

He sat up at the top of the bed and lit a cigarette and looked at her.

'Look at you. How come you're here? In New York?'
She didn't know what to say.
'For a laugh.'
'What's your family like?'

22

'Nice.'

'Nice?'

'They're fine. I can't stand them.'

'Poor little Maria,' he said, so she told him that her mother was dead.

He smoked on.

'I don't remember my mother,' he said. 'I mean she's still alive, but . . . I remember her sitting in a cupboard and crying, that's all. I must have been about four. Fucking cupboard.'

The next morning he left to see a guy about a job on a roller coaster on Coney Island. He laughed and told her all about it; about standing there with a hose and sluicing out the kids' pee in time for the next ride.

He talked while he was dressing; joked his way into his trousers and muttered through the buttons of his shirt. He grabbed his jacket and threw a 'See ya' over his shoulder, while she lay there watching him. She did not get up. She lay there naked and turned her back to him, just before he left the room.

When she heard the door shut, she reached for his pillow and balanced it on her face, feeling the weight and the dark smell of his hair.

Anton said she had sad eyes and funny eyebrows. He said she had a familiar face. He said that, when they kissed, he could see her cheeks flushed out below his eyes and it always made her look like she was smiling.

Always.

He was always describing her. He never asked her to describe him back, but, if he had, she would have found it easy. She would have said, 'You are a mistake.' The kind of mistake that drove you mad in bed, trying to put it right.

His mistaken legs with their mistaken thighs, the long mistake of his stomach and the bitter mistake of his mouth.

Maria took the pillow off her face, wandered across to the kitchen and poured some water into the coffee machine.

She leaned her bare haunch against the cupboard door, waiting for it to bubble through. He would not come back.

It was August in New York. So hot. The sound of the city was everywhere: you were swimming in it. She looked at the mirror, cool and mute on the far wall. After a while, she went over to it and touched the glass.

'What are you like?' she said, checking her ordinary face and the marks of her tan. She turned around and clenched her bottom, looking for cellulite, then stalled a moment, caught by her eyes.

Anton said she had puzzled eyebrows, Buster Keaton eyes. He said she dressed well but her underwear was a hoot. He said she was more clever than she knew.

Maria wanted to take the mirror and throw it across the room.

She went back to the bed and sat beside it, not wanting to disturb the dent in the sheet, the faded cotton roses where he had lain. He would not come back. She traced the cut-out shapes of green and pink, ran her finger around a stain they had left there, remembering things she could not name.

When the knock came, she could not believe it was him. She looked out of the spy-hole at the comic bulge of his face and did not want to open the door. He was wearing a different shirt and had a bag slung over his shoulder.

He sat at the counter while she made him coffee. He looked tired. She touched the back of his neck as she set the cup in front of him.

He said he had seen a man that day, preaching in Times Square. He was thumping a small keyboard and yelling, 'Remember me, my God, for my happiness. For my happiness. For my happiness, my God, remember me.'

Life slowed down again, and stopped for a while in the room.

His hands came round from behind to feel between her thighs, like a man rooting in the pocket of a coat he had just picked up.

He had come back.

When he fell asleep, she closed her eyes and tried to remember him exactly. She would forget his body. When the mortuary drawer was pulled out, she would not be able to tell by the toes that it was him, or by the knees. She would be pierced to the heart by the hair on the leg of someone she did not even know. She would not be able to look at the face. She would nod and turn away, and Anton would be gone clear.

Maria pulled back the sheet and searched every inch of him, trying to memorise the way the hair grew, the swirls and shifts, the pattern of the follicles. She took his shirt and felt the fabric and smelt it. She lifted his trousers from the floor, with their weight of keys and small change. She took out his wallet and opened it. She checked through his bag.

It was a small bag but it was important. There were important things in it. If he left her now, he would not come back again.

At the bottom of the bag she found a navy-blue hardback notebook, done up with an elastic band. Inside, she found a photograph of herself when she was twelve years old.

Maria saw her own eyes. She saw her own teeth, the two extra incisors that were taken out when she was fourteen. She saw her own smile. She went over to the mirror to check if it was still there.

She had been completely robbed.

In the photo she was surrounded by strangers, she was wearing a blue grandad shirt tucked into a pair of white jeans, she was wearing a pair of red espadrilles. In the photo, she was wearing her own smile.

On the Bias

Dublin, 1971

But whatever she wears, the child is clothed in silence. Silence seems to stick to her: whatever she touches lies still under her hand. On the day of her First Holy Communion Maria wears white, and a quieter white you could not imagine. In the photographs you see her, the extra inch between her and the world. Evelyn stands apart. The ice cream will not reach. The high-wristed monkey drops his hand over his face and, in the background, a man is caught in contemplation, the double vents of his jacket splitting over his rumpled backside. Here is Jesus, in Maria, in the Zoo, so quiet the toucans forgot to shriek.

A silent breeze lifts her veil and drops embroidered shadows on her neck. The dress is broderie anglaise, with a petticoat, so no one can look through the little holes and see her knickers, which are white and edged with lace. There is nothing special about her vest, except that it is new, but her ankle socks are stretchy lace. She can feel the pattern, pressed into her feet by her white shoes. It is a black-and-white photo so her shoes look grey – though under them, her feet might secretly be . . . the colour of feet!

Berts smiles out of her face like an old woman, wicked and shy. And a strange pair of eyes, which don't belong to anyone, look at the camera and dare it to guess what colour they might be.

When Berts was called in to help make the dress he brought a paper bag with 'Lyons Tea' written on it and his own tape measure, which Maria prefers to Evelyn's soft one, because of the way it runs back into itself with a whirr and a thump.

'Would you look at her,' says Evelyn. And it is true. She stands on the dining-room table in her pants and vest, with bruises slowly rising red and blue to the surface of her legs, or sinking back down in yellow and green. A big fresh graze from the garden wall runs in parallel tracks around the inside of her knee, and at the padded top of her arm there is a faint oval bite mark around a sucky welt she brought up with her teeth and tongue.

'What are you like?' says Evelyn. Maria looks at her plump sticky feet, while Berts scribbles in the waxy paper, trying to get the biro to work.

'Don't have an accident whatever you do. What would they say in Casualty?'

Berts starts to measure her, waist to shoulder.

'Go from the belly-button,' says Evelyn. 'Or everything will be out.'

'Up to where? Armpit?'

'Armpit?' says Evelyn. 'Where did you get armpit from? Up to her shoulder.'

'Right. Belly-button,' says Berts. 'Where's it gone? Oh, she's lost it,' and Maria sticks her finger in through her vest and laughs.

Berts balances a ruler on Maria's shoulder, 'Hang on to that, now,' and he runs the tape measure up to it. He looks around for Evelyn, but she is hanging on to the chair, laughing.

'It's a dress,' says Evelyn. 'Not a box.' She draws a line with a finger along Maria's shoulder.

'Front half, back half. Like there's a mirror down through her middle.'

'Except that her bottom sticks out behind,' says Berts, and Maria kicks him in the chest.

'Plié, now. Plié!' he says, catching her foot and twisting it high.

When Berts has all the numbers, he draws the outline of a

girl on the Lyons Tea bag; cut into sections and crossed with lines.

'Rump steak, round steak, gigot chop.'

Evelyn cuts it out and they pin her into it; with tissue for her front half, and newspaper for her back, so the births, marriages and deaths are all down her bottom.

'I don't know,' says Evelyn.

The picture on the envelope is of a blonde girl with a white patent leather handbag hanging from her elbow. She has smooth knees and her eyes are rolling blue, with a pie slice of white where the light hits.

'It's swimming on you,' says Evelyn and pins like a maniac. She sews faster so she won't run out of thread – and still the top is too wide. So she puts in some piping and then a lace collar to hide the seam staggering around the neck.

'The hours of work', she says, 'I put into that.'

'Lovely,' says Berts.

'Lovely,' says everyone. But Maria doesn't know if it is true.

When she wakes in the morning the dress is hanging on a nail, a white cut-out girl floating up the patterned wall. Maria tries to imagine being inside it. She lies in bed and tries to tell what size she is. When she closes her eyes her tongue is huge and her hands are big, but the bits in between are any size at all. When she opens her eyes she is the size of the dress. Or she might be.

Maria follows Emily Boles into the line of girls going up the aisle. Her soul is white after confession, and light as an ad for margarine. It floats out over her like a balloon. She walks quietly, pulling it along behind her, her solid white shoes tapping the tiles of the floor. Under her dress the scrape from the garden wall is a nice brown, lines of little beads that she wants to pick off but can't. So she rubs one knee against the other as she walks, and tries to stop her bag banging. It is in broderie anglaise to match her dress, stuffed with a prayer-book that pokes through the satin rope that Maria threaded in herself.

When they practised, the nun used a spoon, wiping it on the sleeve of her habit after each girl's mouth. So the taste of the metal is still there when Maria sticks her tongue out – so far that the thread on the underneath hurts. Then she has to take it back in again to say 'Amen' because she forgot, even though Sr Eulalia had drilled it into them.

'What is it?'

'The body of Christ. Amen. Tongue,' said the class.

'Amen. Tongue,' said Sr Eulalia. 'Amen what?'

'Tongue,' said the class.

And even still Maria has her tongue out before the priest has finished 'The body of Christ', because she wasn't expecting any altar-boys. So she is gagging on it, trying to swallow it and speak at the same time, as she says Amen.

She walks back with her head down, her stupid tongue wrestling secretly with the host, until her throat clutches it and she swallows Jesus straight into her heart. Jesus did not go into your stomach, which is why you couldn't use your teeth. He isn't a sweet, said Sr Eulalia, or a pork chop, but God, and you don't chew God. He chooses you.

'And don't panic', she says, 'if He sticks to the roof of your mouth.'

He is there in the church, hanging on the cross. He is sitting in the chalice and secretly clinging to the roofs of girls' mouths, for fear of their hearts, and eventually He is in everyone except Brenda Quinn who is crying because she said 'Tongue' instead of 'Amen'. He is watching Maria as her soul falls back into her, until she is a little vessel in the perfect shape of herself, full of Jesus. He is looking down on her as He fills her; His eyes so sad and His body all bruises and scrapes and nail marks.

'Don't have an accident,' says Maria to him. 'Whatever you do,' then she eats a bit of herself to keep Him company, picking the scabs off her knee, then pretending to pray, so she can lick them out from between the base of her thumbs.

The zoo is full of girls in white dresses, opening and closing their little white bags, counting their money. They take off their gloves and put them back on again, sliding a finger into the seam at each fork. They push their veils back with their gloved hands. Sometimes they forget and touch things by mistake. They grab the railings at the sea-lions' feeding time and the keeper pretends to throw a silver fish at them to make them scream and resettle along the bars. The chimpanzees throw their doings; very accurate, like boys. The clods of gick fly past your face and it would be a game except that this is the wrong day for it. Emily Boles is upset and even Maria says nothing, but walks away, her veil drifting lightly at her back. She finds Berts and stands beside him. He is talking to another man and he doesn't even know whose father it is.

Maria pulls his trouser leg and says, 'Come on.'

'Come on where?'

Which is how she ends up in the reptile house by herself, dreaming of the snakes that lie there and never move behind the glass. She is looking for bats because they hang upside down. She is looking for something to stuff down her little brother's neck, because he is whining all day, pulling out of Evelyn and getting ice cream. She is looking for Jesus in with the ring-tailed lemurs, a piece of fruit in His outstretched hand, while the lemurs bounce all over Him, landing on His head and peering down into His eyes. She is looking for the Virgin Mary in with the lions.

When she goes into the lion house the smell makes her want to pee, so she holds the top of her knickers tight through her dress and watches a lion working at a bone with his dirty teeth. The bone isn't really white; it has dried blood on it and is a complicated shape with bits flapping off the end. The bits are full of sawdust. Maria tries to think what part of a cow it came off, when she sees that the lion is a lioness. All the others are outside in the sun and Maria is alone with this one and her bald head and the smell. Her animal eyes meet Maria's, and then she looks away.

Maria is afraid that she will have an accident, but if she goes to look for Berts she might cry and wet herself at the same time. But she is having an accident anyway. She fluffs up her skirt really quick and sits in a trough full of plants. Then she watches the bald lioness. When the place is empty, she takes off her pants.

Maria puts on her gloves and walks away from the cage; a little clot of lace left behind her in the ferns. At the door, a man she didn't see bends over her and says,

'You're a dirty little thing, aren't you?' He holds on to her shoulder and roots in his pocket for something that Maria is afraid of. But when he finds it, it is a two-shilling piece, which he gives her for her bag.

'Say a prayer for me, now.'

This is her fourteenth two-shilling piece and her bag is getting so heavy, she gives Evelyn her prayer-book to carry.

'What about the money?' says Evelyn. 'I could carry that instead.'

They are sitting on the grass beside the big bird cage.

'I thought you were with your father. What did you see?'

'Monkeys,' says Maria, and she starts to cry.

'I lost him,' she says, while Evelyn hugs her and says, 'Oh dear. Oh dear.' But it's really her pants she lost and not Berts at all.

Then a peacock walks past, and Evelyn tells her about a peacock she saw once that was all white, up to the tips of its big wide tail.

'Just like you.'

'When did you see it?' says Maria. 'Before I was born?'

Which is when Berts walks back across the grass. There is a girl with him, and she is wearing a communion dress. Maria thinks that she must have been with him all along. Except that it isn't her. It couldn't be. This girl's dress is longer and she even wears tights.

'Another stray,' says Berts, taking out a cigarette and sitting down on the grass. 'Aren't you?' It must be a girl from another class. She looks at Maria's dress and her shoes, then she waves at someone, and runs away.

'Before I was born?' says Maria again. But Evelyn only smiles and looks over at the birds.

They go to the hospital on the way home to visit Granny Delahunty. Auntie Joan is there and some old people sitting around on plastic chairs.

Her granny reaches up under her pillow and squashes paper money into her hand.

'Say a prayer for me now,' and Maria can see all down the front of her nightie.

'Now, Maria,' says Evelyn, and Berts says, 'The child.'

'Sometime,' says her granny. 'Anytime will do.'

'Hail Mary,' says Evelyn. 'What harm?'

Maria bows her head and joins her hands. All the old people look at her and mouth the words.

The hospital smells of accidents – the kind where you wet yourself, and the kind where you get knocked down by a bus. Maria is fine until the Holy Mary, when she realises that she isn't wearing any pants. Then she is back in the middle of the first bit again and someone has to help her finish. But they all clap when she gets to the end.

'What's that you have there?' says a man. 'Let's have a look at the bag. Oh, there's a lot in there.' He clanks all the money.

'Can I look?' He pulls open the cord with two old fingers and peers inside and says, 'Can I have some of that?' and Maria doesn't know what to say so she says, 'No,' and everybody laughs except her granny in the bed, who has fallen asleep.

'Come on so,' says Berts.

Maria walks down the corridor. She has had an accident. She is in the hospital. A man walks past her in his dressing gown, with a hole in his throat. She isn't wearing any pants and Jesus is trickling out of her, all along the floor. Maria takes her veil off and doesn't care. The man smiles at her while a nurse goes down on one knee, says, 'Long day, huh?' taking the veil and fluffing it out and letting it drift back down on to her head. Jesus has leaked out behind her, all along the corridor, and all the prayers she has to say, for the man in the lion house, and her granny and the old people on the chairs – none of them will work and she doesn't care. The nurse is dressed in white, too. She smiles at Berts who says, 'I'll take you home again, Kathleen.'

Evelyn doesn't say anything when she finds her pants are gone. She says,
'Who were you talking to?'
'Emily Boles.'
'Are you sure?' and now Maria can't remember talking to Emily Boles, or what they said.

They hang the dress on the wall, even though it is finished, so Maria can look at it as she goes to sleep. Berts, even, comes in. He sits on the edge of her bed and smokes, using the cup of his hand for the ash. His palm is hard and the ash doesn't burn it and he sits there and they both look at the dress. He doesn't say much, he says,
'Tough day?' And Maria says,
'The nurse's name was Siobháin.'
'Was it?'
'It was on her badge.'
'And you could read it?' he says. 'All that b, h and a fada?'
'Yes.'
'Fair enough.'
On his way out the door he says, 'You weren't talking to anyone?'
'No.'
'Good girl,' and the smell of his cigarette is in the room after he goes.

In the morning Maria puts the dress on for Mass, but it isn't the same the second time around. When Auntie Joan comes, she runs off with her cousin Frankie. They are halfway up the road before Mrs Quinlan catches them.
'Come in,' says Mrs Quinlan. 'And I have a look at you.'
Maria has never been in Mrs Quinlan's house. When she

33

walks in she realises it is the same as their house, except it is the wrong colour. Except it is the wrong smell. Except it is the wrong way around! The kitchen goes to the left instead of the right and when you try to go into the dining room there is a massive blank wall. Maria lifts her hand as though there might be a handle in the wallpaper, then turns around in fright, because there is a door open behind her back, like a room in a dream.

Upstairs someone comes out of her bedroom, but it is the wrong bedroom and it is not even a girl who comes out of it, but stupid Ben Quinlan.

'Say a prayer for me now.'

'I don't want to.'

'You do of course.'

Maria starts to make the sign of the cross, but she does it with the wrong hand.

'Turn around, sure,' says Mrs Quinlan. 'And try again.' So Maria turns to face the other way, and this time she gets it right. She says the Hail Mary from start to finish and Mrs Quinlan drops on one knee in front of her. When Maria is finished, she pushes her veil away from her face and kisses her at the corner of her left eye. She goes into the kitchen and comes back with a sixpence for her bag.

'What about this little heathen?' says Mrs Quinlan, and Frankie says, 'I have four thumbs, but they cut two of them off.'

'Not off the same hand?'

'No!' says Frankie.

'Well that's all right then,' she says, and she gives him sixpence and lets them go.

When the photos come, Maria gets her crayons out. She colours the legs yellow and the eyes blue, even though her own eyes are brown. She does the curtains green like Mrs Quinlan's curtains, and the carpet blue. She leaves the dress white.

Because this is a colour picture. All pictures are *taken* in colour. Some of them *come out* in black and white. This, finally, has come out in the colours it was taken in, though they are not the same colours as Maria's house.

This is the other girl. Maybe it is the girl in the communion dress that she saw with Berts. She lives somewhere else, in Mrs Quinlan's house maybe. Or she lives in America, or England, where they have colour cameras all the time.

The girl stands beside a high, narrow table; with a vase of flowers elaborately pink. She rests her hand on the wood and looks coolly, a little bloodily, out of the picture, where her mouth is crayoned red. It is hard to say what she is looking at. There is a different room in front of her, with a purple carpet and different people. It has jugs full of clotted cream, perhaps, and bowls full of floating rose petals.

Maria decides to scribble on her face and then does not. There is a woman watching, who wears a hat, even in her own sitting room, and is full of pity.

Maria rubs the colours until the girl is grey again, looking out through a blur of crayon. She looks sad now, so Maria tears the photo, very gently, and puts the pieces under her mattress, for later.

Her Own Smile

New York, 1985

Maria had never seen herself so clearly. She looked like a perfect stranger, like a girl you would pass on the street.

She crouched on the floor and went through Anton's notebook again, looking for more clues: a ticket for The Clash in the Lewisham Odeon; a ticket that said 'Welcome to Yellowstone National Park', a receipt for a bar in New Jersey that listed 'Cocktails $2.50' seven times in a row, a piece of paper scrawled with the words 'I O U my entire life'.

She looked at the photo. Anton and herself in a sunny garden, with two people standing on the other side of him. They looked like parents, but it was hard to tell. There was a paddling pool behind them, shaped into a duck's head at one end.

It took her a second to realise that the boy was Anton. Though when you looked at it, no other face was possible for him now. As for herself? She had changed. She tried to extract her own face form this girl's face, but when it came down to it, she could have grown up sixteen different ways.

In the photo she was wearing a blue grandad shirt and white jeans. She was wearing red espadrilles. She was wearing her own smile. There was something sinister about it – happy and cruel at the same time.

Maria did not have a grandad shirt when she was twelve, though she remembered wanting one. Maria had never worn white jeans, not even once. And the espadrilles she had, the summer she was fourteen, not twelve, were denim-blue.

But, more than all this, there was the fact that she looked different, even though she was the same. It was hard to put your finger on it. She had the right mouth, but the wrong voice might come out of it. She had the same eyes, but they had seen other things. Her hair was the same, but the parting was on the other side.

Maria looked at her and wanted to laugh. She had always felt like someone else. She had always felt like the wrong girl.

Anton slept on, his face delicious, like a child's.

She knew nothing about him. She knew that he used to like The Clash. She knew he could whistle without moving his lips, that he chewed his fingernails, that he always went into the bathroom before sex. She knew that he did not believe in birthdays, that he was afraid of drowning, that he wanted to hurt her sometimes. She knew what he felt, but not what he was thinking. She knew nothing about him at all.

'What was the best thing you ever ate?'

When he was fourteen, Anton said, he ran away from home. He ended up walking along the side of a motorway with his thumb stuck out. In a petrol station a man in a white MG had pulled over and given him a lift. He changed gear a lot, hitting Anton's knee with the side of his hand. After an hour or so, they pulled into a layby and Anton jumped out of the car, ran up a bank and disappeared into a field. He walked along hedges and ditches for the rest of the day. He nicked some old man's clothes and a pair of wellington boots from an outhouse, and walked on, and slept in a barn.

In the morning he was so desperate he knocked on the door of a house. The woman who answered did not question him, or ask who he was. She brought him into her kitchen, which was just an ordinary kitchen, and gave him ham sandwiches. He had never tasted anything like them in his life; white sliced pan, butter, cooked ham and mustard. He did not remember the woman speaking much, or even smiling. She was just deliberate. He remembered her breasts, he said, and a cloud of sweet pea along the wall when he left.

Soon after, he hit the sea. At first he thought the noise was another motorway, but he walked up a slope and, just before he reached the top, realised what he would see on the other side.

He talked about a Kilburn squat, about buying kif in Morocco, he talked about the housing estate outside Dagenham where he grew up, his father sitting in the window, drinking, while the kids ran wild outside. She could picture him playing Cowboys and Indians on a piece of waste ground; the kind of place where the bulldozer tracks froze and softened from winter to summer, and still the estate was neither built nor healed.

His father was a refugee, he said, from Czechoslovakia. The only women he could meet were public women, so he had married a barmaid, because no one else would let him in. She let him in as best she could, but he still hit her. And his English children, he wept over and thumped, as though they were history itself. He could not bear the distance between people in this country, he said. We are a family, he said. He said it to them in English, and also in Czech. He said it to the team of social workers who tried to stop him pouring a bottle of vodka over himself and setting it alight, as they took the children away. The kids sat in the car, staring at the waste of alcohol, wondering which one of them would get the blame when he realised it was gone.

He told her this on the third day. They were lying in bed, and Maria could not believe the distance they had travelled, each of them, to this small bed, this rectangle of space. She wanted to rip out the pages of an atlas and plaster them over the wall.

She kissed him. Anton said that he could see her cheeks

flushed out below his eyes, and the shape made him think that she was smiling, even though her mouth felt sad.

So Anton kissed with his eyes open. He kissed with a smile on his lips. There was nothing confusing about it, but Maria was confused. She straddled him and apologised every time she came, coming and stopping and saying sorry, until she realised he was in no hurry, he could look at her all day and smile.

It was nearly dawn. The yellow light from the lamp made her room look dingy and lost. Maria found herself standing over him as he slept, with a saucepan of water that had just come off the boil. She held the saucepan over him and tilted the water to the lip. Then she made tea with it, drinking it cup after cup, taking her hatred like a lesson and swallowing it down.

His lashes swept down from lids that barely closed: his mouth was a smile that nearly happened. She could not believe he was really asleep. He must know she was sitting there beside him, a replica of herself. She saw the bulge of his iris move from side to side, as though checking some place out before he could dream there. And the bulge started to dance.

Anton was dreaming, and there was such a tenderness in the sockets of his eyes, his flesh under the sheet was so warm and private, that Maria could only lean back and watch. His head was full of saxophones that turned into fish, and ordinary matchboxes filled with dread. This flat, these walls, did not exist for him, as she did not exist for him, sitting there beside the bed.

Maria wanted to be with him in his dreams. She wanted to break him open, or slip into him, somehow. She wanted to turn towards him, smiling, *Yes, it's me.* It was the kind of want, she realised, that could make you kill someone.

She twisted in the chair and, gently, switched off the light. There was a knife in her hand. It was quite blunt – a landlord's knife. She sat there naked and wondered which part of him she would mark. His torso was very white.

Maria sat half-lotus, with one foot on the other thigh. She tested the knife above her ankle and, after the cut, there was a pleasure so clean it make her eyes close. When she opened them again, she could feel everything, even the pain.

Berts' Heart

Dublin – Donegal, 1976

One evening in spring, when Maria was eleven years old –
the last year she would climb the cherry blossom in front of
the house, the last season of spitting contests and hide and
seek, the last months in which she would prefer the dusk to
night and her body would be easy to her – Berts looked out
the front window and was astonished by his wife's death.

It was not that he had thought of her often, or even in the
last years, at all, but what he had not been thinking of was
finally true. She had been alive. She was not alive any more.
And suddenly he loved Maria for the eyes she had, in which
the generations that made her regressed like opposing
mirrors and from which whatever portion of heaven there
was looked out on the world, confused by the light.

The tree was planted the year they had moved into the
house: a spindly stick that put out three clumps of pink, in a
row with the other trees on the road – like a TB clinic's
annual ball. His wife had such a want for it. She wanted the
winds to be kind to it and the years to surround it; she
wanted the blossoms to come and to fall. And Berts was
caught in the bandaged light of the curtains as, out in the
dusk, the children called to each other and Maria swung
down from a branch, showering the grass with pink and
white.

Berts lost his breath, pushed his head against the window,
and tried for air. Too much smoking. Something else as
well. The cries of the children left him and the sound of the
radio receded or switched off – he could not tell. You can
drown in a saucer of water, he said to himself; you can

drown in no water at all. He swiped the curtain away from the window, as if the clear glass would give him clear air – if he could see, he could inhale. Outside, the children were playing, and something about their dashing and twisting caught his breath and would not let it go. The colours of the dusk ticked in his eyes, from pink to grey, from violet to black, and back again. Evelyn was frying onions in the kitchen and the smell seemed to be coming from inside his head, from the very centre of his head, not from the kitchen at all.

So this is it, he thought. No pains shooting down your right arm or your left. No rugby team sitting on your chest – just fear itself, which took your breath and waved it in front of you. Fear pulling the breath out of your mouth like a piece of chewing gum that stretched and stretched away from you and would not snap back.

Berts rolled his eyes upwards and tried to look through the glass at the children clambering up the tree trunk and slithering back down again. He wanted to hold in his hand their small fresh hearts, wanted to lay his head on the narrow, springy chests where their pink lungs rose and fell. And he thought that children kill you just as much as anything. They get you, one way or another, and that was what they were for.

Maria swung from the tree to the wall and balanced there. Eleven years old. She let the branch go and steadied herself, walked a few steps, then jumped down into the front garden. This big-arsed child of his, who walked walls like they were ropes wound with flowers, who jumped into the garden like it was a trench full of bones. She kicked them out of her way as she ran to the front door. Berts did not want to frighten her with his forehead pressed flat against the glass and his eyes rolling towards the last of the light. He tried to pull himself away and found that he already had. He tried to breathe and found that he already was breathing. Her steps thumped over the lino in the hall and Evelyn shouted 'Take it easy!' from the kitchen as she ran into the front room and stood behind him. He could feel her eye on him.

The net curtain fell to Berts' shoulders and rumpled there, then fell again to the centre of his back. Maria watched him for a while – neither in the room, nor out of it. She looked at his back, made mysterious and womanly by the veil between them. Then she ran and poked him in the backside with an awkward, pointy fist and ran back to the door.

Her father was still at the window, still behind the curtain.

'What age are you?' he said.

'Eleven.'

'Eleven, is it?'

And she ran back and stiffed him another one, saying, 'Eleven!' and ran back to the door.

'Isn't that a bit old to be poking your poor Da on his backside?'

'No.'

And he turns and lifts the net curtain and says, 'Isn't that a bit old to be poking your poor old Da on the backside?'

'No.'

'It's not, is it?'

'No.'

And he is halfway across the room in two great strides and she has slammed the door on him; she is pushing up against the handle, while he turns the metal slowly, inexorably down, unhinging all her joints, until she abandons the door and runs out to the garden, as the door rushes open and her father strides down the hall and stands at the front door, his breath singing in his lungs.

'Pax?' she says.

'Fair enough,' he says.

And the next day at tea he tells her that they are going down the country for a couple of days, to see her mother's parents, and they are called Kennedy, and how does she like that?

43

Maria is too old for the four stomachs of cows, or for their five teats and the last one the hind tit. She is too old to dip her fingers in the milk and let the calves suck. Though when she does, a feeling she has never had before goes straight up her arm and into her right nipple. Hello, farming.

Most of the day she doesn't know what she wants to do and there's nothing to do anyway. So she lumps around the kitchen where Berts reads the paper, while her dead mother's father sits and says nothing and her dead mother's mother sets the table all day for her dead mother's brothers, who might come in any minute and want their tea.

Maria's Uncle Ambrose is the first grown-up man to talk about her bottom. He says, 'There's meat and two veg,' and he gives it a slap that might as well have been on her face, except nicer. He slaps the rumps of the cows too, as they wander into the yard looking lost, even though it's the only yard they know. The cows' eyes are so female, but the haunches are lean and loose under their hides, like an old man's bottom. She hates their huge bellies, slung over the ridgepole of their spines, fit to break. She hates the muck that squeezes up between their hooves as they slip and splay. And the udders make her sick, the pink veins wriggling under the white down, and the too-low teats that squeeze out between their back legs at each step; leaky and helpless, waiting for the machine.

So she ignores it all, ignores their gentle eyes and the power of their pissing, as they stand thinking about the suck and gasp of the machines that hang off them, and tick, and swing. And when Ambrose milks one by hand she does not see, as he eases his cheek against the huge bulb of her belly, that same thinking, unthinking, look come into his eyes as into the eyes of the cow he milks, the muscles on his forearm switching and swopping as the milk, with a pinging hiss, hits the side of the pail.

Maria is just bored. All she wants to know is how to become less bored as she feeds the calves in the haggard, hitting them on the skull with a chair leg when they've had enough. All the wrongness of the farm does not strike her, the calves sucking each other's ears, the cows who mount each other as they crush together in the gateway of the yard. She wants to know something, but it isn't this. She doesn't know what she wants to know. They're just cows, that's all. She is so bored she can hardly speak.

It rains all the time.

She goes over to the milking parlour.

'Scat,' says Ambrose, who is talking to a man in white wellingtons. Maria waits until they are gone, then she goes in to the lone cow that is tethered to the wall. There is a cigarette butt beside her and, in the trench behind, a clear plastic shoulder-length glove. The glove was pulled off inside out so the fingers stick back up into it. It is full of blood.

Maria hunkers down to take a look. There are five rings of pink where the fingers run back up themselves. The tips are squished into a pool of blood gathered in the palm. The plastic clings to itself through the pink bubbles and brown clots; a sticky map of meniscus pulling reluctantly against plastic all down the forearm. Maria reaches over to touch it and one side slides across the other. She pulls back and watches the blood turn brown, sort of interested but mostly bored. So bored she could die.

Berts talks about baling machines and the EEC and doesn't seem to realise how much they despise him.

'A baler?' says her grandfather. 'That's a thought.'

They switch the radio on for the news. Then Ambrose comes in, changes the station and makes Maria dance, holding her wrists, pushing and pulling each arm forward and back. And just when her feet begin to move with them, from side to side, he falls back into his chair. Maria is left to walk to the end of the table by herself. When she sits down her grandmother runs a dry hand over her cheek and her grandfather gets up and leaves the kitchen altogether.

Then John comes home with his knives in a leather

45

pouch. He has a bib of chain-mail, thick with fat and blood; so clotted and greased you cannot see the links. It looks like a flap of living hide, it looks like a bit of leather ripped off a cow that is still running away from him. John shows her the scar curling around his arm, shows her how to slit a cow's throat with her own throat to the ceiling, he calls the people at the factory 'Fuckers' and no one reproves him. So he says it again for her and her grandmother throws the dregs of the dishwater over him, with a fork still in it.

At night she hears it, the same cow roaring, all four stomachs of her and her grassy breath, all half a ton of her, rump steak, round steak and gigot chop, emptying itself into the black air.

What was wrong with her?

'Mastitis,' says Berts. Or a dead calf maybe. But,

'She didn't take,' says John, and Ambrose goes out the back door and spits.

'See that little window,' says John. 'At the back of the shed. A cow came out through that once, when the mood was on her, tore herself up to her back end.'

'What mood?' says Maria. And her grandmother says,

'Lay the table now quick before your Uncle Amby wants his tea.'

'Moooood,' says John.

And Maria bashes the fork down and makes the knife spin.

'I'm from Dublin,' she says, and they all have a good laugh at that.

'You don't have knives in Dublin?' says John, and he shows her one.

'That father of yours.' They hated him. Not just for his accent and his talk of balers, or for the back of his neck that is more eloquent than what comes out at the front of him, but for something else as well.

'Will you come to the dance?' says John. 'Are you dancing?' and Maria says nothing.

'Wise girl,' he says. 'Get yourself a man with a job.'

'You have a job,' says Maria.

'All in the wrist,' he says, and the scar on his forearm shimmies from side to side.

Maria lies in the tall grass and looks at the sky and thinks about John fencing with the dead bodies of cows, their blind eyes looking at the roof, their guts oofing and slithering out on to the floor under his old one-two. And then the old three-four that splays their legs back against the wall.

'What about five and six?'

'I gave them up for Lent.'

Ambrose says not to mind him, all he does is dump guts in one bucket and brains in another, because he has neither himself, while John whittles the edge of the kitchen table with his knife. The next morning he gets the call again and he is gone, swinging into the mini-van with one clean bag and one stinking, but before he goes he kisses her and Maria knows it is not her he is kissing but his big sister that died and she feels her mother flower inside her and is proud for him and wishes she could be with him all the time.

Maria spreads her anorak and lies down in the front meadow, although it is wet. Easter has come and gone. It was on Spy Wednesday she saw Ambrose leaning against the belly of the cow. On Holy Thursday the AI man came – before the holiday, which was probably why it was too early. It was on Good Friday that John had the dishwater thrown over him, and on Easter Saturday he told her about the old one-two.

Sunday was an insanity of table setting and table clearing, of dish-dusting and napkin folding, until Maria felt like throwing the lot at the wall, but there was a panic deep in her grandmother that meant she couldn't. John didn't swear or even talk much and Ambrose read the newspaper like it was a real pleasure, shaking the whole thing each time he turned the page.

John carried the roast to the table, his hands raw with blood that would not wash out. The bone-handled carving

47

knife sighed as the meat shivered and dropped in slices. Then he used the flat of the blade and the bare tips of the fork to lift and dip a heap on each plate – a movement so formal and gentle it made Maria hungry for something she couldn't name, and happy when she ate.

'Lovely,' they said.

'It's underdone,' said her grandmother when she saw blood by the bone and she half-rose, before they pushed her back down with,

'Lovely.'

'Perfect.'

The blood of the joint was salty-sweet and pink, the same colour as the roses on her grandmother's delph. There were roses on the cloth as well and roses on the wallpaper and modern roses blocked out in triangular petals on the new plastic breadboard. The men ate their way through to the china, mashing potatoes to sop up the gravy, shaking the salt, their movements obliged and tragic as they picked their way through the teacups and the tiny jug for milk. The tattered joint sat in the middle of it all, like a tear in the cloth, the only thing in the room that had no shape.

Suddenly the plates were dirty, though it was the same food that was on them as had been there a minute before – perhaps that was what the roses were for, so you could tell the difference. It was the first time she noticed it, at any rate, this disgust that made her rise and stack against her will. But she hated her grandmother as she passed her in front of the sink. She hated Amby's throat as he bared it to swallow his tea, before holding the little cup out for more. The others saw the cup but did not find it relevant and Maria stopped; caught by the sight of it sitting in the air like that, the absence it implied.

'Your uncle wants another cup of tea,' said her grandmother, shocked. And blushing, big-arsed, she, who was not let near the teapot at home, crossed the room and poured tea for her uncle, who did not notice and waited for milk.

She was in the middle of strangers. Maria looked around the table and no one took any heed. She looked at the jug. He could squeeze the milk out of a cow's wrinkly teats, but he couldn't squeeze it out of this. She picked up the jug. She poured, and the milk smelt of everything. Behind her, she felt her grandmother stir with relief.

All of that before he wanted sugar. All of that before she was left drying the dishes by the sink with her grandmother, who said,

'They'll be yours, someday.'

'Thank you,' she said, wiping the plate and grateful for this, the one cracked reference they had made to the blood between them and her mother who had died.

When Maria gets into the car, pride of place beside Berts, her grandmother sprinkles the whole lot of them with holy water for a safe journey, and her grandfather turns his face away.

'Don't leave it too long,' says Ambrose who shakes Berts hand and waits and watches until they are gone.

During the drive back, she asks Berts where he met her mother.

'We were climbing the pigeon house chimneys one Sunday afternoon, she was on one of them and I was on the other, and we waved to each other when we got to the top.'

'I'm too old for that,' says Maria.

'So I see,' says Berts and he switches on the radio.

Maria looks at the flooded fields. The Shannon has burst its banks and spread like a mirror around Athlone. The fields are full of sky, pierced with grass like frozen, upside-down rain. She sees a swan sailing into the dark mouth of a shed, and the sun comes out at Ballinasloe.

Maria closes her eyes and remembers the cow. She was lying in the front field, tracing a tree on the inside of her eyelids, when she heard a monstrous chewing sound, a broken-hearted swallow. There was a cow leaning over her – four more were swinging their way across the field, their heads lowered, apologetic and huge. The cow dipped down to her bare legs and snuffled – vast quantities of air sucked up through the meat of its nostrils, then blown back out again, wet.

'Ghkgh!' said Maria. Because you need to draw breath, before you can scream. The cow flinched back, like a house in a nervous breakdown. Everyone paused. Then they all wandered forwards again.

'Hup,' said Maria and she lurched back, sidled forwards. Curiosity mixed with dread – as if Maria was some kind of atrocity, a terrible truth that this stupid cow just had to see.

'Hup!' They could do this all afternoon.

That was Monday. On Easter Saturday, there was the rain.

Maria had never seen rain before. She had never seen rain that started a mile away, a high smudge under the clouds. It looked different to everything – like the bit of a drawing you tried to rub out with your finger.

Soon I will be inside that rain, she thought. I will be there.

When she turned round, it was closer again. It was hitting the ground now, a curtain of water slicing, drop over drop, towards her across the land. She raced into the barn, climbed into the high hay and watched as it whispered up, spattered, then loosed itself like a thousand pencils dropping on the roof. She turned and sprawled on her back, flinging her arms wide.

'I am the king,' she shouted. Then she jumped up and ran to where the hay met the back wall. If I fell down there, she thought, I could die in the hay. Ambrose would pitch me out with his fork. His fork would crunch into the hay and then into something else. The corpse in the hay. He would pitch me out over his shoulder and shout as he saw me flying over him in the air, grinning and floppy. She stuck one leg down to try it, all the way to her thigh, then she pulled it out again. She ran down the hay, high up under the stunned roof, shouting 'La lah lah' while the rain glazed the sides of the barn in three wet sheets and the smell of dead grass began to rise.

Maria buzzed around the barn, and itched where the hay caught her. If you had asked what she was then, she would not have been able to tell you. Out in the rain she would have been wet, she would have been a girl from Dublin caught in the rain, but here in the barn she was anything at all.

Then she saw Ambrose, his shoulders slumped in the wet, his cap pulled down. Ambrose was the patron of bees and the rain dropped around him, grey and golden in the light. Ambrose was the beekeeper, he was sweet and stingy, and when he moved he moved altogether, in a swarm. His skin was warm and tiny muscles danced under it, and when he walked in the rain, the drops fell between all the separate pieces of him, and kept him dry.

He stood inside the barn, pushed his cap back and wiped his face with his hand while Maria watched him from the top of the hay. This is what people are like when they are on their own. She waited for him to do something strange, but Ambrose was always on his own, even when he knew you were watching him. His eyes did not get glassy and happy, like Uncle John's, pretending you weren't there.

Maria took hold of the swing, leaned back, then swooped across the barn. She saw Ambrose jerk past. Then she saw him break into a run, so that by the time she had slithered down off the high hay, he was there to take her by the collar, and swing her around. His free arm chased her, then hit her like a board on the backside. Maria stopped laughing. Ambrose hitched her up by the collar until she was standing, and for a moment she knew exactly what was going to happen, before his hand caught the back of her head, sending her sprawling into the hay.

'Shush now,' he said. 'You gave me a fright, is all.' Holding his hand away from his side, and shaking it, as he walked to the cowshed door.

But, as far as she could tell, Maria wasn't even crying.

That was Saturday. On Sunday there was the book.

After dinner, Maria opened the door of her uncle's room by-accident-on-purpose and looked in at the two beds. One bed was not made, the sheets wrinkled and exposed; pink brush nylon, and 'Oh,' she thought, 'oh.' The room was full of her uncles' lives, years and years of it. Ambrose asleep night after night – there wasn't a single night that he didn't sleep. John at the weekends, coming in after a dance maybe, his brother stirring at the sound of his shoes dropping in the dark.

Maria walked in and opened a drawer. It was full of brown envelopes and bits of paper done up in elastic bands. She realised that she was looking for a picture of her mother so she went to her grandparents' room instead. But there was a chair inside the door, with a potty fitted into the seat, and there was something in the potty, so she could not pass.

Maria went into the front parlour and checked the china cabinet. She found a Bible with a thick page at the front, printed in red and gold. Along the dotted lines, someone had written a list of names and dates, in spidery black ink.

Valentine	born: 1928	died:
Anna	born: 1929	died: 1965
Brendan	born: 1929	died: 1934
Ambrose	born: 1935	died:
Catherine	born: 1936	died:
John	born: 1938	died:

Maria whispered the names aloud. She tried to learn them off by heart, but they kept sliding around.

'Who's Valentine?' she said to John.

'Where did you pick that one up?' he said.

'Who's Catherine?'

'Catherine,' he said and sighed. 'It was Katie. She's your Auntie Katie in London. Or she's in America now.'

'And who's Valentine?'

He slashed at the grass with his scarred left hand.

'Will you come to the dance?' he said. 'Are you dancing?' but Maria said nothing.

'Where is he?'

'Lost,' he said. 'Don't worry. He was no good.'

Maria sits in the car with her eyes closed, the hot trees flicking across her eyelids. She is on the road to Dublin. Two days ago she could not even imagine school, now she remembers the homework she has to do. Hard stuff: the Aimsir Gnathchaite. We always used to. Didn't you always used to? The Past Continuous – always, always, in the past. Or, at least, all the time.

'Mammy, didn't you always used to? Didn't you always used to walk down that road, when you were little? Didn't you always used to clear the china, and stand at the back of the milking parlour at night? Always like that? Always, when your father did the milking? And wasn't it always by hand?'

'Yes, always.'

'And what else did you used to do, always?'

'I always used to go into the front field. I always used to like it.'

And Maria is on her way home, the road unravelling behind her.

Because her mother was there once, but now she is gone. Her mother walked down the avenue once, in her summer dress, or once in her coat, or once with her schoolbag: she walked in her bare feet or her Sunday shoes or her winter shoes, sad or happy or singing or silent, but always down the avenue. And each time she walked, she was already gone. There was no 'always' in it – just a kind of repetition.

Nothing happened in that place that had not happened before, that would not happen again. The lifted teacup. The joint sitting there, like a tear in the cloth. The four fingers and a thumb sticking back into the glove, tickling the blood, like an udder that had run back into itself and would not come right.

Everything there was like a memory, even as it happened. No wonder they didn't talk about her. No wonder they didn't talk about anything at all.

Her grandfather leaning his face towards her.

'You might have died inside her. You have your father to thank for that.'

He said that on Holy Saturday. On Easter Sunday, they went to Mass.

Berts stops the car for lemonade. They eat the sandwiches by the side of the road and he takes out the bottle of tea her grandmother gave them, with the milk and sugar already in it. He slings the bottle across the ditch.

'They wouldn't know a flush toilet, that lot,' he says. 'If it jumped up and bit them on the backside.'

Maria laughs, but when they get home, something unfair starts to happen to her. Her chest starts to go all stupid and so do her eyes. She has a feeling like there is someone always coming around the corner, who never arrives. The sight of crockery makes her so mad, she would smash a dish sooner than wash it.

'No one said it was easy,' says Evelyn, who gives her a plastic bag full of meshed-up cotton and safety pins for no reason at all. But her little brother Cormac is delighted.

'Girl,' he says. 'Girl, girl. Girly girl girl. Girl girl, girly, girly, girl, girl.'

The Country of the Lost

New York, 1985

Outside her window, the city started to hum. It wasn't so much a noise as a tightening of the air that you forgot and lived in for the rest of the day.

Anton seemed to make a decision in his sleep, he turned on his side and Maria held her breath. It was bright now. He was sleeping the thoughtful sleep that day brings. He was back in the room.

If he opened his eyes now, he would see her sitting there, a bloody foot, a stained thigh. A blunt knife. A dark crotch.

Maria wanted to leave this picture for him, somehow, when he woke, but she didn't want to be there herself. She slipped out of the chair (leaving herself in the chair) and put on yesterday's dress. Her bloody foot slipped and stuck to her sandal as she made her way across the floor.

She looked back at him, before she shut the door, and at the melodrama of the empty room. What a joke. She listened for the soft thunk of the cross-bar as she locked him in. Then she walked down the stairs.

It was 6 a.m. in New York. People were on their way to work, their faces heavy with the night before. They seemed so real and automatic. Maria walked by them, dizzy in the thin light, all those brute human beings, with their muscle and lymph and bone. They walked down a street in Manhattan like a herd of bison, quiet and astonishing in the fact of themselves.

Maria floated by, checking the ghost of her reflection in shop windows, looking at the fragments of her face that bulged and swung past in the fat bonnets of cars. She expected, at any moment, to see herself – her real self – turn a corner and wave, and say hello.

In Washington Square, she sat down on a bench and waited and watched. A woman walked by with a Spanish greyhound. She was expensively dressed and running to fat. Behind her the dog barely touched the ground. It was spring-loaded, a grey question mark. The arch of its loins was so high it looked like its bollocks hung down from its back.

Later, she found herself outside an Italian bakery on Bleecker Street watching a film being shot on the other side of the road. A man stopped at a vegetable stall to check out a melon. Another man passed by. A couple came out of the shop door, laughing.

They did it four times and still Maria couldn't tell what the story was. She couldn't tell who was really in the film and who would just keep walking out of frame.

It started to rain and people ran around with sheets of plastic. The actors rushed together under the canopy of the vegetable stall. They chatted, as though they had known each other all along. The smell of fresh pastry rose from the shop behind her. Maria turned around and walked in the door.

Inside there were three small tables and a high glass counter the length of the room. The people behind it were laughing, as if no one was there. Maria pointed out a pastry to a middle-aged woman who reached for it, and swung her backside to the left, dodging the tea towel a younger man flicked at her backside.

Outside, the street began to fill with water.

'Everything floods in this town,' said a man at the table behind her. 'Everything floods.'

The cake was warm and savoury, melted through with ricotta cheese. It was the best thing she ever ate.

She watched the rain slice down in mirrored sheets. It was so heavy the drops shattered, as they bounced back up, into a knee-high haze. Maria walked out into it, feeling the weight of the water on her shoulders, and the lightness of the drops that trickled into the hollow of her back. The cut above her ankle started to sting, and the blood ran again, under the arch of her foot.

By the time the rain had stopped Maria was somewhere else. She was walking on new streets, full of different people. The sidewalk began to steam. She had to pause, to remember what she was doing here, and which was the way home.

She began to spot the other people, stalled or stopped, who stood there and wanted the crowd to wash past them. A man endlessly studying doorbells under the swelling stone breast of a sphinx. A regulation drunk, sitting on the sidewalk, his face working in slow motion, as though every emotion was a puzzle to him, and the solution always a surprise.

Maria was in the country of the lost. They were everywhere – a small man with a chair strapped to his back walking down Varick Street, a woman in the middle of Broadway, going through the contents of her handbag as the cars swerved past. It was a parallel world. It was just over the other side. Maria had always known it was there, but, now she was in it, she did not know how to get back out again.

The city was full of doors that led to God knows where. She opened one of them, and was back in her own room.

Anton was walking towards the door as she opened it. He stopped when he saw her face.

Maria sat in the chair and Anton looked out the window. Anton sat on the end of the bed while she stood by the counter, gathering crumbs with the side of her hand. Anton went into the bathroom and came back out again, too soon. The row was like a marriage after the affair – so clichéd it couldn't be real. Except, somehow, it was the wrong way around.

'Who is she, Anton?'

57

'What are you doing, going through my things? What are you doing?'

'Just tell me.'

'Give me that, that's mine.'

He had packed his bag.

'Who is she?'

'What do you mean? She's a girl.'

'No she's not. She's not just a girl.'

'Jesus. Give that to me, will you?'

'She's me.'

She swept the crumbs off the counter, slowly. He looked at the floor. He said, 'Any chance of a cup of coffee? Do you want coffee?'

After a while he raised his head and looked at her. His eyes stayed the same but his gaze seemed to widen.

'Hang on.'

'She's me.'

He came back into the room. 'She's a girl I knew. For about two seconds in, Jesus, in 1977.'

'Why did you keep it, then?'

'She was a girl.'

'Did you fuck her?'

He started to laugh. Other things happened. He picked up his bag.

'You don't believe me,' she said.

'Believe what? There's nothing to believe.'

He walked over to her with his hand outstretched and gestured for the photo.

'Why did you fuck me in the first place?' she said. 'Why did you fuck me at all?'

Later he said, 'Will I ring Cassie?'

'Why?'

'I'm going out. Do you want me to ring someone? I'm going out for a while.'

She said, 'You haven't listened to me. You haven't listened to anything.'

He touched her shoulder. She flinched away. She threw

the coffee pot at him, she picked up the knife. He was stained with coffee. She threw a newspaper at him and the sheets separated as they flew through the air. He caught her arms and her wrists were bruised. She turned to the wall and hunched over. She faced him and smiled. She pulled her shirt open and leant towards him, jeering. He walked towards her and she whimpered.

He put his hand on the latch. He let his hand drop. He sat down on the chair and looked at her. He said,

'Jesus. This town.'

Then he left.

3

Dublin
21 April 1987

Electricity

The only way Evelyn could meet Maria, when she came back from New York, was by going into a shop in the centre of town, taking some clothes off a rail and going into the fitting room where she worked. Maria spent her day handing out plastic numbers to women who came through the curtain, saying 'That's really nice' every once in a while, 'That really suits you'. It wasn't much of a life, unless the child was a lesbian, but she was glad to have her back in the country. God knows why. Just in case there was a funeral to attend. It would save the cost of a flight.

Maria said she wasn't actually home. She wanted to work in an airport, she said, and this was the next best thing. She was waiting for something and Evelyn did not know what it was. Every couple of weeks she came in to see if she had found it yet and each time she came into the shop she hoped to find her gone.

Evelyn hated the centre of town. There were security guards to pass and the girls behind the cash registers picking at bits of themselves. One day she would steal something by mistake. In the meantime she took real clothes into Maria's fitting room, in her own size. She even tried them on. Once, she bought a dress.

It was one of those communal changing rooms, a smelly, underwater sort of place with mirrors the length and breadth of opposite walls. There were three cubicles at the far end, with scraps of doors – you might as well be in the middle of Grafton Street for all they hid. You had to come out anyway, to see what you were trying on. Evelyn tried to take decent things in with her, so she wouldn't look like a

63

fool as she stood there, exchanging a few words. It wasn't easy.

'Any news?' she said, in a red, raggedy, tart's dress, with handkerchief ends.

'Anything strange or startling?' in a houndstooth hacking jacket, very Protestant, her big backside sticking out the vent.

'Are you all right for money?' in the palest blue. The things she had to do to see a girl who was not even her daughter, who was barely polite.

'Cormac's moving up again. He's decided to specialise.' This in a gathered floral thing that made her look like an alcoholic. 'I am a barrister's mother,' she thought. Even if he was still a student, she should try to look the part.

'So how are you?' she said, in a fluffy cardigan, in a pair of Capri pants (quite nice), in a Nehru jacket with a peacock sheen.

'How are you?' she said in a skirt with her top off, in a blouse with her legs on display. While Maria stood there, in a plain white shirt and black skirt – the only one who never had to change.

'Suits you,' she would say. 'No, really.' The little bitch. She wouldn't get rid of her that easy.

When they first met, the child had tried to strangle her with her own jewellery and Berts had kissed her neck. And so it went. Evelyn knew, for the first time, what it was to be wanted, and that it had nothing to do with her. Another woman would have done just as well, a woman in a houndstooth hacking jacket, a woman in the palest blue. Never mind. Evelyn made her own clothes and she was good at it.

She made wedding dresses for the neighbours' daughters for pin money, working in cotton gloves so her sweat would not stain the silk, tacking and stitching their agitated flesh into the rolling sea-calm of the dress. They all wanted ruffles. No innocence without frills, no love without a fuss. Someday she would dress Laura, her youngest, plain as an

64

arctic fox with her red hair; in the meantime she fussed them up good and proper, all shriek and suspenders.

'So, how's the love life?'

'Sorry?' She would not be making one for Maria, not at this rate.

'Is there anything you need?'

'Like what?'

And Evelyn would change back into her own clothes with a grim smile. Because this is what they shared – they owed nothing to anybody, not even to each other. And this is what brought Evelyn back through the streets full of young people with their longer legs and better skin and loud deflowered voices, to see a woman who wasn't even her daughter, but who had the same embarrassing laugh – they were free. Life had put them in the same room, they might as well take a look at each other now and then. Though you got the feeling from Maria that she did not even look at herself, with that acre of mirror in front of her. And although freedom made Evelyn kind (because you might as well) it made this woman who wasn't her daughter unimportant and small. Evelyn was not important, but she knew how to pour someone a cup of tea like it was an important thing to do. How did other people grow, when Maria just shrank?

'She's got a job.'

'Has she?' said Berts. And there was no use getting annoyed with him. She was in charge of things like that, family, the telephone, Christmas. While Berts – well, Berts was just in charge. Evelyn felt the unfairness of it. Because Maria had always been hard. The child did everything on time, from sitting on the potty to going on the pill, like she had read the book on how to grow up. But she never had the gift of liking things. She would love you if she had to, but liking was another matter.

'As a shop assistant.'

Berts took a piece of gristle out of his mouth and laid it on the side of the plate.

'So what do you want me to do about it?' he said, and his silence spread and became unpleasant. Evelyn decided not to embarrass him with her trips to town, but she still went back, for the barest of reasons. At least she was able to hold her head up in front of the neighbours and say, when asked, that Maria was between things. That is what you said about children these days, that they were between things – you did not say that this was the place they had ended up.

Evelyn checked the knobs of the gas and the lock on the back door. She went from room to room closing what had been left open, unplugging things. The harsh spring sun cut through the windows and bleached her furniture. Everything in this house was clean, and nothing was new. Tomorrow was her fifty-third birthday. If only she liked shopping, she thought, they would have led a different life.

A woman on the radio was talking about electricity. She could not suffer it in the house, she said, she was allergic to the static. She sat ten feet away from the television, and kept a cat on her lap to absorb the rays. And what was the reason for all this?

'My father worked in a power station. He was an older man, Marion,' she said. 'He was fifty when I was born. You know, he'd come home in the evening and I was his little girl. I'd sit in his lap, and really, he'd be just crackling with the stuff.'

Evelyn sighed. The country was falling apart. She stood in front of the hall mirror to do her lipstick. If Evelyn was allergic to anything these days, it was probably the radio. Hundreds of people talking over the airwaves about being ignored, or hit, or loved, or raped. Evelyn had never met a woman who was raped but they were queuing up on Radio Eireann. Raped at seventy, raped at seven. Ireland was packed with men with the strangest lumps in their trousers and still Evelyn couldn't go out the door without a bit of lipstick on.

The house was humming around her, the sockets leaking into the rooms. She left the radio playing, to keep the burglars company, and went out to catch the bus.

The clothes in Maria's shop were for girls who were two sizes smaller and twice as young again. Evelyn settled for a loose batik dress with a bit of shape to the waist and pulled back the curtain to the changing room.

'How'ya,' said Maria.

Evelyn checked the room for other customers. There were six of them, half in and half out of their clothes. They looked stuck.

'One? Is it?' Maria handed Evelyn a blue plastic tag and the women started moving again.

'What do you think?' said Evelyn, holding up the dress.

'Lovely.'

'So how are you?' she said, hanging up her coat and draping her scarf around the hook.

'Fine,' said Maria.

'How's the flat?' as if she had been over there, twice at least, to help run up some curtains or just take a cup of tea.

'It's a bit musty. There was a flood next door,' and they talked about that while Evelyn dived through the hoop of the dress and let the fabric fall to her waist. Maria smiled.

She looked in the mirror.

'What am I like?' she said, looking at the pattern that flowered and cut against her skin.

'No, it's lovely,' said Maria.

'Right,' said Evelyn, letting her tweed skirt drop, but keeping within the rumpled circle it made on the floor.

A woman burst a cheap zip in the corner, with a soft, plastic sigh. She looked at the gape like it had happened in her own stomach and Maria watched as she worked herself out of the trousers, her shoulders and breasts rolling loose. She did not look away. As a child, thought Evelyn, she rarely cried.

'So when are you coming out to see us?'

'That really suits you,' said Maria and she started to unzip.

'Your father says hello.'

'How is he?' said Maria.

'How do you think he is?' Evelyn turned to face Maria. 'I don't think he's well.'

'What's wrong with him?'

'I don't think he's himself.'

'Really,' said Maria. 'How can you tell?' And Evelyn was suddenly fierce. She didn't know everything, this child. What it was like to sleep beside a man all your life and count the breaths he took in the dark. She pulled the dress off her any old how, showing the long sad line of her cleavage, the armpits she had never shaved now sparse and grey. Maria looked away and Evelyn felt that she had won something small, at least. A sense of shame.

'He misses you.'

As soon as she said it, she realised that it was true. When Berts went for walks, Evelyn checked whether she should go with him, or let him go alone. When he came back, she made tea. Later she would ask how it had gone and he would say, 'All right,' as if it was her fault.

'Does he now,' said Maria. Sometimes she thought the child was unnatural. Sometimes just the sight of her, half in the country and half out of it, put Evelyn in a rage.

'Throw it away,' said Evelyn. 'Why don't you?' her voice suddenly too loud.

'Throw what away?'

'You know what I mean,' she was actually shouting. 'I don't know why you came back. I don't know why you bothered. All the things you put us through, and look at you.' They were all watching her now, a copse of women, a mirror full.

Maria made a small gesture, as if for her tag, and the whole place went quiet as Evelyn tried to get the right buttons in the right buttonholes. She pulled the scarf down from its hook and threw her coat across her arm, then she walked along the line of the mirror towards Maria.

'Well?' she said. 'Well?' And she handed the tag back and

68

pushed her way through the curtain into the shop. She walked past the rails of clothes, shrugging herself into her coat, hitting a skirt by accident and knocking it to the floor. She did not pause to pick it up and when she was out the door and into the street, she heard the sound of the alarm go off behind her. This was it, then. Evelyn checked her bag for the dress that she didn't even like, but must have stolen anyway. It was not there. Maria was behind her, swinging her around.

'Sorry,' she said. She had a bundle of trousers in her arms, the hangers dangling and rattling. It was raining, hard.

'You're sorry? What age do you think I am?'

'What's that got to do with it?'

'You'll come out?'

'No, I won't come out,' she said, the rain hitting her face. Evelyn sensed the pain of the child and her vanity.

'Why not?' said Evelyn. 'What are you waiting for?'

'Just.'

They stood in the street, looking at each other like a pair of tinkers. Evelyn wanted to slap her in broad daylight, but she did not. She turned on her heel and walked away. Someone switched off the alarm.

The One-eyed Man is King

Berts crumpled up the wax paper around his sandwiches and threw it in the bin. 'Brennan's Bread', said the wrapper.

'Sufficient unto the day,' said Berts. 'Sufficient unto the day.'

He lit up a cigarette and waited for his insides to ease. After a while he got up and walked across to the window. He had to go out, and the thought did not appeal to him. There were some dirty-looking clouds hanging over the centre of town, and they weren't shifting.

The door opened behind him and Carney's narrow little face slid through the gap.

'Seventy-four grand?' he said. Berts opened his mouth to reply but Carney was gone. Carney was a waster. Lash it out, said Carney, like he was scattering Smarties. The world is a droll place.

Seventy-four grand was nothing; the irony, as always, was in the details. When it came to the details, Carney was a connoisseur.

James Anthony Murphy, welder, of 174 Shandowen Park, had tripped and fallen on a piece of pavement laid and maintained by Dublin Corporation at the corner of Parnell and Cumberland Streets. He had sustained, he said, a bang to the head. In evidence, Mr Doney Sheridan, medical consultant, had stood up on his hind legs and discussed the non-linear transmission of information in the brain: he talked of parallel connections, of recursive connections, of feedforward and feedback. Mr Murphy, in short, had a leaky head. He suffered a range of symptoms: a speech defect that affected the 'K' sound, a problem with the *meaning* of colours (which had ended his welding career) and a strange helplessness when it came to the sense of smell. His patient, said Sheridan, was continually swamped by fragmented scenes from his childhood, which had not been happy. Freshly laid tar was a torment to him. Toast made him cry. Grass cuttings rooted him to the spot. It was not known when or if the symptoms would abate – until they did, his patient lived in an emotional state so heightened as to be disabling. Even in these modern days, the brain was a mysterious and, perhaps fortunately, a private place. Thank you, Mr Sheridan.

James Anthony Murphy stood up, and said that as a C . . . C . . . C(atholic?) . . . C(ream bun?) C . . . areful man, he was not in the habit of tripping over holes in the ground but that this one was a very devious hole in the ground and the street lighting was inadequate. The joke was of course not the stutter but the way he slapped his barrister on the back after the jury came up with seventy-four big ones and said, 'We did it, Corcoran. We creased them,' before walking into the pale blue yonder. Was it true? It was true because it had to be.

Notch it up.

Berts did not have an opinion. It was not his job to have an opinion but sometimes the sheer weight of it got to him. He looked at the stacks of files, heaped on the windowsill and even on the floor. He looked at the map of the city on the wall, stuck with the flags of small disasters. He lived with them. He breathed them in.

The Murrays. Every member of the Murray family had a claim in somewhere. Berts made sure they had the safest path in the city outside their front door. He had checked it himself, a path like silk, poured with love and finished with the workmen's own spit. And here was the latest: an 'incident' with some traffic cones and pram on the South Circular Road. A pram no less. Throw the little fecker down a pothole, why don't you? Start them young.

Berts' stomach was at him again. There was something coating the back of his mouth – pure distaste. He cleared his throat a hundred times a day as he sifted through damaged ankles, whiplash, lumbar strain. Most of it nothing you could put your finger on, not a torn ligament or a decent-sized scar among them – just aches, lots of aching. An occasional swelling. And distress, of course. Buckets of distress.

The city was a vague, shifting injury that did not yield to X-ray; a stiffness, a pain, a relapse; a misalignment of the knee that was putting pressure on the hip that was pulling the lower back out of line. It all ended at the back. Get a good back case and you were made.

Sometimes Berts stood at his window and imagined he could hear the soft sound of bodies hitting concrete, all over town. The world was full of people who fell and gravity was not on his side. None of them ever caught their balance. None of them floated away. They tripped and fell, or pretended to fall, and every day of his life, he fought to make them safe.

'Sufficient unto the day,' he said. 'Sufficient unto the day.' It was one o'clock. Berts lifted his raincoat from the stand by the door, checked the corridor, and slipped along it. Tomorrow was Evelyn's birthday and he had to do the decent thing. He had to, that is, go outside and walk the length of Dame Street, stepping over the cracks.

The weather was soft and electric, threatening rain. Berts hopped over cables that trailed from a television van into the Olympia theatre. He ducked under some scaffolding beside Nico's restaurant and skirted a gas board sign that might as well have said, 'Flash burn'. On Grafton Street the new herringbone red brick looked lovely, but Berts could not face it. He doubled back up to Nassau Street along the walls of Trinity College – full of Japanese tourists digging up the cobblestones.

The granite kerbstones were slipping into the gutter, the gutter was falling down the drain. Today, despite all his work, the city was a subsidence, a slow-stirring trap. The city was full of holes.

What could he get her? Last year he had ended up with a bunch of flowers and the promise of whatever she wanted herself. The year before it was chocolates, but chocolates were wrong, apparently – he didn't even notice she was fat.

'Whatever you want,' he said. 'Anything you want, yourself.'

The worst was the year he put the money in an envelope. It was not the amount, she said at last. It was the raw notes. She had thought it was a card. Could he not give her a blank cheque?

As if, Berts said, they were the kind of people who walked around town waving blank bloody cheques.

This year, he could get her a book maybe, and whatever she wanted herself. He went into Hannas and looked at the cookery section, but the illustrations brought the egg sandwich to the back of his throat. He considered an atlas and put it back down again. He knew what he had to do. He had to go back to the big shops on Grafton Street and buy the wrong perfume. He had to pause over blouses that were too see-through, or too nylon, and examine cases of jewellery that she would pretend to love, and never wear.

Back on Grafton Street, Berts walked under more scaffolding and into the most expensive shop of the lot. He found himself beside the bags: all shapes and sizes like different words – they might as well be talking Japanese. He picked up a kind of purse that said 'money belt' on the label. It was a clever thing. Maybe he coud buy her a 'money belt' and put the famous blank cheque in that.

At one of the perfume counters a woman sprayed her wrist for him and held it to his face. Lovely. They all smelt lovely, he said. But the smell of Evelyn was something else again. He paused by the gloves and tried to remember the size of her hands. He remembered them as milky and freckled and young, but Evelyn was nearly fifty-three. He looked at his own hand, then turned to face the jumble and smell of new things. For ten minutes solid, he looked at blouses and dresses and whatever else they were called. He felt fabrics like a pervert and lifted things off the rail, then the humiliation got too much for him and he left the shop.

There were other places further down the street and Berts tried to move towards them. It was Evelyn's birthday tomorrow and he needed Evelyn. He needed her to laugh at him for the stupid thing he had bought. He needed her, even if he could not remember what she looked like, from time to time.

He pushed through the smell of roasting coffee outside Bewley's, paused, and finally passed the shop where his daughter worked; the mannequins in the window blankly accusing, with their grey, plastic flesh. Warm air ballooned out at him from the open threshold and his whole body was edged in heat. But the security man was smoothing his lips with an unthinking fingertip and his eyes were blank.

On the junction with Chatham Street he found a new tear of black tarmac. The bricks were gouged out around a manhole cover, leaving a bare hole. And sure enough, there was a blind woman walking straight for it, tapping her cane. Over and back, over and back – the cane swung and tapped, as the herringbone brick ran towards him like a closing zip.

She was almost smiling. She lifted her foot over the hole in the road, stepped down, and landed on air. Then she fell the extra two inches, and hit bottom. Her face jolted. She tapped twice, and stepped high, and walked on.

It started to rain.

Suddenly, Berts felt the unfairness of it all. He pushed back down the street, overtaking the blind woman, passing the open door of his daughter's shop. All the brains she had, spoiling away in there. She had shut herself up like an accusation. But he would not be blamed. All the mess of her coming home and her small face like flint.

When she looked at him she did not see him at all. She did not, she could not, see the truth. Because the only truth of it was that every day of his life he had fought to make her safe.

Berts swung in through the doors of Brown Thomas's

74

and sank into the deep pile of the grey carpet. He passed the lipsticks and potions, with the girls like psychiatric nurses in their white coats. He stopped at the handbags and disentangled the money belt from the heap of hollow leather with their clasps and straps. Then he went up to the assistant, with her fake accent, and her smile.

When he got back to the office, of course, he realised he had no wrapping paper, and had to send out one of the girls.

Spilt Milk

Evelyn had a cup of coffee and an almond bun in Bewley's to calm herself down, moving the cup from the saucer to her mouth and back again; coaxing herself, like a baby, to take and measure and spit nothing out. She gathered her things around her once more: the strap of her handbag wound around her ankle, her scarf on her lap, the old woman she had chosen to sit with, chewing away on the other side of the table.

'Desperate rain.'

'. . . the like of it.'

She lifted the cup and set it down again, wondering if the iron had eaten its way through the board by now. The radio was still on, leaking into the kitchen, people talking about allergies – allergic to their own ear wax, allergic to the spit in their mouths.

She thought about Cormac wheezing and scratching as a baby, wondered was that what had made him vicious as a child. She thought about Maria, allergic to the sight of herself in a mirror. And Laura eating bits of herself like she could whittle herself away. Evelyn had wanted to make a go of her children, to make friends of them, but they were all strangers to her still. If you thought about it, it was the loneliest job of them all.

Evelyn sighed. She checked the woman opposite, to see if she had been talking out loud.

Thyroid. There was a goitre hanging out over the brooch at her neck, lopsided, like testicles. Evelyn should have been a doctor, she'd have had her out of the surgery in three minutes flat.

The woman was wrapping a paper napkin around the

uneaten half of her bun. She put it into her handbag, glanced at Evelyn, and snapped the bag shut. Mad, obviously.

Evelyn closed her eyes and wished that she, too, could be odd. She wished she could be the kind of woman who said, 'It's the electricity gives me headaches, Marion, I know it is.' But she was not. Of course she was not. She had loved her children too much, that was all.

She remembered a trip they had taken up to Turlough Hill – Berts driving them up to see it one Sunday afternoon. The electricity station built under the mountain; an artificial lake at the top and a real lake spreading at its root. At night they pumped water up the slope, then let it run back down to spin the turbines during the day. It was like pouring milk from cup to cup, over and back with nothing spilt, and it eased Evelyn to sleep, the thought of the electricity spinning out all day, the water flowing uphill while she slept.

They had gone out to see it in the new Ford Cortina and Evelyn, three months gone, still did not know if she should sit in the front seat or the back. The younger women on the road knew these things, knew absolutely you should sit in the back after the second month, or in the front with no seat belt, when you got the new car. But Evelyn had no one to ask. She had come to this road too late: with too many clothes and a habit of going to the theatre. There was too much of the spinster left in her. She sat in the front of the new Ford Cortina with Laura on her lap, and didn't care.

They drove up the military road, past the bogs of the Featherbed and over the Sally Gap. They sat in the car and looked at the mountain brim-full of water. The line of pylons straddling ditches, and clambering hedges, all the way home.

This was being married. Berts' profile beside her. The ease of a car. This was the difference.

They climbed the slope by an Aztec path and, when they reached the top, stared into the concrete crater and its lake. It was huge. Evelyn looked at the sheer sides of the basin.

She imagined the workmen hanging there on ropes, the wet concrete spilling down the slope towards them, their boards patting and sucking it smooth.

'A very Irish volcano,' said Berts. 'All water.' He said it like 'wa-ther' so that Evelyn would know it was a joke.

They took out a plug at the bottom, during the day, so the wa-ther rushed down to make the electricity, then they used the electricity to pump it back up again. It didn't make sense to Evelyn; surely something was lost along the way?

Berts said maybe it was rain that made the difference.

But she pictured it at night, when she was frightened and thought, with this baby, she could just leak away. The rest of her life could just leak away. She thought of the economy of it, the buildings humming in the heart of the mountain, the pool at its foot, and the serene cup set in its tip.

But she could not hold on to it. Evelyn already had her babies – not enough of them, and too late. Laura was the last, and after Laura came the unmentionables, the clots and spoils in the bath or toilet that told her how old she really was. In her head she tiled the bathroom blue-for-a-boy, pink-for-a-girl. Finally she settled on Scandinavian pine, because there was something heartless about grouting, the way it told you how liquid the body was, inside.

The woman opposite was wrapping up the remains of the jam and the charms on her bracelet jumped and shook. There was something wrong with her husband and Evelyn was not wife enough to know what it was.

She had always felt like an impostor.

But Berts had carried Cormac on his shoulders that day at Turlough Hill, and they had looked so fine. Laura in her own arms, Maria running ahead. Who could say they had not been happy? Or done their best?

Evelyn unwound the strap of her bag from around her ankle. It was time to go home, to switch off the radio, then switch it back on when the silence had settled. She would go down to Hickey's for a packet of interfacing and catch the bus. She shook out her scarf as the woman opposite put the jam into her handbag. Evelyn was worried about the lining, smeared and unhygienic. She rose to leave and saw that the bag was already full of loose sugar. The sight made her halt halfway, like she had a twinge in her back.

There was something she had forgotten and she did not know what it was.

'Has it stopped raining?'

Perhaps that was it. The rain. Maybe the rain was the thing she had forgotten.

'I think so,' said Evelyn. 'It must have, by now.'

That night Evelyn dreamt of sperm and the smell maddened her. It lingered in the morning and made her ashamed. It was her fifty-third birthday. Time to throw things out, she thought, and started with a plastic bag full of shoes that had taken the shape of her feet. Ghost steps, and all the wanderings she had never made, knotted at the top and left out for the bin men, waltzing in the quiet, in the rain.

Eeny Meeny Miny Mo

Sr Misericordia bought a bunch of freesias on Grafton Street and decided that they were for herself.

'See that woman?' said the flowerseller.

Every time a stranger talked to her for no reason Misericordia thought they knew she was a nun. It was true that her shoes were sensible and her tights a little too thick, but she had been plain Maura for years and sometimes, on a Friday, she had too many gins for the hell of it. So,

'What woman?' she said, in her 'kind' voice.

'That one. The one with the cane.'

Maura looked at the blind woman tapping her way through the scent of the flowers, rising in the rain. Her coat was a sad, vivid, blind-woman's blue.

'What about her?'

'She's not blind,' said the flowerseller.

'What?'

'She's not blind at all.' They watched then in silence, as the people parted ahead of her. She certainly walked very fast.

'Really?'

'Look at her,' and there did seem to be something more than real about how she made her way. Maura smiled. Yes, it could be nice, all those people scuttling out of your way, the famous white cane, your eyes rolling in your head. A man she passed looked back to see her safe and Maura felt a pang at his kindness. She looked at him for a second, then back at the 'blind' woman as she walked into the iron upright of some new scaffolding outside Brown Thomas, face first.

'Would you look at that?' said the flowerseller. 'She heard me talking.'

It spoiled the freesias, of course, those innocent, small flowers that brought Maura back to the May altars of childhood and to country weddings. That brought her back, if she was honest, to her own wedding, lying face down on the church floor. Sometimes she thought she had married a set of octagonal marble tiles.

Maura stood back from the small crystal vase and sighed, asking forgiveness of Jesus, whom she still loved for all kinds of reasons, though none of them the marrying kind. She took the Foot Spa out from under the bed, filled it with water at the sink, pushed off her shoes and, deliciously, pulled down her tights. She sat on the bed and lowered her feet, so the skin sucked at the hot water and let it go. Then she sank them in and switched it on.

Bliss. After a while she flopped back on to the bed and flung her arms wide, thinking about nothing while the Spa hummed and sloshed on the floor. The peppery, childish scent of the freesias drifted towards her and she found herself laughing, a giddiness at the base of her stomach that caught and spread, until it burst outright into the bare box of her room. Such a big, intimate sound – laughing on your back – the sound that babies make, the sound of summer parks and probably of sex. Maura tried to stop herself but couldn't. She rolled over, finally, her feet dangling and dripping over the carpet as she pulled herself up, her stomach sore.

'Look at that. She heard me talking.'

Well, she hadn't lost it, anyway. She always had a big laugh, never mind the name. Sr Misericordia, Maura Reynolds, The Misery, picked up her small towel and started to dry her feet, toe by toe.

Eeeny meeny miny mo.

She emptied the Foot Spa into the sink. She threw the rumpled balloon of her tights into the tepid water and they collapsed into strings as the water drank them down. Maura could not stop watching them. She reached up under her skirt for her knickers and dropped them in too. Then she looked into the mirror over the washstand and said the Our Father slowly and out loud.

What a life.

Dressed and spruce, she walked out into the corridor, Matron Maura Reynolds, wide, capable mouth, big bust, strong waist, warm grey eyes, barely a nun (she would have to do something about that), washed up, sort of, in the Stella Maris Nursing Home.

'And how are you today?'

The woman in the bed said, 'Lovely.'

'Good for you.' Maura checked around the room, saw the dentures fallen on the floor, and gave a reproving glance to the nurse standing beside her. They were useless without their teeth, something hard in the middle of their face.

'What's my name?' the woman gummed as Maura turned to go.

'Bernadette.'

'That's a horrible name.'

'Good girl.'

'Who called me that?' she said. 'It's a horrible name!'

Maura closed the door before the woman got excited. What she had really wanted to go for was tropical medicine, all those fevers and romance. She opened the door again.

'What would you like to be called?'

'Get out!'

'Good girl.'

She had chosen her own name outside the Mater Hospital, when her father was dying. Facing the gathering arms of the steps, she looked up and saw the words written on the portico – MATER MISERICORDIÆ. What she liked best was the way the A and the E stuck together. She was ten at the time.

Of course, when it came to it, she had to lose the 'e' – it wasn't grammatical, apparently. Her first act of humility, when humility was all the rage.

Now, when she thought about what it was that kept her going it was nothing she could mention. The veils were gone, the skirts shortened, all those big names lost or thrown away. Maura stayed in her room in the Stella Maris, with forty lay people and ten dying nuns all in a row. Someday, she would take her own place in one of the beds. In the meantime, she did her job and said her prayers, and who could say it was not enough?

Maybe she had taken the easy way out. Maura had seven brothers, had loved them all too much ever to choose between them. She was a general sort of girl. And death had made her pious, of course, like it was some great secret.

She tried to decide whether to go up the steps on the right or those on the left. She looked up at the portico and, as she spelt out the letters along the base of the triangle, she knew what she was going to be. She knew what a nun was.

Mater Misericordiæ. Mother of Mercy.

'And how are you, Mrs Doyle?'

'Oh yes. Oh certainly.'

Maura pressed the forearm of the woman who was sitting in a chair by the bed, waiting for her mother to die.

'Mrs Doyle?'

'I'm just fine.' The morphine was shining between the surface of her eyes and the faded pigment of her irises, like she was wearing contact lenses that made everything ecstatically clear.

'And how are *you*?' she said.

Maura looked at the daughter and nodded her sympathy. Mrs Doyle should have gone last night or the night before, but her dying was too much of a revelation to her. It was too much fun.

'I'm fine too, Mrs Doyle.' Maura leant over her with a serious face, watching the fear fall into the pupils of her eyes. 'Will you try to relax now?' She found the place where Mrs Doyle was entirely herself, and terrified.

'Will you do your best? For me?'

'Oh.'

Then the fear was gone and the joke was back — something hilarious was just around the corner, which Mrs Doyle could not wait to see.

Maura wound down the morphine to bring back the pain — just a little. Then she changed her mind and racked it back up again. Let the old woman dream.

The parquet was loose and the skirting board needed a coat of paint. Maura made her matron's list as she walked the main corridor, gathering and losing staff as she went. It was a surprise round, at the wrong time of day. The few flowers that found their way into the Stella Maris were set on the windowsills along the corridor, in case they smothered the patients in the night. She passed them in the dusk and caught their scent and found herself flinching before a thing she could not see.

When she looked in on Agatha, the old nun was telling her beads and just nodded to her; the white down of her face glowing golden in the evening light.

'Goodnight, my dear.'

For the first time in a long time, Maura wanted to pray. She went back to her room, scrubbed out her underwear and draped it over the radiator. Then she went through a few files, unwilling to face the task in front of her, which was: to take off her uniform and hang it up and put on her nightie and get down on her knees, stretch her arms across the bedspread and say nothing, in English, Latin, or Irish, but wait for the knowledge that God was there, if she could just reach out to him.

The words on the page were a blur so she closed the file and began to undress, dreading the moment, knowing that when it came she would give a quick Hail Holy Queen and jump in between the sheets. God was just there, if she could reach out to him. But she would not. It would break her in two.

'O clement O loving O sweet,' she finished in jig time, got into bed and pedalled her legs along the sheets to warm them up. She settled herself on her back and, deliberately, started to fall asleep, starting at the tips of her toes. She was all the way up to her neck when she jolted awake, catching herself from falling down a flight of steps that was not there.

At five o'clock Maura was awake again, without knowing how. She was fighting with Agatha about washing. Agatha telling her not to walk so fast, for a hundred reasons, from modesty to dignity and back by way of the suffering Christ. When the whole convent could hear the laundry sister shouting about sweat. The laundry sister was from Gardiner Street and suffered from winter nerves when the drying was bad, and that was the whole fact of it – never mind the suffering Christ. So was Agatha lying? Who could tell? Agatha was a saint. A woman who said three novenas before breakfast and had various disgusting ways with the contents of her nose. She would outlive them all.

Maura groaned as she got out of bed and started the night walk. Five paces to the far wall, which was cool to the touch, then five paces back to the door. In recent years this circling just made it worse, so she sat down at her desk again, and tried to bore herself to sleep.

The file was one of Agatha's. The bishop's secretary had brought them to her room, in an unhygenic heap, because Agatha was old now, because she (of course) would be discreet.

She flicked through and made notes. Hogan, Byrne, O'Brien. She stopped at one name. Albert Delahunty – what Catholic in their right mind would call a child Albert? There were Delahuntys in Mayo but she doubted he was one of them. She looked for his signature – Berts. A Dublin address. She checked for the Birth Cert, found it and stopped. Then she stared for a moment at the wall.

Maura pulled off the rusted paper-clip, spread all the scraps of paper across the table. She felt sleep, and the longing for sleep, come for her in a wave.

She remembered him.

He sat there, twenty-four years old, perhaps. Her own age,

or younger. There was something about him that annoyed her and it took Misericordia a moment before she figured it out. The man's wife had just died in very painful circumstances but he still kept his hat on, even in here, in the heat of the hospital. He was tall and thin, with a stoop that made you want to slap him between the shoulder blades, in a friendly sort of way. She went over to him and lifted him gently by the elbow.

'Come and see.' She led him down to the baby unit where the children were placed in their rows of incubators – that looked like a graveyard under his stupid dreadful gaze.

He walked slowly towards her, his eyes fixed on hers, refusing to look in the box.

It's just a baby. She wanted to reassure him. Just a lovely little baby. Or in this case – thank God – two. As he stopped, she reached out and pulled over the other little mite, so that their incubators were side by side.

He looked from one to the other. There was something very slow about his grief. All babies look the same, but even a man could see that these two looked more the same than most.

'Jesus,' he said. 'Twins,' and she thought she might bring a bit of decency back into the room.

'We baptised them as soon as they came,' she said.

'With no name?' he said.

'No,' she said. 'There was no need.'

'How can you baptise them without a name?'

'You just can.' But he seemed annoyed by it. He reached into his pocket and pulled out a box of cigarettes, then realised where he was and stuffed them back in again.

'So what do you want to call them?' she dipped her hand into the first incubator, as if to teach him that babies can be touched.

'Maria,' he said, abruptly.

'Maria,' she said with a rub of her tummy. 'Lovely. And this one?'

'I said "Maria".' Her hand pulled away from the second child he had blasphemously named, not named at all.

'Well, I can't take them both.'

'Later,' she said. 'Later.'

'What's later? There's no later about it.'

She left him then, trying to switch the name from one to the other to see which one it fitted, and which to leave behind. She walked back along the rows of children: the hundreds of tiny feet, the thousands of tiny toes. By the time she had reached the swing doors he was behind her, grabbing her like she wasn't a nun at all.

'Sister,' he said. 'Please.'

The next day she met him in the same waiting room, lifted him again with a touch on his elbow and led him, down corridors and around corners, into a small courtyard where the spatchcocked building had forgotten a roof. They walked across the broken concrete, in through an old green door and into the secret part of the hospital, the nuns' part. It wasn't used to men. He lumbered along behind her, following the squeak of her shoes.

At Agatha's door, she looked at him long and hard, trying to get him to take off his hat. He didn't want to understand, just took hold of the knob and pushed on through.

Agatha sat surrounded by her files in stacks, a crucifix in front of her and one behind. There was a cupboard with soft drinks and some sherry.

'Some brandy perhaps?' A whiskey. Agatha was one of those Sisters who always gave men drink – in case they might explode maybe, or hit them. Poured it in like lemonade.

'You are right, to do it soon,' said Agatha. 'If you are to do it at all.' She bent her head and Misericordia followed suit. Delahunty lifted his glass, then blushed to see that they were praying. He set the glass back on the desk and did not touch it again.

Agatha lifted her head.

'We will take them both,' she said.

'No,' he said.

'It is God's will, Mr Delahunty. It's not something we can slice up, just to suit ourselves.'

'But I could manage one, Sister.' He wanted her to undo it, this joke. He wanted her to make the world simple again. Just like a man.

But Agatha knew her stuff. By the time he signed the form Delahunty looked like he had been given a child, for which he should be grateful, not like he had just handed one away. Agatha tipped the wink as Misericordia opened the door. She walked ahead of him, chatting about weights and feeds until they were back in the main building and the first Exit sign.

The twins cried all night. Misericordia finally dumped them together in the same incubator, to see if that would quiet them down. She thought about their father, the feel of him at her back, his stupid hat. His first daughter slept with her face to the ceiling, and his second daughter slept with her face to the first. Or perhaps it was the other way around.

Misericordia found herself pausing beside these children through the long shift, breaking her heart with the need to tell between them. She stood in the hospital dark, her two good hands placed on the corners of the incubator. She looked at them, a scrunch of features, a little mess, and all of it twice. And suddenly she doubted the God who made this symmetry – too lazy, suddenly, for difference. He has counted the hairs on our head, she thought, but now and then, he just couldn't be bothered.

Agatha was good with mothers, firm and kind. But there was no one to cry for these mites, or plead for them. No girl who would be grateful, in the long run, that her baby was gone. Because they had no mother.

No mother. It was like a gash on your soul, and Misericordia prayed for the Virgin to protect them, and the whole, motherless world. She prayed until she could see her, standing with her hands placed, as her own hands were placed, on the other end of the little glass box.

The blue veil, the slender wrists, the tear that stayed on her smooth cheek and did not fall. Misericordia closed her eyes and the Virgin was imprinted like a negative on her eyelids. It was not a true vision, she knew that – it did not move, did not amaze, or relieve her. And she knew it was for herself she prayed and not for the children at all.

So when Delahunty came to get a baby she looked away, so as not to see which he took and which he left behind. She doubted whether he could tell between them, anyway – which he had marked, and which left blank. And when she registered the remaining child, the word she went to write was 'Maria' because, quite simply, she did not care. Either or, she thought. Either or.

When she registered the child, the word she went to write was 'Maria', but her heart failed at the last letter. Because one slept facing the ceiling and the other slept facing the first, and this was all the goodness that God allowed, a difference between one breath and the next, a lapse of the heart. When she registered the child the word she finished writing was 'Marie'. Knowing that A for E and E for A, she had named them for the hopes she used to have, and not to honour the Virgin at all.

Mater Misericordiæ.

Maura Reynolds looked at the file spread over her desk. It was all there in front of her: a set of adoption papers; a birth cert; a faded request from a girl living in England. She looked at the child's handwriting, all grown up: she looked at her own handwriting, from when she was still a child.

Innocent days. Six months later they had moved her into geriatric care, and no wonder. E for A. It was an act of the imagination, more pragmatic than real. It was the kind of thing she had lived for, in those days.

Maura slipped the paper-clip back into its U of rust and felt something welling inside her. What was it? She twisted in her chair and appealed to the room, to the knickers on the radiator, to the freesias and the crucifix and the four bare walls. What was it? It was a sort of silent roar. It was herself.

It was what she had turned out to be – a fifty-year-old, God-hating nun, patient and raucous and hungering for mankind.

Maura Reynolds was running down the corridor – an impossible thing. The matron in her nightie. Of course she never got ahead; she took risks like this and didn't care. She slipped through the rectangular pools of light, ducking the shadows as they came up to hit her. She was on her way to Agatha's room, the words she would say rushing through her head. If it weren't for you Agatha, that's what she wanted to say. If it weren't for you I could be matron of somewhere like the Mater by now, down to the portico, down to the words over the door. Every day you thwarted me. Every day. You old saint. You nose-picker. Every day you told me that this was what God wanted. And I stayed down while you rose up – all the way.

She reached Agatha's door and caught her breath. When she opened it, she saw something she had never imagined possible. The old bitch was asleep. The moonlight shimmered in the white down that covered her face, even to the tip of her nose. Maura placed her hand flat on her chest. She dipped her head and was turning to leave when she saw Agatha's eyes open, and a wide-awake voice slip from her face.

'Yes, my darling. What is it this time?'

4

Rose

Rose floated up from the bottom of the pool, face first. She broke the surface, then rolled back in again. She swam underwater all the way to the rail, before hauling herself out into the shouting and the noise. Then she stood on the edge, while everyone looked at her huge bottom and her stupid breasts. She knew they were looking by the way her nipples tingled and bruised in the moment she took to straighten, and draw breath, and dive again.

Did she close her eyes as she hit the water? There she was, back in the thick blue, pulling herself all the way down to the floor. She tipped her fingers along the tiles, until she saw the deep central plug, matted with hair and hung with a spiralling, spent elastoplast. Slowly she stopped, curled in on herself and stretched out, already rising.

She looked at the view.

The surface of the pool was hung with legs. She loved the way they dangled and opened, the white heels jabbing down. She loved the secret, flat space boys had, under there.

The new one was over by the wall; she caught sight of his trunks that were underpants really, even though they had pictures of mermaids on them in purple and green. She thought about yanking them down, but she was rising faster now, and lighter. She was pulled up mouth first, her lips swelling, a space opening in her head.

The break was gentle. Rose let the water suck away from her face, pulled in the chemical air and rolled over on her side. She lay there a second, then bobbed into a duck-dive

93

and swam underwater to where the new boy's legs hung by the rail.

He was breathing hard. She could see his stomach bulge and suck. One arm circled just under the surface, grabbing the water. His legs were skinny and white. His head was gone.

The underpants were too thin, really, for getting wet. Rose looked at the mermaids and laughed, a clutch of bubbles loosening from her mouth. She found the floor with her feet, shot out in front of his face, took the top of his head and pushed down. The boy's body loosened in the water below her and she wrapped her legs around his neck, wedging her shoulders under the rail. She could feel his thin little face panicking into her stomach, then he went still and punched up close, between her legs. Rose didn't hear the whistle. The lifeguard pushed her down from the rail, grabbed her under the arms and lifted her out clear; her legs still clamped around the boy's neck. He dumped her back from the pool and the boy's head bounced on her stomach, belching water. Then it clunked against the tiles between her thighs, and did not move.

She looked at him.

This was the new boy. This was the one who would not give up.

You would think he was simple, but Rose knew that he was not, because he would not touch the cats. All her life there had been boys who came and went, but first and last, there were the cats. They filled the back kitchen, rubbing against things, hoiking their horrible pink holes into the air. Her mother fed and petted them, talking low and silly. She had a weakness for strays: toms with broken tails, boys who chewed their lips so their mouth was just a rash. Her mother fed everything and everybody. She smelt of cat's piss and Camay and it was sometimes hard to love her.

The boys were always twelve, or thereabouts. They never could tell what they had done wrong, though there

94

were lots of re-enactments with the cats in the back kitchen. Annoying the cats was the only crime in this crime-free house, where people were just as good as they could be. Where Rose was expected to sit up straight and get her peas on to the slope of her fork and chat about school, while some cretin chewed with his mouth open and scratched his crotch. Her mother saying 'Seconds?' in that chirpy polite voice that made Rose just scream. Nothing they did was bad. Smashing, stealing, spitting – all these she was supposed to Understand. But annoying the cats was a different matter. Teasing the cats, damaging the cats, experimenting on the cats in a scientific fashion, meant just one thing – the social worker putting you in the back of a Fiat with the child lock on and driving you off to the Home. Annoying the cats was Rose's favourite game, though she never touched them herself. It stopped the boys annoying her and it taught the cats a thing or two about the big bad world. It also, if she was lucky, shamed the boys from coming back, as they did come back, for money or a bed, while her parents believed them time after time, and were robbed so often they didn't bother replacing the telly any more. Rose was the only girl she knew who never saw *Top of the Pops*.

Rose locked her bedroom door, opened her drawers and rearranged her things: dolls on the bed, beads in a bowl, the windowsill paved with shells and stones. She sat on the bed and tickled her face with a gonk's blue hair. The room was so silent – the dolls were dead plastic, the stones were just stones. She wondered what she used to play at, or who she used to talk to, in here.

Twelve years old. No telly. A sore chest. Outside, the wind sent the leaves of the beech tree slapping against the glass. The more she grew, the more chance Rose had of catching the boys up. She couldn't tell what might happen when she passed them out.

She looked at the picture of Adam and Eve that had hung on the wall as long as she could remember. Her long fat stomach, those flabby legs, the weak little hands. Eve was just born. She never had to grow up, never had to be a child, she didn't have to wait for her first period, or watch her breasts to see if the left one would ever catch up. She just woke up in the garden with her finger stuck in Adam's belly-button, and was madly in love.

Above all, she didn't have parents, like Rose had parents. These people with their old bodies and soft, stupid words. These people who really LOVED you. Rose's father was a doctor, but that was no use to her − he would say 'mucal discharge' as soon as 'pass the teapot', she couldn't invite anyone back. In school, she told people The Facts of Life and no one believed her. When she came home the basement was full of smelly people with their diseases, the back of the house was full of cats. And upstairs, banging his head off the wall or picking his scabs, was The New Boy, waiting for her.

The secret was to let them stew. Rose would go into the drawing room and play a few simple tunes on the piano, then go humming through the house. After a while she might look in the door of his bedroom, wearing something simple and girlish and very frightening. Or she would leave him until dinnertime, say 'Hello, you' as she came into the kitchen, then stoop to feel the thin, light skull of the nearest cat.

It always worked.

In the weeks that followed, she would feel him circle her, while she sat, her hands folded in her lap. She sipped her tea, she chattered gaily, she skipped down the drive singing 'la la la'. And just when he was about to lash out − to pull her hair, or mark her white arms − she would pick up a kitten and say 'Oh, poor pussy'.

It always worked, though the waiting was hard. It was hard to sit still with your legs crossed and your mouth curved in a little smile. It was hard not to speak. While she waited, Rose told herself stories. She was the child of a

96

ballet dancer, she was the child of a spy, on the run. But she knew there was no need to explain herself to them. That was what the waiting was for.

Rose came in from school with her gym bag over her shoulder and checked the hallstand. An anorak, dirty blue, with quilted orange lining. She decided to go out into the back garden and play on the swing. Rose hated the swing. She was too old for the swing. But her mother had trained a clematis down the sides of the chain and it was in flower, so she went out to play on the swing.

After a while, she ran back into the kitchen and poured herself a glass of orange juice. She took a straw and sipped while she walked through the garden, swaying slightly from side to side, bored, bored as hell.

She ignored the face at the window, a white shadow behind the black pane. She emptied half the orange juice into a flowerbed and skipped back into the house, so bored she could die.

After piano practice, she changed into a pale yellow cotton frock with a white yoke and patent leather shoes. She was twelve. She could vomit. She didn't know why she did this any more.

When she came down to dinner, he was sitting there, eating like a maniac. He glanced up at her, then went back to the food on his plate.

'Hello,' she said. She didn't expect a reply.

Her father walked in and squeezed the back of her neck.

'Squeeze,' he said.

'Squeak!' she said back. He settled *The Lancet* beside his plate and picked up a spoon.

'I think you're pregnant,' said her mother to a fat grey Persian. 'I think you've slipped through the net.'

The boy finished his meal before anyone else and pushed back his plate.

'That was lovely, Mrs Cotter. Thank you very much.'

'Mother!' said Rose. 'Do you have to?'

97

'What?'

'Let the tissue go,' said Rose. 'Just let it go. You've been waving that tissue for the last half-hour. You've been eating with it.'

'Oh,' said her mother, looking at a scrap of tissue she had clutched to her left palm.

'I think I'm going to throw up,' said Rose.

'Don't be silly,' said her father.

'Do you know where that's been?' she said.

And so it went. On day two, he asked her mother what the food was.

'Ratatouille, dear,' and Rose swallowed a smile. She decided to wind him a little tighter.

'Daddy, what's a hermaphrodite?' And azzakazhaam, there he was, spilling salt on to the table, drawing a diagram with his index finger.

The problem was getting the little bugger on his own. Usually the boys hung around after dinner as if they expected a telly to materialise somewhere – out of one of the cupboards maybe, or from behind one of the chairs – but this one just set his chair back flush to the table and went up to his room. Rose finished the dishes and listened to the silence. She decided to have a big long soak with her 4711 bath salts. When she passed his open door on the landing, he said something foreign.

'Sorry?'

'It's Czech.'

'Sorry?'

'As in, Czechoslovakia.' He was sitting at a little desk over by the window that was too small for him. His face looked peaky in the yellow lamplight and his eyes were blank and grey.

'Oh,' she said. 'Fun!'

The next evening he looked into one face, then the other, as they ate, then cleared his throat and started to speak. He asked her mother why her forehead was so smooth and pale at the top, when the rest of her face wasn't.

98

'Africa, dear. I always wore a hat.' Her father looked up. 'Ultraviolet,' he said, and Rose despaired.

By the end of the meal, they had been through Nigeria and Sierra Leone. They had talked about Yoruba and Ibo, and the Leopard Claw Murders of bloody Calabar.

'Do you miss it?' he said.

'Yes,' said her father. 'Yes, I do. Yes, I do miss it,' and Rose was amazed. He had never said as much to her.

'Of course it had fallen apart by then. It's all a question of when you leave.'

'Yes,' said the boy. 'I can appreciate that.'

When she went upstairs he was sitting just under the first landing with his legs propped up on the wall. Rose turned around, like it was a game, and came back with a young calico cat that jerked its back into every stroke of your hand. She sat on a step below him, setting the cat between them.

'Randy little bugger,' she said.

He said some more of his Czech words. They made his tongue sound soft and thick and muscular. Rose kept pulling the cat's tail.

'What's that mark on your arm?' she said.

'My uncle tied me to the radiator.'

'Didn't know they had radiators in *Czechoslovakia*,' said Rose, despite herself.

'Well, now you do.' He picked the cat up and placed it on his leg. He straightened his knee, lifting it into the air, and made a creaking sound.

'Have you ever heard of Isambard Kingdom Brunel?'

'Sorry?'

'Clifton suspension bridge. Six-hundred-and-thirty-foot span.'

The cat jumped and ran.

Her parents came up the stairs and stepped over each of them in turn. They let the dark fall and told time by the hands of his fluorescent watch. It was hard to tell what they

99

talked about by the first landing in the dark: Radioactivity, Time, Cats.

He said that, in his head, the alphabet was all colours. D was pink, O was white with a sort of halo of blue. No matter what words the letters came in, the colours never changed. He said it was genetic. He showed her a roll of money and Rose did not ask where he had got it from. He said his grandfather was a White Russian. He said his grandmother was a Jew.

At four in the morning they dropped out of the bathroom window, on to the garage, then climbed on to the roof proper and sat there until the light broke. The tiles fell black and steep to either side of the house. If you squinched up your eyes, you could see the back garden and the front garden, both at the same time.

The morning came, grey and faintly pulsing. Rose saw their street change into a coloured map of the street – greeny, leafy, Bellingham Close, Leatherhead, Surrey.

They climbed down at six, their legs trembling. Inside, the house was huge and hilarious. It took them ages to get up the stairs. Rose fell asleep like she was taking off a runway. She dreamt of a story written in a secret language, whose colours changed even as you looked at it.

On Saturday they got into the Volvo and sat on opposite ends of the back seat. When they arrived at the shopping centre Rose realised her mother was wearing old plimsolls under her floral skirt.

'See you in half an hour,' she said.

They stole some dried apricots from a bin in the Health Food shop, then ran across the car park, making faces and throwing the lot away, like scattering money.

Inside the supermarket, they walked the two cross aisles, hiding and finding each other from Soap Powders to Paperware to Pet Foods. Rose started to laugh. Then she saw her mother by the delicatessen, getting free samples and talking loudly to the man behind the counter.

The boy nudged her, showed her a packet of Jaffa Cakes hidden under his anorak.

'We've got those at home,' said Rose. They followed her mother secretly through the shop and up to the till. She unloaded the trolley, squeezing and feeling each item of food as she placed it on the conveyor belt. But her face looked so thoughtful that Rose nearly forgave her the stupid shoes.

Back home, there was a woman sitting on the doorstep, in a shapeless camel coat and a dust-pink headscarf. She had a plastic bag gathered beside her on the step and a cigarette in her hand.

Her mother went up to the door while Rose stood beside the car and looked up at her beech tree for a while, the bonnet ticking beside her. When she looked around, he was still in the back seat so she opened the door and pulled him out low on to the ground.

'Tony,' said the woman, when she saw him. 'Tony!' He walked towards her. When he was close enough, she reached for the back of his neck and pulled him down and kissed him. He stood back and pushed his hand through his hair. She reached into the plastic bag and took out a book. It was called *The Seven Wonders of the Ancient World*.

The woman started crying. Her mother brought her into the kitchen to make a cup of tea and Rose went into the front room to practise the piano. Between pieces, she listened while the boy stood in the hall – her mother opening the kitchen door and whispering, while the woman said, 'Tony. Please. Tony,' over and over again.

Finally, her father came home and got the creature out of the house.

As soon as the door closed, she went bananas. She walked up and down the path, shouting at the street. Rose watched from the front window as she wrote with her lipstick along the top of the wall. When the lipstick broke, she threw the stub at the window and cracked it.

Rose's father disappeared into the surgery, then he went

out to her with a pill and a glass of water. Her father was so tall. He had a really gentle body and he had to stoop over her to offer the glass. The woman looked at him. She steadied herself against the wall for a moment. Then she walked away.

After dinner the boy came into the front room and sat on the floor. He leant his back against the armchair Rose sat in, and stayed there until the moment for speaking had passed.

The ebony men and soapstone men were arranged on the sideboard where the television used to be, before it was stolen one last time. Rose liked their long slim lines and the smooth oval holes, like handles for picking them up.

Upstairs her parents slept. Her father twitching at mosquitoes in his sleep, mending black people, sewing them up. His own flesh like wax that, when you cut it, did not bleed.

'Thought your name was "Anton",' she said, finally.

'That wasn't my mother,' he said.

Rose sighed and closed her book.

'Who was it?'

'Just.'

Rose slid down from her chair and sat beside him. She took his arm in both of hers and hugged it.

'Fuck off,' he said. He rolled her on to the ground and straddled her. She punched him in the stomach and he fell over on to her, still crouched, his arms on either side of her head. He rested his forehead on the floor and started to make a noise.

Rose pushed the fleshy side of her hand against his mouth, to hush him. She put her fingers against his chin, and his mouth followed her hand into the air. He was eating at her fingers, she could feel his spit slide down the sides.

This was not how it was supposed to be. His legs were on top of her now. One of his hips pushed and ground into her stomach. Rose realised she had been imagining something like this all along, but something different. She tried to remember what it was, as she pulled her hand away and

102

stroked his sides, trying to calm him down. There was a muscle like a turned rope that wound down to his waist. His face was moving against her neck, still making the noise. Rose could not shape her lips to say 'shush', her mouth would not close. She realised she was going to cry and, as her body gathered for tears, he stopped.

'Shush,' she said. He looked at her, surprised. His mouth came down again, quietly, and pulled at her bottom lip, his heavy skull swinging down to the floor.

Rose kissed him. And under the high round of her pubic bone, a pain started to spread. It rose like dough, clinging and tearing from the bowl of her pelvis. Then the pain shot down like a needle and she pressed it against the leg of his jeans. She moved it against him but he rolled away from her, leaving her body open to the air. He stood up.

'Jesus!' he said. And paused. And left the room.

They ignored each other for a week.

Her mother took out a pack of cards on Friday night to cheer everyone up. Rose hated cards, the sight of her father with a Jack of Spades stuck to his forehead was just excruciating. But the boy played quietly and after a while she was shouting at him and trying to sneak a look at his hand.

The next morning she decided to cut his hair. She wasn't very good at it, and started to laugh at his face in the mirror,

'What are you doing to me?' he said.

'It's a Czech haircut,' she said. 'It's all the rage in *Bratislava.*'

Then he was on top of her again, wrestling her to the floor,

'"Anton",' she said. 'Oh, "Anton".'

His knees dug into the dip at the top of her arm where the tendon met the bone. He was light and tough. She could see up the sleeve of his T-shirt, to the hollow under his arm. She stared into his eyes and he picked up a handful of the cut hair.

She kicked up, lifting him off the ground, while he rode

bronco, with his hand held high. When they dropped back down, the air was smashed out of her chest. She rolled her head from side to side, trying to bite through the denim of his jeans. When she lunged at his crotch, he got some of the hair into her open mouth. She tried to spit and he stuffed in more, so she clenched her teeth and looked him in the eye.

Her throat was full of hair. She started to dry retch and her eyes filled with tears.

They stayed like that for a long time. She hawked, tried to push the dry stuff forward with her tongue. She kneed him in the back and when he lost balance, she spat, then scraped her tongue along the seam of his jeans. They looked at each other for a while.

He caught her chin with his hand and tried to squeeze her jaw open. When he pushed a finger between her teeth, she bit down hard. She thought he might hit her then but he just leaned back, folded his arms and started to whistle.

Rose didn't care. She could stay like this for ever. She knew she would win. He could kill her if he wanted to – she would die winning.

Then her mother came up the stairs saying 'Anyone for a swim after Mass?' and he swung off her and walked out on to the landing.

'Oh dear,' said her mother. 'Never mind.'

Rose floated up from the bottom of the pool, face first. She lay there a second, then swam underwater over to where he was hanging on to the rail. Of course he wouldn't go out of his depth; he just splashed around a lot, making noise. She thought about pulling his underpants down but dunked him instead. When she wrapped her legs around his neck, she could feel his hands grab and slip from her back. He punched her crotch and the pain was remarkable. The lifeguard yanked them from the pool, still joined together. His head bounced on her stomach, then clunked on the tiles.

'He started it,' she said, but the lifeguard had already

flipped him on to his front and was pressing the water out of him. He shook his head like a dog, crawled over to the edge and vomited into the pool.

'You could have done it on the tiles,' she said.

They laughed all the way home.

That night she threw a marmalade kitten into the tree outside her bedroom and called him in. When he went out to get it, she shut the window. She got his book on the seven wonders of the ancient world, tied a scarf under her chin like his mother, and made boo-hoo faces at him, until he lobbed the kitten at the glass.

After he left, her father came into her bedroom with a chainsaw. It was so unfair. The tree was hers. Ever since she was little she had watched it grow up towards her, as she leant out the window; then meet her and pass her out.

'No!' she said, but her father just smiled at her over the noise of the saw, like it was all a big adventure.

Rose could not believe the branches fell so hard. She leaned out the window and watched them crash down between the trunk and the wall of the house.

That evening, she stayed in her room and arranged her things one more time; the tree lopped outside in the dark. Stones on the windowsill, gonks on the dresser, dolls on the bed. She took down Adam and Eve, stuck up a picture of David Essex, and tried to believe in it.

'I didn't know you missed Africa,' she said to her father, after dinner.

'Ah,' he said. 'But then we got you.'

'Why didn't you pick up a little nigger instead?' she said. 'A little black one?'

Her mother went silent at the sink and her father looked at the table. He lifted his head.

'Where is your liver?' he said. It was their old game. 'Where are your kidneys?'

'Oh, shut it.'

'Where's Africa?' He reached out to her, and tickled her

under the arm. 'Is it here?' He tickled her stomach. 'Is it here?'

'Daddy.'

Her mother smiled at the sink. 'Leave her hormones alone.'

'Is it?' he said, lifting her arm into the air. He peeked under it.

'Oh look,' he said. 'It's the Queen of Sheba.'

But she was too old for all that. Anyway, the next boy they got was just a kid.

Music

New York, 1984

Maria went up to the fourteenth floor where the woman sat, terrified of her own body. She was always in the same place, sitting with her back to the window so the light would wash past the creases on her face. Sometimes Maria saw her move, a tiny pleasure in the turn of her wrist, a sweetness as she straightened and stretched her neck, and then it was gone. May-Ann Bell was frightened of her legs, and no wonder – she had the sharpest knees you could ever want to see. Bagged in skin and sheathed again in the most expensive stockings that Maria had ever seen. Sheer, sheer, the legs of a sick old girl, as she crossed and uncrossed them for a thousand men and never left her room. Her ribs hung with little pouches for breasts, her thin arms just something to hang a muscle off, meat swagged over a curtain rail.

Maria had no idea how much of her was real. Though, 'I'm all me,' she said. Everything she had was old, so maybe her prosthetics were too. She was from the South, of course, though she never spoke about her father, or hummed to herself a winsome tune. Still, Maria had seen her before; and heard before the childlike lift in her voice as she asked for the weakest tea.

'Just show it the bag.'

Maria was afraid that May-Ann would shatter as she cleaned around her. She surrounded her with flesh, rolls and heaps of it. She gave her bursting thighs, a triple layer of bosoms unrolling down to her waist, a belly that forced her legs apart and sat for her on the seat of the chair. When she vacuumed around May-Ann, she gave her plenty of room.

This woman's meat was amazing. She was not a doll. May-Ann Bell – a woman Maria had known about long before she came to America, a woman she had heard about in so many different ways – was real. Maria swept her nail clippings off the bathroom floor, shook her skin from out of her panty hose. This woman, who sat alone in a Manhattan apartment and said,

'Oh good, you're Irish. I had a Polish girl last time and she couldn't figure out the juicer,' was real. Maria was in America. She was really there.

'And where are you from?' said May-Ann, as though her own history were well known.

Maria thought about a line of three-bedroom semi-detached houses in the suburbs of Dublin – that would really cheer her up. She invented a farm, added in some rain that slanted across brown – no, *lilac*-coloured mountains.

'Lilac?' said May-Ann, like why was she confusing a hair-rinse with a lump of rock.

'Heathery,' she said.

'Ah,' said May-Ann, who could relate to tweed. 'And how many children in your family?'

'Three,' she said.

'Three?'

'That's all,' said Maria. 'God was not good to us.'

Most of the apartments were empty when she came, and that was the way she liked it. There was something embarrassing about meeting people when you were so intimate with their things. Though, it had to be said, they didn't seem to mind. They stood and explained themselves to her. They took time for it. Maria couldn't believe it, this level nonsense they came out with, like life was a corporation they were trying to run. All their names sounded invented and lost.

Wendy Shower, a writer with five white rooms on the Upper East Side, was suing the hospital where she was born because they had induced her mother early and so messed up her horoscope. She was delivered during an opposition of Saturn and the full moon in Virgo. If the consultant hadn't had a golf date, she said, the moon would have made its transition into Libra.

'And you know how beautiful a Libra moon can be.'

'Really?'

Wendy swept her arm around the four white walls and said, 'Don't you see?'

'What?' said Maria.

'Exactly,' she said. Her walls were practically bare. She was drawn to the wrong men, she ate Japanese, she could never splash out. They had played with her luck and turned her into someone else – someone she was not, had never wanted to be.

'So how is it going?'

Her lawyer thought she had a case, once they had cleared the Time of Conception argument. She had been conceived in a boathouse in Maine, under a Cancer moon.

'Cancer nothing,' she said. 'I'm not fat.'

'How do you know?' asked Maria. 'I mean, where you were conceived.'

'Don't you?'

Maria slopped the Ajax around the sink, thought about the bed that Berts and Evelyn now shared.

'I don't really want to.'

'OK,' said Wendy, slowly. 'But. Well, my parents were very much in love.'

No one in this town lived straight. Outside were the streets of Manhattan, numbered and cut, but everyone was still looking for the map. Even her boss Cassie, who was from Galway, was getting involved in cosmic convergence and the *Tibetan Book of the Dead*.

'But that's because I'm Irish.'

And Maria could never figure out what people actually did. One client said he was an inventor.

'My job', he said, 'is to sit in this apartment, for as long as it takes. My job is to live, that's all. The remote control was invented on a settee.'

But she did not believe him. Besides, there was something uncomfortable about the way he sat there, as though there was a something in his trousers that he had invented just for her. She mentioned it to Cassie, who dropped him from the list pronto, then told her about a Latvian girl she had once, who didn't get out of a client's bathroom for three days.

Maria loved New York. She slept with a couple of guys, just because they were in this town together and both at the same time. Saturday nights they ended up in tiny apartments in TriBeCa and Cassie explained who was into what, and where they were moving on to from here. But the only thing that Maria understood was gay or straight – and that not fully either. Sex seemed to be the easiest solution, when you were the new girl in town.

She didn't tell them she wasn't used to it. Maria thought that maybe she was no good in bed. The bit she liked best was getting up as the city relaxed into dawn and mooching her way out into the street to get a cab. She liked catching sight of herself in someone else's mirror, surrounded by their things. On the other hand, she could have a good snoop on the job and didn't have to sit around afterwards, waiting for them to call.

Maria wandered the empty rooms of the rich with her dustpan and brush, and had their lives, down to the shower gel. There was nothing surprising about them after all, these people with blood-smeared diaries and clean smiles. The pornographic magazines were only remarkable once, though seven pairs of jeans, the same make and size, gave her a fright every time. She tried all the cosmetics in the bathroom cabinet. She cocked the guns and smoothed the sheets with a feeling hand.

The only thing she stole was the music, and even then she left no trace. Each disc she slid out of its sleeve was a different room to clean; the melody curving into the corners, making a joke of the gaps. She hummed as she went, imagining herself into a cleaning woman with a taste for Bach. Imagining herself into a woman who had, somehow, grown into a complete box set of Wagner's *Ring* cycle and a scratched half-hour of Al Stewart's *The Year of the Cat*.

Meanwhile her visa was running out. May-Ann Bell switched to autumn wear; trim suits in air hostess colours, ancient bouclé with big sophisticated buttons; a ring of metal around a bobbled woollen heart.

'What do you mean you're going home?' she said, looking betrayed.

'Well, actually, I'm in the middle of an engineering degree,' said Maria and immediately felt that this wasn't true; that someone else might be in the middle of an engineering degree, but she was here in Manhattan with her foot on a pedal bin and a limp lettuce in her hand, which she was trying not to throw at Ms May-Ann Bell.

'Oh my,' said May-Ann.

Nights, as she tried to sleep, Maria wove her way over and back across the bridges of New York, from Brooklyn Bridge to the Triborough Toll. The idea was to end up back on Manhattan itself, but she always lost her way up by Harlem, until she had to put on the light and find the map. She shuttled across the nameless bridges of the north all the way round to the wide Hudson and the George Washington Toll. Then she started over again, including the tunnels. Then she started over again and took the ferry rides. The week before her first lecture was due to start, she took the phone off the hook. She said to Cassie, over a couple of joints, that she wasn't sure who she was yet, or who she might turn out to be. Cassie agreed, up to a point, and passed the cherry ice cream. She asked was there a guy involved in all of this and Maria said – well, yes – and the two of them laughed like horses.

But the fact was that Maria just liked being nothing. As though there was something coming out in her now that previously she had not allowed. Because she was a treasure. They left notes on the refrigerator to tell her so. She set flowers in their vases and ornaments according to height. She never cleaned the same way twice. The music changed the order of the rooms, made her shift a book from one shelf to another, arrange the chairs parallel or diagonal to the wall.

The guy she was seeing was Irish. He had ended up on her floor one night after a Pogues gig. Maria looked at him in the morning, chewing bread, and she realised that he was mad. He even smelt mad – a girlish, soft smell, to go with his messy eyes. There was no telling what was in his head. When she took her clothes off, she might as well have been a swarm of bees, the way he looked at her. It all depended on the light. It actually all depended (and she could barely admit this to herself) on how she was feeling at the time. Maria walked towards him and saw things flitter across his irises and she knew what they were. This was the exact extent of her own madness, at the time, a kind of understanding. Which isn't so mad, she thought, which isn't so mad. As she shape-shifted in and out of his arms.

It was only when he spent the night looking at his hand in the dark and they woke up the next morning and it was still in the air that things began to get a little strained. Maybe it was just the whole question of anyone staying the night, not just Jack. A good name for a madman, she thought, 'Jack'.

'Do you want some breakfast, Jack?'

'Yes.'

Stone mad.

The airplane took off without her on a still night of thunder. The sky over Battery Park lit up like a low, flat movie screen. Maria looked up in New York, wondering which passing plane held the life that she had let go. She went into a phone booth and punched a random number. A man's voice said 'Hello? Hello?' while the city spread about her, crackling with connections she could not hear.

May-Ann threw her a set of keys that she had stored in her dreadful lap, bandaged today in turquoise Chanel.

'My husband. Or should I say ex.'

Maria looked at the keys.

'I don't know why I do it for him,' said May-Ann.

His apartment was in the same building. It was a mirror image of May-Ann's, the same chrome in the kitchen, the same rack of appliances. He came in as she was clearing out his fridge, Thelonius Monk hesitating and hustling on the hi-fi.

'Ah. The help,' he looked too packed, too fleshy and healthy – though now that Maria thought about it, May-Ann could be any age at all.

'Tell my wife I'm doing just fine.' He wandered off. After a while Maria followed him, opening door after door. She found him sitting at a desk in the den, with his back to her.

'So do you want a cleaner, then?'

He smiled at her over his shoulder.

'I'll leave your money on the little walnut table. In the hall.'

'That man,' said May-Ann. 'I don't know why we bother. I told him you were coming. I said to him expressly.' She sat there, vividly ignoring the new intimacy between them. Maria could feel her hunger, but there was little enough to tell – no fluffy slippers under the bed, no rubber gear in the wardrobe, no big secret. A photograph of a woman in a plain silver frame. A moisturiser in the bathroom, which was the same brand as May-Ann's. That was all.

For the next few weeks she had a free play of his record collection, and wondered at the exact difference between a man's dirt and a woman's. There was more hair, which was grey, and the feeling that things gathered in crusts. The hair could have come from any part of his body. Otherwise, he was neat enough, almost shy, and stripped the sheets before she arrived.

One room fed into the next, a series of double doors that could be flung open, until blocked by a final wall. May-Ann had hung a painting there – the most beautiful heap of rust you ever saw. He marked the end of the line with a black baby grand.

When she dusted along the keys, Maria wanted to bottle the notes, she wanted to take them home and drink them down. The slow stroking scale brought him out of his den, and he watched as she put down the lid and picked up the picture in the silver frame.

'She looks sort of mean, don't you think?'

As far as Maria was concerned the woman didn't look anything, except maybe a bit sad. She ran her cloth across it.

'What age is she?'

He listened to his own silence for a moment, then laughed at it.

'You know, for a moment there, I thought you were insulting my wife.'

He left a message, 'Please come up to iron Thursday, if you can, 7 p.m.,' and when she came for the extra hours' work he was, as she expected, waiting for her there. He leant against the kitchen table drinking Scotch and water, teasing the corner of his lip with a blunt finger as she shook out a linen sheet and ironed it on the double, wishing she knew more about starch.

He watched her for a while, then ducked into the living room. The apartment filled with the high-wire wobble of Callas singing Tosca. She could hear it fill the distant rooms.

'I have a faggot's taste in music,' he said. 'Don't you think?'

'I couldn't really say,' said Maria, knowing she had been discovered; grateful for the ironing board between them and for the iron that was now just a prop – though the shirt she was running it over, the armpit she nosed it into, were altogether real.

'Well, enjoy,' he said with a tight smile, and went back to his den.

The music ended and the smell of hot cotton drifted down the hall. She picked up his boxer shorts and rubbed the thick cream silk between finger and thumb, feeling slightly hilarious. Then she heard his door open, and reached for another sheet.

'What a nice smell.'

'Yes,' said Maria, and noticed the slight hissing you got from good linen, the slippery feel and the shine.

He leaned against a counter, crossed one leg over the other, and watched her. He wasn't embarrassed. He wasn't even drunk. Maria wanted to laugh, but she realised that there was nothing in this man's pants that liked jokes. He stood there until she imagined it too, the simple feeling of his cock sliding in, just twice. Then he smiled, drained his glass and went down the hall.

He brought back a dress in a dark lime chiffon that Maria had not seen before.

'Could you do this before you finish?' and laid it across the board.

'It's very fine.'

She turned the iron right down, realising that every rich man in New York had laundry that just arrived, that she was here for no reason, except for this moment, when he would stand behind her as she ran the iron over lime-green chiffon and caught the rising smell, first the perfume and then the sweat, of an unnamed woman, who had not worn this dress in a long time.

'You know, May-Ann nearly had an affair once,' he said. 'She could have slept with him and told me. But she didn't sleep with him, and she told me that instead. I'd rather she slept with him and said nothing.'

He waved his glass. 'Women just *love* the truth, don't they? They think it's simple.'

So he was drunk, after all.

'For a woman, a lie is the same as an infidelity; an infidelity is as bad as a murder. I mean, come *on*.'

'And what is it for you?'

They had ended up on a sofa in the living room. It was the first time Maria had had sex with someone she did not like, and she found she quite enjoyed it.

'Listen. Every morning I woke up with my wife, I thought I was beside the wrong person. I go to a shrink, the shrink says, "Maybe you're the wrong person. Maybe the wrong person is you."'

'And was it?'

'"Defensive doubling," he says, "castration anxiety, that'll be fifty bucks." Don't ever go to a shrink.'

She picked up her clothes from the floor.

'Not much use if you don't have a dick.'

He snorted into his drink. He was a man not used to laughing at other people's jokes. Maria could hear him repeating the remark to someone in a tasting, droll way, just because she had caught him off-guard.

'Fuck you,' she said.

She said she had another guy at home, and *truth* didn't come into it.

'The week before Christmas,' said May-Ann. 'Oh my.'

Eighty-seventh Street was misting up behind her, all the way to the park. It was snowing in New York, the slowest snow in the world – every flake seen and known, long before it hit the ground.

Maria did the bedroom and wiped down the kitchen. She took a scrubbing brush to the grouting in the shower. She switched on the tap to rinse it down and looked at the water pulsing in from every side.

'That's it,' she said.

'I'll tell Mr Bell you said goodbye.'

'Thank you.'

The windows were fully steamed up now. The ghosts of old words were emerging on the glass. The last time the windows were wet, it seemed, someone had scribbled on them with their finger. Maria realised that the room had been invisibly written, all that autumn and the summer before. She looked at the scrawls and drawings – which were not exactly nice. Though some of them, it had to be said, were quite funny.

She looked at May-Ann, who looked back at her, with an amiable dislike.

'The heating needs doing,' she said. 'Oh my. How many times?'

Maria walked out into New York. In front of her was the line of Fifth Avenue, cutting into the city. In the dizzy silence of the snow, she could hear the whole goddamn symphony. Back in Dublin the class was stuck into Hydraulics & Metal Fatigue – but she was inside it. Maria was inside everything she could ever know. And she decided to lose herself here, disappear into the music, bone by bone.

Hands

London, 1980

Rose had come too late to the violin. She could read
anything and play it on the piano, but she could not
improvise and her tone was too polite and dry. People
envied her precision but it was not what she wanted, not,
not, not. She ended up bashing the keys; she damaged her
hands while chopping carrots or moving a bookcase against
a wall. Because when she was playing, she could never
stumble. Even when she was exhausted, she would pause
rather than fall. And she always felt that she was falling.

Her father said that it was just her age – later, the emotion
would start to tell. Rose was fifteen and she felt as old as the
hills. Besides, it was not emotion she wanted. It was the
feeling you got when something complicated was suddenly
clear. It was,

'Bliss,' she said.

'I see.'

'Like Notre Dame.'

Her father pushed his glasses up and leant his forehead on
the heel of his hand. She saw that he was smiling down at
the wood of the table, or wincing, and Rose was suddenly
mortified. She turned out of the room, slamming the door
behind her.

They had stood there together in the centre aisle, the two
of them, almost father and daughter. She had looked at the
astonishing space, and seen them both in it; a girl in a
summer dress with her mosquito bites fading, and an old
man by her side. She saw him clearly, his long belly hanging
from under his ribs, the tremor of his hand that dabbed

118

back, as though in irritation, from his side. While above them both, the cathedral gave its huge, silent roar.

Rose listened to it – a thrilling, high chord that she could not name. She looked at the stained glass, the columns and grace notes of stone and for a moment she knew what it all meant. Bliss. Something so big, you got it and forgot it at the same time.

Then her mother was back beside them, telling her to light a candle under the statue of Joan of Arc.

'Oh, Mother,' said Rose. 'Would you please grow up.'

Rose wanted to play the violin because it was the hardest thing she could think of: it sounded so awful when you played it wrong. And she loved the flexible, singing sound of it, the way it soaked out into the room until that moment of solid release, like the top of a yawn. She liked, she said, its acoustic shape.

Her father paused over his dinner. She had spent the afternoon battering through Bach and had decided on an adult approach.

'Is that so?' he said, tilting his head. He was listening for the echo of her music teacher in what she said. Rose was in love with her music teacher, but that was not the point.

'Because I'm not sentimental,' she said. 'And it is.'

'And why aren't you sentimental?' he said.

'Don't be silly,' she said.

'Show me your hands.' She held out her hands.

'How much did you say it would cost?'

'Please, Daddy.'

'When I was her age, it was horses,' said her mother.

'Your mother's right,' he said. 'You should get out more.'

So she got the violin and she put in the hours and was good enough. But it was all too late. When she got to college Rose was surrounded by girls with hands as tough and flexible as steel cable. Not one of them could play, she thought, but they still played better than she did. Besides, she was worried about her chin, which was doubling as she looked at it, no matter how far she stretched her neck each time she settled the damned thing in. Her room at college was a brick box that bent every note into a right angle and fired it back at her. Sometimes she liked to close her eyes as she played and let herself cry; the tears mixing with the rosin and sliding on to the wood.

Rose checked the lines on her palm under the anglepoise light at her desk: lifeline, heartline, fate. She pinched the muscles at the base of her fingers and examined the white splits when she stretched them apart. She hated her hands: their Victorian tapered look, the quiet crook of the smallest finger, the cushioned, upholstered backs. She wanted hands that flew and tore; not these soft cats hanging off the end of her wrists, with a dodgy octave, and a secret tension between thumb and index finger that she had to shake out every half an hour.

After practice, she swung out of the lintel to stretch her tendons and went shop-lifting. It was the only thing she could think of that was exciting and funny at the same time. Sex didn't seem funny, and music was only funny when you played it in your sleep. One day Rose went into Tesco's and was so disgusted by an old woman's warty hands feeling up the fruit that she turned and walked out of the shop with a vacuum pack of salami still tucked under her arm. She looked at it in the street outside, six fluorescent rounds of meat, lurid with fat. Then she tucked the lot, hands and meat, into her pockets and walked away. It was only when she turned the corner that her heart started to go.

She told nobody, not even William, who was her boyfriend – who really was her boyfriend, now they had started sleeping together at the weekend. Though they did not have sex, because they weren't ready yet. Sometimes Rose wondered if she just liked his flat, it was so much better than her own brick room, with a decent double bed, lots of space, and three framed pictures of men unloading fish at a dock.

'Lithographs.'

'Sorry?'

'Not "pictures",' said William. 'They're lithographs,' and Rose asked herself if her virginity wasn't worth more than a man who was prissy about bad art. Or was it worth anything at all? Every man you met said something stupid, sometime. She lay beside him in her T-shirt and knickers and they talked in the dark, not knowing how to stop and fall asleep. She thought she loved him when the light was off but she did not tell him about the salami, how good the stuff had tasted when she got it home. And she hated wearing knickers all night, it made her feel dirty when she woke, made her want to swim with William, or shower with him – get it over with, somehow, before the whole thing went sour.

'Tell me if I snore,' she said and unclenched her hands and slept.

She saw him first playing viola, in the quartet that he organised. He had the brilliant Andrew Mew for first violin, but the bass was a dork and the cellist was a boring bitch, with a nervy, sentimental rubato. She should have fallen for Andrew Mew, but Rose fell for William instead. She liked the way he nodded as if the music was something he allowed. She liked the control in his face, while Haydn surrounded him with such helpless sweetness. She kissed him, drunk, and for the next few weeks mulled him over, falling in love with him piece by piece.

His legs were too short and his face too heavy for nineteen. He sort of sniggered suddenly, when people gave their opinion, and he hated to dance. But, somehow, Rose was jealous of all these things. William had what she always wanted – he had never been a child. Her day turned into a conversation with him, as he judged the clothes she wore and the people she passed in the street. He commented on

121

the food she ate and tut tutted her out of bed in the morning, even when he wasn't there.

When she saw him in the flesh again, she was always a little disappointed. William's face looked like it had been stuck together by someone else, like he was waiting to grow into it. It was this bruised, blocky feeling that she sensed beside her all day, drawing attention to the lecturer's pop-socks or the wonderful brickwork on that Victorian façade.

They talked about sex a lot. It seemed to be something you talked about, like Scarlatti, or working with period instruments. Apparently William had already done it with the boring bitch cellist (as if Rose didn't know), but she had run off with Andrew Mew. He pushed himself against her and,

'Not yet, William,' she said. But she could not shake him out of her mind.

After the episode of the pink salami and the old woman's warts, Rose realised something strange. From the fruit and veg, all the way into the street, she had been completely alone. William was gone. It was only when she looked at the vacuum pack in her hands that he returned to her side and said ... Well, he said nothing, actually, for quite a while.

Now when Rose walked up the aisle and lifted the odd half-pound of sausages William would turn away and burst like a bubble, leaving an irritated 'ping' behind. The more she took, the longer it was before he came back – until he was so far away that she thought she might sleep with him now, quite easily.

And there was no doubt about it, her playing improved. She walked past the old dears using their trolleys for zimmer frames, a tin of Bird's custard stranded on the wire, and her heart sang. There was no other word for it. The singing got her through the map of the shop, made her timing easy when the moment came, to stoop, reach, put it away. She did it allegro. She did it easy easy. She sang her way past the tills and out into the street and then down the street and around the corner, until she reached her brick room and the silent round of applause.

Sometimes she went back twice in the same day. Plink, pingeddy pong – addicted to the muzak and the aisle full of breakfast cereal, something really big and light. Everyone was watching her, and no one actually saw. It was like escaping and being locked up, both at the same time.

She imagined what it would be like to be caught: the humiliation of the security guard's hand on her shoulder, something sexual about the way he would not let her go, made her feel like trash. 'I am a music student,' she would say. 'My hands, mind my hands.' Her nifty little, nimble little hands, which floated over corn on the cob and packets of frozen spinach and forgot themselves entirely. Her criminal little hands, who knew just what they were. She saw them before her on the dock, and liked them: liked the edgy, raped feeling when she lifted her head and looked the judge in the eye.

At least, if they caught her, she would have something to talk to her mother about. Finally. Lots of earnest discussions about the pain Rose felt about being adopted, the unfairness of it all. For the first time she understood all those boys who casually stole from and betrayed her parents – not because they wanted to, but just because they could.

By February she was getting B plus for expression and William was even more cautious. When they slept together at the weekend, he swallowed over and over in the dark and left her plenty of room.

Rose knew he was right. He would have to catch her now, or lose her, once and for all. She walked out of Safeway's with a full trolley of groceries. She started stealing clothes: stockings, tights, a dreadful pair of jeans. For a while she went around in her mismatched, snatched, anything-she-could-put-her-hands-on, until she got sense and stuck to tops that were a reasonable and roomy size twelve. She wore them like an open secret, the lumpy bras, the culottes that looked too butch and fake, and the skirts that trailed the ground.

One morning in spring when she was cycling to her harmony class, her legs started to itch and burn. She hopped from foot to foot as she locked her bike and walked like a cowpoke through the door of the hall.

Rose sat there watching the lecturer's hands swirling through some nonsense about the tritone of C# − G, while the rash spread from her thighs down the back of her calves. For the first time, she knew what her skin actually was, so she picked it up and walked it out of the hall, leaning slightly backwards, looking straight ahead. Her skin was fighting against her. It was trying to jump off her. Rose looked out through the holes of her eyes as she walked down the street, and hoped the rash wouldn't travel to anywhere strange.

By the time she reached Boots, she was quite frantic. She passed the shelves without lifting so much as a packet of aspirin, went to the prescriptions counter and placed her white hands on the wood; a patch of red already creeping out from under her cuff. The pharmacist took one, unhurried look and gave her some antihistamine tablets with a glass of water, and some cream for later. The cycling might have something to do with it − the sweat and friction.

'Change your washing powder,' she said.

Rose sat naked in her room and tried to study. She stood naked at the music stand playing Poulenc and feeling foolish. Someone came to the door, who might have been William, but she ignored his knock. After a while, she put on a pair of rubber gloves, and an old dressing gown, ventured down to the bathroom and started to rinse out her clothes.

The next weekend they were sitting over William's special omelette, made with fried potato and chopped tomatoes that shed their skins into the yellow of the egg. She was gathering the skins into a pile on the side of the plate when William stopped eating and pushed his food away.

She was talking about the boring bitch cellist, the way she quite liked playing with her legs open, the way she swayed so her chair creaked, in a way that was always, somehow, out of tune.

'That's enough,' he said.

'Is it? Sorry.'

Rose wondered if there was something wrong with him in the trouser department. There was a thing her father used to say about boys pulling their foreskin back or it wouldn't work properly when the time came.

'Enough,' he said again and she thought about the rash subsiding from her thighs.

'Maybe we should get drunk,' she said. 'People get drunk.'

He came around to her side of the table, and placed his head on the shoulder of the white cotton shirt she had lifted from Marks and Sparks men's department. After a while, he creaked down on to his hunkers and pressed his cheek against the space above her breast. This was it, then.

They started to kiss, the dinner getting cold on the table. Rose felt the muzak start in her heart – plink, pingeddy pong. She felt like giving poor, perfect William the fright of his life. She felt like stealing the breath out of his mouth. But the fright, when it came, was hers.

They spent the rest of the year, Rose's second in college and William's last, practising sex. Practising and practising, and still not getting used to it. Her music may have improved 'emotionally', but her technique went to pot, so it was hard to tell. She did not stop stealing, although the things she took got odder: shoe polish, when she never polished her shoes. Toilet brushes. She had a light bulb phase. She started to bring home clothes just to try them on, taking them back again when they did not fit. Once, she got a refund.

At Easter, William suggested that she come to his parents'

for the long weekend, and Rose packed carefully, taking only the things that she had bought herself.

When they got there, Rose couldn't believe the house. She had the strangest sensation that there were more rooms in it somewhere, which she just couldn't find. It was terribly clean, and the doors had silly pebbled glass in them instead of wood.

William's mother was in the kitchen when they arrived. They sat at the table and had their cups of tea in china that matched, while his mother chopped vegetables on a counter that had nothing on it but the vegetable to be chopped.

'Good journey?' she said.

Rose tried to be relaxed, but William's mother did not seem to want relaxed. She went very quiet when Rose described the other passengers on the train, the man with the corset, and the deaf couple who made the filthiest signs.

When she tried to wash up, his mother intercepted her at the sink and Rose nearly dropped the cup out of her hand. There was William's mouth, sitting on a woman's face. It was older and plumper, pleated with wrinkles and slightly wet. It was revolting.

Over dinner, she realised what it was that made William old. She looked at the dreadful mess of his mother coming out through his face, listened to his father discuss the lawn – as though a good mower was early Baroque, and dandelions were those fools who wanted to play it on period instruments. William was lived in: by his father's bluster, his mother's sexual response; by these dreadful, banal, living ghosts.

'William says that you are adopted,' said his mother, and Rose felt all her features jumble and strain. Her face was full of people she did not know, and they were fighting their way out of her. Some woman's mouth, some man's nose. Even the way she chewed might come from someone else, the tiny muscle that gathered on her chin. She cut into the overdone roast beef and felt her body fall to bits.

'Yes, apparently.'

Her own mother would have said, 'How very romantic,' or 'Do you mind?' But William's parents did not feel they should say anything at all.

That night William came into her room and they made love, in silence. He was very keen, but she could not concentrate. She felt a baby catch in her stomach. She could feel its stare. She turned into it, and found herself falling into its plum-like, foetal eyes.

She jolted away and William came out at a funny angle that nearly did for them both. He laughed, all angry and flustered like he had pulled his head out from under a waterfall.

'What's wrong?'

'I'm sure your parents heard.'

'Don't worry about them.' He seemed almost proud. He rolled on his back and looked at himself with regret and said, 'Is that it, then?'

Rose decided to marry him then. She straddled him and kissed him for ages and made love to him again for real, her heart sinking.

At the end of the year Rose went home and announced that she was giving up music. The family were having dinner. Her father was reading up on a new ulcer drug and squeezing the flesh under his ribs. Her mother was talking to Gareth, a foster boy with bin-liners on his hands who had lasted all of six years. He had a hygiene thing that kept him away from the cats.

'I boiled your plate,' her mother was saying. 'For ten minutes. You timed it. You were there.'

'Did anyone hear what I said?'

'Sorry, dear?'

'I have decided to give up the violin.' Her father closed the medical journal and waited.

'Because I'm not good enough,' she said.

'I see,' he said.

'Well, if you can't be good, be useful,' said her mother, then looked at Rose and regretted it.

'You could always become a composer, dear,' and Rose slammed her fork down and shouted that it wasn't that bloody easy and there was nothing left to fucking compose, was there? while Gareth sat upright and started to sweat, filling the room with the smell of bleach.

Her father went back to his reading.

'So what's this chap's name?' he said, turning a page.

'What *chap*?' she said, feeling betrayed.

Rose sat at the piano, picking her way through a Chopin nocturne she found in the stool, pausing just before she got it wrong, starting again, pausing again, her hands completely still and gentle an inch away from the keys. In the pause was a pain so acute, so timid, that nothing would cure it except the next right note, the perfect one that she knew was there, and could barely find.

She was four when she picked out her first tune on the piano, and 'Oh, she's musical,' said her mother. 'She's musical!' as though she was wonderfully unknown, full of surprises. All orphans are musical. So Rose was musical. That was what she was.

She broke into a piece she used to know blind, the adagio from Mozart's Sonata in F that she had once dreamed would grow into the Concerto in A with a full orchestra behind her, herself plunging and weaving over the keys in a perfect black dress.

The music rolled and sadly lifted, just tipping the melody before slipping away. It barely reached, then lost itself again, over and over. And as it yearned and caught and let the melody go, Rose started to make mistakes, dreadfully, one after the other. One mistake after the other, until she felt like she was beating herself up.

Just beyond all the wrongness was a place where she could actually play this thing. She pushed on, flinching and fighting through the slowness of it all until, for a few phrases, gone as soon as she had grasped it, she was there. Bliss.

She finished the piece simply and rested her hands on the keys.

This was why she played. Because she was musical. Because somewhere out there, her real, musical mother was listening. Somewhere out there, her real, musical mother was singing into the dishes, to the child she loved so very much but had to give away. This is why she paused and played, and paused and could not fall. She had switched to the violin because she thought it would make the falling easy – but there was nothing easy about it.

Because her mother was not in the music. She was in a room somewhere, she was riding in a car. She was cutting her toe-nails in a bedsit, or stroking the head of another child. She was not in the music, and every time Rose found her there, she was already gone.

That night, she thought it over as she fell asleep, listening to Gareth next door, soaking his room with fly spray.

She had the wrong kind of mind. She did not know where it came from and there was no one she could blame. It wasn't exactly a man's mind; it was something different again. It was the kind of mind where nothing was ever enough.

She would have to make do.

'So what have you decided?' said her father a few days later, when she met him in the hall, ushering a man with a spongy nose out of his consulting room.

'Oh,' she said. 'Nothing yet.'

Love

New York, 1985

Maria looked at the menu. All she wanted was a sandwich.

'Genoa salami, mortadella, Black Forest ham, provolone, balsamic vinegar and olive oil.'

It looked like a dinner party slapped on a slice of bread. Maria tried to imagine what it might taste like, what kind of person went to parties like that.

'Pâté Croissant'. That was more like it. It was not a sandwich you had to dress up for. She had just put in her order when a man passed her table, in a green shirt and a pair of black jeans that bagged at the base of his spine. He worked the lock on the big window, sliding it back on one side. And,

'Oh shit,' said Maria to herself, as he stepped out into New York.

When he came back in again, she knew it would be easy to talk to him. He had been out in the wind and the weather. The café was like coming home.

'Thought you were going to fly away,' she said. And he laughed.

I am twenty years old, she said. It is time I fell in love. For the next week Maria set her thoughts on him. She looked at the same sky as he did, rode the subway in his head, and when she went back to the café he was there, as she knew he would be, because now she owned the map.

He sat down and smiled.

'So what have you been up to?'

'Nothing much.'

They talked for a while, and Maria was amazed at how clear it was, this thing that was happening at their table, how anti-social. It had nothing to do with Manhattan at all.

It was not the ordinary way of things that you saw in the street and in the bars, women flirting with their foreheads, the men leaning back. It was not the anxious door-opening, body-dodging, how can we get through this building, being differently constructed down there. The problem of getting anatomies through architecture, the problem of getting anatomies through the streets. How can we get through this conversation even? Laughs and coughs and sudden clearings of the throat because we can never be the same down there. It was desire itself, when the map is your blood, and the room becomes so big it disappears.

'I was talking to an Irish girl, says she knows you.'

It was easy, it was horrible to watch.

'Don't tell me, I don't want to know.'

'Why not?'

They would sleep with each other, tonight or the next night, sober or drunk or in the middle of the afternoon. All they could do was try to keep speaking until the time came. It was as simple as that. As simple as men walking on the moon.

They went down to the skateboarders in Central Park, then over to a bar on St Mark's and then back to a bar near her place to hear some Haitian Creole. It was a fake journey, a fake afternoon. In the cab home they were already disappointed. They looked out the windows or smiled deliberately when they caught each other's eye.

But inside the door of the apartment Maria said,

'This is what the Polish girl left behind. Look.' She pointed at a picture of a girl sitting in a field of daisies in a see-through shift. And he laughed.

He stayed for a week.

It was August. So hot. Maria set three fans around the bed. She went out to the shops now and then, came back with things like pumpkin pie ice cream. They laughed all the time.

He liked to dress her before she went out, to undress her when she came home. He pulled a red dress and a pair of heels out of her wardrobe, and danced a close, chunky salsa with her, naked from the waist down. She looked over his shoulder as the room lapsed and lifted around them and the sweat on his chest stained her front.

It was so hot. Her hands leaked on to the bag of groceries, turning the base into a brown pulp that gave way as she opened the door. They ran around picking up bagels and half-spilt cartons of salad. They laughed as they shouldered the door shut and spilled the food out over the counter, eating it in no order at all.

She fell in love.

His name was Anton. He couldn't remember his mother. He remembered a woman sitting in a cupboard and crying. His grandfather played the piano along the edge of the kitchen table. His father tried to set himself alight.

It amazed her how like grief it was – this desire for someone's story, and the flesh it came wrapped in.

Anton had a circular scar on his arm and two pearly patches on his shoulder blades. He had leant against the stove as a child. He had taken a tow from a friend's bike, on his new skates, and the twine bit into his arm, when he tripped and fell.

One night he started to cry. They were having sex enough to make you mad. He was coming softer and softer, until she thought her heart would break. Anton lay there looking at the ceiling and talked about his mother, sitting in a chair for hours and hours, and when she finally got up, there was blood on the back of her dress.

'When was that?' she said.

'What do you mean, "when"?'

It was so hot, she did not know if they slept or not. They slid over each other in the bed, so she could not tell which

132

bit of him was under her hand. When she finally fell asleep, she felt herself slipping between the mattress and the wall.

What else did he say?

He said he slept with a girl in Tucson, he slept with a woman who turned out to be a whore, he slept with a girl who had lost her foot as a baby, during a protest against the Vietnam war. He slept with a man once, just to try it. He saw a man in a urinal, who pulled his dick out on a ribbon and pissed holding it like a dog on a leash. He went into a urinal with his father once and could not believe the size of his thing, or the hair.

So how much of that was a lie, and how much was true, in a way?

It was always so hard to see him. Every bone in his body was twice the length it should be. They lapsed into a shape on the bed, stroking the length of each other, losing themselves in a dent or a curve, surfacing again to the bare cube of the room and their bodies in it, lying on the bed.

Anton said he was in a motel once in the middle of nowhere, Arizona, listening to the sound of sex coming through the wall, shifting over in the bed, those thin sheets, getting a hard-on, the noise going on all night. Finally he walked out into the desert wrapped in a motel blanket, and sat there and smoked until even his lungs got cold.

The next morning they were gone. No idea what they looked like: they sounded like a porn movie, but they might have been ugly, they might have been fifty years old. The door to their room was open, he could see the bed and a half-empty bottle of Tio Pepe on the locker. So he walked in, and lay on the used sheets, and drank it all.

'Tio Pepe?' she said.

'You know what it tastes like?' he said. 'Metal.'

Where was the lie in that? she thought. Which part of that is a lie?

The light shifted on the walls, making them more solid. Then it loosened again and the room began to give way. The light read and re-read them and dusk fell because it suited his skin. His face shifted into night as she lay beside him, trying to match her heartbeat to his.

He said he never knew his mother. His grandfather played the piano along the side of the kitchen table, he said. His father had laid his dick across his shoulder once, said, 'Feel the weight of that.'

He said she had a familiar face.

The Abortionist's Restaurant

London, 1985

William was very excited by the fact that Rose was Irish. This she discovered when he took her out to dinner and said, 'This place used to be an abortion clinic,' for no reason at all. Rose looked around at the white-tiled room and back at William – who did not seem to realise. Bless him. William had a job now. He had taken her out to dinner just because he could.

So I am Irish, said Rose to herself, sitting in the abortionist's restaurant and eating Tagliatelle alle Vongole. So this is what it means. Perhaps he wants me to order potatoes, say, 'Oh holy God, fuck me, fuck me,' when we are having sex, which, from now on, will be in the dark.

No. She should not have told William.

'Really?' he said. 'Irish?'

When she was thirteen, Rose read *Anne Frank's Diary* and decided she would be a Jew. She would have fine eyes, a deliberate approach to things. She would be a small point in the present with history howling at her back.

She still thought of herself as being conceived during a war, somehow. A father home on leave, a mother who rushes to the door while trying to undo her print apron, her hands wet from the stone sink.

But the Irish didn't have A War, they just had a mess. They bred like something in a petri dish, each generation scraped off the top. Rose had been dumped by a mother, not because she was interesting or tragic, but because she just couldn't help it. Never mind the clouds, the cliffs, and the rain.

She was conceived in a shed, born in a ditch. She was started in a priest's fumbling, or an old uncle pulling down his fly. She was made with a difficult soft grunting: a young woman crying silently, as if she were somewhere else in the room.

'What about James Joyce?' said William. 'I always thought you were good with words.'

She looked at him across the table. Rose still slept with William, but she had not put her tongue into his mouth for a long time. And now, she knew, she never would again.

She watched him work over his pasta, forking it up over and over until the sauce was mixed in. Why did men do that? They mashed potatoes into gravy, and mixed the rice into vindaloo, while woman just picked out one vegetable at a time.

'Why do men do that?'

'What?'

'Mix everything up like that. With their food.'

'Do they?'

Most of the time, Rose did not know who she was. She was a woman. But, until now, being an English woman had not come into it. Maybe it was time to bring in food.

'Yes.'

'Are we talking about men again?'

'I'm not saying "men". I'm just saying it's true, that's all.'

'Probably because we're a bunch of shits.'

She took a baby clam on the end of her fork and looked at it. So this was who she was. She was a person who picked at her food. She picked at her food because she was a woman. She picked at her food because she was English, because she was Irish. She picked at her food because she was a Capricorn, because when she was a baby she had choked on a spoonful of puréed parsnip, because she had a famine gene, or a food-picking gene, or because when she was young her mother told her to sit up straight and not wolf her food. She picked at her food because she was middle class.

136

'So how's college?' said William, after a while.

Rose did not say that she had started staying up all night. That her brain was racing all night. She did not say she was in love with the dark outside her window, or that she had become interested in silence, addicted to it, so that when she put on some music she felt as though something vital had been broken. She did not say,

'I think I'm losing it.' She said,

'Oh, you know.'

William took another forkful. He lifted his spaghetti high and dipped it into his mouth. She watched his jaw muscles as he chewed.

It probably was a gender thing, actually. Less time at the breast if you're a girl. The thorough, satisfied boy child. The fearful, precise girl child. The knife-and-fork man. The anorectic. Rose was very interested in psychology these days. On Thursdays she slept with a man who was married to a psychotherapist and said it was driving him mad. It was driving Rose mad too. She wanted to go into therapy for a start, if possible with his wife. Not that it would be much use, lying on a couch and talking her face off. Tearing her dreams apart. Recovering her childhood, those first months, that blank.

But she had to do something. Her brain was whirring. There was too much inside her now. There were all the things she did not say to William for a start.

Like, 'Who am I, William? Who do you think I am?'

'So how's work?' she said.

William had taken to blue stripey shirts with plain white collars. He spent his days in a legal office listening to pop songs, slowing phrases down in his head and speeding them up again, trying to prove they had been stolen from someone else. He loved the job, convinced, as perhaps he always had been, that the whole music thing was a con. Perhaps because it had fooled him into feeling something, once.

'What do you expect?' she did not say. 'Ten years of the fucking viola.'

No. William was happy, finally, exposing the lie. Pulling apart phrases by Stock Aiken and Waterman to see if he could squeeze a couple of K out of them over an ascending series of dominant sevenths. Everyone was copying someone else. If Puccini were alive, he was fond of saying, he could get some shitload out of Andrew Lloyd Webber.

'But that's what music is,' Rose did not say back. 'It's a game. Like throwing the ball.'

Tonight, he talked about money. All he needed was fifty K for a computer that would take a melody and transcribe it for any number of instruments you chose. Think of it. Think of the fees, not just the Royal Philharmonic, though it could be the Royal Philharmonic, but the Ta-Rar-A-Boom-Dee-Yay for the panto in the Leeds Playhouse, or more likely, all the gloopy strings when Cliff Richard decides to do a cover of the 'Londonderry Air'.

'The bank', he said, 'is keen.'

'Terrific,' she said.

William had discovered money, like the discovery virgins make that everyone fucks, that they fuck all the time.

Is money dirty? Only if you are earning it right.

Rose was back at college for her last year. After that, she did not know what to do. Down in the career guidance office she looked up short courses in psychology, ethnomusicology. Late at night, she read research on whale song. But what was the use? Everything she tried to listen to just got in the way of the noise in her head.

William caught someone's eye and made a little signature in the air. She wasn't even finished dessert – he just could not wait. It gave him such pleasure to lay his credit card on the little tray and ignore the waitress who came to take it away. Rose remembered the first time they had dinner, on her nineteenth birthday, when he stared at his plate and said,

'They're raw.'

'What?'

'The oysters. They're raw.'

Never trust a man who won't eat seafood. They never went down. This she got from her Thursday man who married a psychotherapist, and told jokes, and went down all the time.

Her brain was out of control.

The waitress came back with the credit card receipt and William signed it, pretending not to look at the price. He clicked his nice pen and put it back in his jacket pocket.

Everywhere you went these days they were playing *The Four Seasons*, or that thing by Albinoni. Rose pushed the tiramisu around her plate and did not say that the whole country was going to pot.

'The whole country is going to pot,' she did not say.

Well, that was something at least. She was a person who hated nice pens, and stripey blue shirts and Margaret Thatcher. That was who she was. She would work with handicapped children. She would do music therapy and ease them into swimming pools. She had an image of a small girl buzzing with her lips against the taut skin of a balloon.

Kissing language.

Out in the street, Rose looked at William and took his complicated arm. Ten years of the fucking viola. She wondered would it be better, after all, not to resent the thing. To let it go, if you were losing it, but all at once.

His new flat was half-finished. The living room still had its old wallpaper and there was a big black hippo of a leather sofa squatting among the violets. William wanted to christen it, so they creaked around for a while. Then he panicked about the stain and went to find a J-cloth. Rose peeled her bare bottom off the leather and knew that she had to get out of this relationship, very soon.

But she looked at him as he slept and thought, 'He is so very sweet.' He was not an immoral man. The problem was her. Everywhere she looked, she knew what it meant.

But she still didn't know what it meant to be 'Irish'.

Her mother saying, 'But that's why we went to Mass, all those years.'

They must have told her. She must have forgotten. Or did they forget? How could you forget a thing like that?

'Did you tell me?' she said. 'Did you?'

Maybe. It was back somewhere with polio jabs, and the facts of life.

'We *must* have,' said her mother.

And perhaps they had.

Now Rose lay beside William and made a list of the things she was — things she could not forget, even if she tried.

She was twenty-one years old. (Probably)

She was studying music. (More or less)

She was a woman. (?)

She was in bed with William/Will/Bill.

She was too full of things.

She was born with a hole in her head, a hole in her life. Everything fell into it.

She started again.

She was Irish.

Her favourite colour was blue.

Her favourite colour was actually a deep yellow, but she couldn't live with it.

She was English.

She was tidy. She was polite. She hated Margaret Thatcher.

She was a mess.

She was someone who gave things up.

She was someone who tried to give things up and failed all the time.

It was all lies. Rose had a hole in her head and anything at all could come out of it. She could be anything, do anything. She could be a murderer. She could go deaf. She could study whales. She could place the balloon against the child's lips, gently, gently, and teach it not to bite.

Eggs

New York, 1985

After Anton left, Maria found herself walking the streets every day after work. He was somewhere in Manhattan, lying or telling the truth, and she looked into the faces of the people she passed, checking for clues.

Hello.

Hello.

Hi.

Some afternoons she developed a system – every second turn a left turn, or every third turn a left, or always on the sunny side of the street. But mostly she just put one foot in front of the other, until she was sucked down some subway steps and a train ride home.

One evening she found herself in Battery Park, at the end of the road. She sat down on the grass, with her back to the cliff of money that was downtown, and she looked over at the Statue of Liberty, a postcard hallucination in the sea haze.

The first month she was in New York, they came here all the way from the Bowery, just because they couldn't believe it was real. They sprawled on the grass and dropped acid and followed the slow arc of the moon.

Maria still remembered the feel of that moon in her stomach, a hard-edged plate of pure light. There was a guy called August lying beside her, so black he looked green in the dark. You could sink into him like moss. Maria took his hand but was frightened by how dry it was.

'The moon,' she said.

'That's right.' Stoned or straight, August said everything

like it was a funny little thing that just slipped out of your mouth.

Maria's tongue was a muscle. She knew that much. But she wasn't sure if she knew how to speak. A guy started shivering out on the edge of things. No one knew who he was.

In those days, everyone had a fantasy on their skin, a way of showing what they knew. Eoin, who was her contact for the flat, had a crown of thorns tattooed around his right nipple. August had a dog lead hanging from his belt with no dog at the end. And Leenane, who just watched, had a baby, a beautiful bump she wore over her skinny little legs.

During the day it was one betrayal after another. There was a girl from California who had all these parents and didn't give a shit. She slept with Leenane, and messed up her head. August just disappeared. He owed Maria money but she didn't care about that. She cared about his skin; about the fact that he belonged everywhere; that he never once thought of her as being real.

Maria had to get it together and earn some money. When she decided to leave for Cassie and a cold-water walk-up in the North Village, Eoin spent all night sitting on her bed telling her how much he hated her.

Now, when she thought of all the drugs, she felt a twitter of horror, as though she had run across the street in front of a car, and nearly not made it to the other side. Whoosh.

But she missed the moon. She missed having it inside her. And she could not read the streets any more, where the good things were, where Anton might be. She used to be untouchable. Now she was a drab little Dublin girl, out to get herself raped. She was a cleaner who might take a job in a bank if the visa came through. She was a woman who mistook sex for everything else. She did not have a talent for life.

This is what he had done to her.

The more she walked the less she wanted to meet him. His tatty little-boy eyes. His thumped face. His stupid lies.

He was on the run from some fuck-up – money, or everything, or maybe a girl like Leenane whose beauty was hard to get away from.

Maria crossed intersections and turned right or left. She felt ordinary, ordinary. She had never been in love, never lost herself in that place where your own face was a mystery to you. She wondered what the girl in the photo looked like now – like someone else again, probably. Still, she wanted to see herself, her old self, or a different self, passing her by and escaping down the street.

At dusk she came across a diner; a metal trailer outlined in neon and tacked on to the side of a fifties highrise. She did not think it could be real, but when she walked in, her stomach clenched at the smell of hash browns and bacon. Over easy, she said to herself. Sunny side up.

'How would you like that cooked?' said the waitress, and Maria tried to remember. She recalled an egg, crisped and frilly at the edges. She recalled an egg she had once with a runny yolk.

'Whatever.' The waitress looked at her with something like disgust and turned away. Maria watched the other customers, chewing solidly.

An egg wasn't just an egg, it was a state of mind.

Everyone in this city knew what they wanted. She turned to the window and looked at the three hundred perfect eggs that passed, runny and hard, and just soft enough. And Maria wondered why she had never seen them before like this, happy in a sort of senseless difference. She looked at the particular cut of their collars, the different colours of their shirts, the way they styled their hair.

The waitress was coming to her table. She had wig-blond hair and was wearing a dolly apron. Maria dreaded what she might find on the plate. She stood up and walked out the door.

'Hey!'

Maria ran and stopped and lifted up her face. She opened her mouth and tried to howl it up into the canyons of New

York. But no noise came. She kept going. Her body bulged as she walked and the pavement hit her step after step. A tramp passed and she smelt his coat in the very middle of her head.

Panic was in front of her, but she could not turn back. It was in the breaths she took and the smells that happened in her brain. She tried to run but there was a wall of it, and she could not get through.

She walked and shuffled into a run and paused and walked some more. Somewhere in TriBeCa she started to recognise the streets again, realised she was nearly home, and that she could not move.

After a while, the air opened up around her. She felt calm. She sat on the ground. She was on an empty lot in TriBeCa, sitting on the ground like the queen of smashed glass. She knew that it was wrong to put her life to the test like this, that it was very wrong. She looked at the weeds and the trash. She looked up at the moon in New York.

People passed. A man said to another man, 'I thought I was going to shit in his hand.' A pair of dealers, dipping at the knee. Six young guys, who stopped talking Spanish as their fanned-out shadows flicked over her. A couple hurrying through, the woman speaking low and hard.

It was a warm, fighting night.

Maria pushed herself up off the sidewalk and went on. She passed a sad-looking woman who ignored her, and recognised, too late, her own reflection. Even she did not know what she looked like any more.

Finally.

She had wiped herself off the map.

Roughly Translated

London, 1985

Rose blamed the man on Oxford Street.

One dismal winter afternoon, a man leaned towards her on Oxford Street, rubbed the tips of his fingers together and said, 'Puss! Puss!'

Rose walked on, checking her clothes. She was wearing a brown suede jacket, a pair of washed-out Levis and a black turtle-neck jumper. She was wearing white underwear, black socks and black flat shoes. She felt her face flush. Everything was her own. She had lost the habit of stealing. There was no reason for men to hiss at her, as she was walking down the street.

She wondered what he knew, what flaw he sensed in her. *Think you're good-lookin'?* Rose did not know if she was good-looking, though there were days, like today, when she was pleased enough. Recently she had applied for a passport and surprised herself by not knowing what to write on the form. Her hair was an ordinary brown, but how to describe the mucky nothing of her eyes. Blueish-grey with gold flecks? A few green bits?

'What colour', she said to William, 'are my eyes?'

At Oxford Circus, Rose walked into Hennes, of all places, and lifted, in quick succession, a chocolate-coloured cardigan and a slim red skirt. She took them into the fitting room, and opened her bag and just did it.

But she had grown up. She had lost her nerve. She was trying to get past the stone balustrade at Oxford Circus tube when she felt a hand running down her forearm and on to the top of her bag. Rose turned.

The woman had grey hair, dyed blond, and lidless eyes set flat into her face. She looked bothered, as though she had rushed out without her coat, left something behind her on the stove. Rose's heart leapt. She opened her mouth to say something, but there was a man on the other side of her now, with a grip that bunched the muscles against the bone of her arm.

They brought her to a room at the back of the shop. A few orange and grey plastic chairs, coffee mugs on a drainer beside the sink. You never thought about shops having rooms like these, the door hidden by a mirror where people looked at themselves and despaired of their old clothes. Ordinary rooms, with the shop assistants' old jackets on a coatstand by the door.

The woman, for some reason, wiped the table with a cloth, then turned to rinse it at the sink.

'I have a sixth sense,' she said. She stood with her back to Rose and dried her hands. 'I'm never wrong.'

'It was a mistake,' said Rose.

The woman turned.

'Of course.'

She sat in a chair on the other side of the table and joined her hands together as though praying. Then she pushed them forward across the damp table, and glared.

'I know you,' she said. 'As soon as you walk into my shop, I know what you want. I know what you're going to do, even before you know it yourself.'

Rose started to laugh. Then stopped herself. The woman leaned back.

'Don't come back, all right? When you pass me, you pass sixteen security personnel talking to me in their walkie talkies, up and down this street. You don't come into my shop. You don't go into their shops. All right?'

They sat in silence then. An assistant came in with a plastic bag, the top stapled with a receipt.

'Here's your change.'

Rose made her way out into the street. She hung on to

the balustrade and laughed. She looked at the stream of people pouring down the steps to the tube; the tops of their heads made vulnerable by partings, and thinnings, and dark roots on show. She turned around and looked into the shop.

The bitch refused to catch her eye, but Rose hung on. She hung on, literally, for half an hour, furious, wanting. Because when she turned and saw this woman for the first time, her heart jumped in her chest.

Rose thought this woman was the answer. And as she glared through the shop doorway, she translated the question for the first time – the question she asked of faces on the street, the question she had been asking all her life, was the simplest one of all.

'Are you my mother?'

The crowd bumped past. She felt its slow patience as it tried to tear her away from the barrier, as it clotted at the traffic lights, and broke free again. Rose held her ground, and tried to catch the women's glances as they hurried by. A start of recognition, that is what she wanted. She checked their eyes for the puzzled look, the mucky everything of her own. Is it you? Are you sad? Is your life better now, without me?

So many people looked as though they had lost something, or put something away.

Two weeks later she went to see Judi Dench in *Antony and Cleopatra*. She felt like running on to the stage and unmasking the woman on the spot. She felt like shouting it out to the crowd.

When she was small she had cut pictures of actresses and models out of magazines. She remembered feeling sorry for them. This was what you had to do to look beautiful, she must have thought, this is what you had to do to make everyone love you. You had to have a secret sorrow. You had to give up a child.

But the secret sorrow grows up. The secret sorrow becomes so famous she plays the Albert Hall and her mother hears her own voice in the music. The dressing room is full of flowers. The mother stands at the door and watches, unsure, as the whole world takes and loves the thing she gave away.

Rose sat in her room night after night. An anglepoise lamp. A desk and chair. A music stand. The black mirror of the window. A wardrobe overflowing with clothes, many of which were not her own. A bed.

She stayed up late and walked in the dawn light, trying to catch them off-guard. She hated the way they hid themselves – under make-up, under sunglasses, or layers of fat. The streets were full of women who dyed their hair. Sad women, and glamorous women: women who gave her away and never got over it, or women who were thriving, because giving her away was the simplest, the most sensible thing to do.

Her mother was on the tube, overdressed and sleek. Her mother was in the supermarket aisle, ducking away from her, and she was there behind the cash register when Rose went to leave. Her mother was standing outside a hi-fi shop looking at twelve television sets, she was writing a letter in a café window, she was pausing at a street corner and checking her left-hand coat pocket.

Her mother sat, finally, behind a desk at the adoption agency. She said that some of the Irish records were distorted. That was the word she used, 'distorted'. She said, 'They didn't want the children to turn up on the doorstep. So they put the wrong things on the forms. Do you understand what I'm saying? They lied routinely. They lied all the time.'

Rose sat on the other side of the desk and stayed very, very quiet. She made no sudden moves. She answered all the questions just so. Her mother had her own life to lead, she said, she didn't want to intrude.

'But it is your right to know,' said her mother, from under her foundation, from behind the pinkish eyeshadow. She had a cheerful twist of maroon hair sticking up from the back of her head. Her glasses were half-moon and full of 'character'. She looked out over them kindly.

'Isn't it?'

Rose knew that this was just a test. She knew not to frighten her, not to frighten any of them.

'Well, she has her rights too.'

Melody, for this, impossibly, was her mother's name, twinkled in a searching manner over the glasses. She lifted her bosom with her folded arms, and settled the lot on the table in front of her.

'By law,' she said. 'You are entitled to know. All the rest is up to you.'

Blood

Christmas, 1985

The sound of the city eased suddenly, and Maria realised it had been there all day. The sound of traffic and of feet, and millions of people speaking millions of words. New York was as loud as a fridge in the corner, switching itself off.

She shook her head slightly, and looked around her room. Two lawn chairs. A round table with fold-down flaps. A rickety bookcase with a small can of blue paint sitting on the top. Her life.

Christmas had come and gone. She had helped it go, by closing her eyes for long stretches of time. She could not imagine where Anton had spent the day. He was on a beach somewhere, he was in a bar. He was with the girl in the photograph. He was in a different month of the year.

She sat in the armchair and tried to fall asleep.

She could hear a child's toy spinning across the floor of the room upstairs. It sounded like a marble. Over and over. First she heard the sound of a winding mechanism and then the sound of a marble, hopping out on to the floor. Which meant that it wasn't a marble after all – there is no such thing as a mechanical marble. Maria listened for hours and tried to figure out what kind of toy it might be.

They were moving the furniture around up there, and every fifteen minutes they put on 'Bohemian Rhapsody'. They were the kind of people who turn up the volume for some bits and down for others, and turn the whole thing off in the middle of the song.

Maria sat in the chair and looked at the door.

What she was waiting for was the sound of the key

turning, that liquid click, whether to close or to open. She heard it over and over again. She could smell the cold metal. She was licking the latch.

When dawn came, she walked the streets to get some light. She would feel the photons hitting the back of her eyeballs: more photons in a second of light than people who have ever lived, or are yet to be born. No wonder Einstein slept for fourteen hours a night.

She was looking for something clean and inevitable. Death might do, but she knew it wasn't clean. A face on the street, perhaps, sudden and sexual. But the face on the street speaks and there is nothing interesting coming out of its mouth, something about shoes, and the rain.

'It was hard to find you,' said the man in her dream. 'I had to look for you in so many countries, across so many times.'

But Maria knows that she is lost. There is no one to find her. No one who even wants to look.

Maria puts her head in the middle of the room and examines the contents. It is full of tatty little thoughts. They keep repeating in no order at all. She should give them numbers. Number Three: Anton lied.

Number Four: Going mad.

Number Two: Staying. Leaving.

Number Five: The wrong things that keep coming out of her mouth every time she opens it to speak.

And finally Number One, which is just a phrase, *We are on our own*, she says to herself. *We are on our own.*

Each of them is followed by a small swoon, a tic, a want. One morning, as she is rooting under the bed for a pair of shoes, she finds a man's sock and the phrase comes to her translated into words, fully formed.

'I want to die.'

Once she has it, she cannot avoid it.

'I want to die,' she says, as she watches the door, as she walks out into the painful air.

'I want to die,' as she stacks the pots on other people's draining boards, as she empties the dust into the trash.

At night, Maria sits in the chair and counts her thoughts, sorting them into bags like marbles, but this one keeps hopping out and rolling across the floor.

'Oh please. I want.' As she swings out of bed and her feet hit the floor. As she touches the windowlatch, or the cold handle of the door.

She does not think of Cassie or of her other friends, the goodness of them that pursues her and tries to shoulder her clear. She does not remember her luck.

She buys a plane ticket home, but she does not know if she will make it. She does not think she can make it.

'I want.'

She has forgotten even the word for death. She has a bottle of yellow sleeping pills from a bathroom cabinet on the Upper West Side. She has a bottle of blue ones from the back of a bedside locker in Eighty-fifth Street. She takes one pill out of each bottle, just as an experiment, and she sleeps for fifteen hours.

Rose sat in her room, back at college. Christmas had come and gone. She needed to be alone. When she was alone, her brain did what she told it to do, just about.

Her parents were in the Caribbean, on a cruise. They left after Boxing Day, very concerned about Rose. Watching them going up the gangplank, her father wearing sneakers and her mother in a powder-blue tracksuit, she realised that they would die, someday. It was the tracksuit that did it.

She told them she was going to spend New Year with William, but the truth was she had kissed William goodbye on Christmas Eve in Paddington, and did not have the heart to tell him it was for the last time. Since then, the phone in the hall rang sometimes, sometimes for a long time.

But she was better off alone. When she opened her mouth, the wrong words hopped out of it. Everything she tried to do came out backwards. She drank from the hot tap. She said things like, *He is the kind of woman who.*

On New Year's Eve, she stuck in a pair of ear-plugs, not so much to get away from the phone as from the noises in the street. Her room became an underwater place, full of sudden frights. Someone was breathing in the corridor outside, someone else stood behind her back and sighed.

At two in the morning, her eye was caught by a lampshade hanging over an archway in a flat across the road. For a second it looked like a body hanging there: the archway as a dark coat, and the lampshade was the head, broken at the neck like a blossom on its stem. Of course, it didn't exist, except in the corner of her eye, but the face was awful, dead and fleshy and somehow pleased with itself, and the coat, or cloak, the shapelessness, was worse. The face was blank when she saw it first, down-looking, perhaps a little sad and surprised by the sight of the floor. It was only when she saw what it really was that it took on this pleased expression, no doubt because she had been fooled.

Turn the light on, thought Rose, Turn on the light.

The flat belonged to a woman who sometimes stayed up late, as Rose did, and sat in a chair and rocked. She might be there at eleven and gone at five past, she might be still there at three.

Rose wondered if she might sense the collusion between the arch and the lampshade despite the different view she had – the inside view, where the arch was on one side of her and the lampshade on the other. Perhaps the way the lampshade hung over the arch was oppressive to her in the middle of the night, when space flattened and arranged itself at angles, as it might for a painter or for someone who was very tired.

What if the woman really did hang herself? What if the woman hanged herself, maybe next week? She would wait until Rose's head was turned and then climb up on her chair. Or she would wait until Rose had gone to the toilet and then she would climb up on her chair and tie the knot.

154

She would wear the coat for effect, or perhaps because, in her distress, she felt cold. (Why would she leave the curtains open? Because she did not want to rot at the end of a rope, did not want the rope to grow wet with her, to creep over her skull and pull her face away at a slow crawl, until she slipped through and fell on the floor, and then the rest of her face dropped off after her – a day later, because gravity is slow, a whole day. She left the curtains open so that Rose could get the authorities on the phone and watch their fumbled *pietà*, in trilbies and trenchcoats, as they caught and cradled and lowered her down, one on the chair, now put to rights, and one standing on the ground.)

The woman knew Rose. She saw her at the shops, or she saw her at the bus stop. And she didn't like her. She would wait until Rose looked over before she kicked away her chair. Their eyes would meet. She would smile and kick away the chair.

And what could Rose do?

I could smile back, thought Rose. I could look into her eyes and say goodbye.

But of course it has nothing to do with Rose, nothing to do with anyone. The woman is very distressed. Space has flattened for her, she does not so much cross the room as crawl up the face of the floor. She is cold even though the night is warm. The rope feels funny, numb, the rope does not feel at all. She knots it carefully, because she is not sure what it is under her fingers. She hopes it will hold. She places the chair carefully, unsure of the angle of the floor, unsure whether it will slide away from under her feet.

And here am I, thought Rose, there is a street between us, stairs to run down, a door to fight, a peculiar state of dress in which to run out into the middle of the night shouting 'No! No!' And then what? The chair is fallen, she is bucking the rope, her face does not bear thinking about. 'No! No!' and the neighbours and the delay and the excitement and no one with any sense (except me, except me) or any keys, or a battering ram, or the calm hands to slip a credit card into the lock, if and when we have run and fallen up the stairs. Her stairs.

There she is. Here is Rose across the road, three floors up, sitting in her socks. She doesn't even have a credit card. She is climbing on to her chair. She looks calm, because once she is up there (and the chair does not slip away) the world is steady again and she has a view. She slips the rope over her head. (It is a just a rope, after all, she can feel the tight twist of its ply.) It is a smooth, clear feeling to let it down over her head and tighten it like a tie, a smart, old-fashioned gesture. Whoops, there's a wobble.

But Rose is thinking fast over here on the other side. She will run to the window, scatter the books from the sill, throw the window open. Throw it! and not feel the wood stick. She will shout 'No!' and the woman will see herself, suddenly, standing on the chair. First their eyes will meet and then she will see herself on the chair. She will look down at her feet and see the distance to the floor. She will pause.

Then what?

'Don't do it!' she could say. But is that enough? 'Don't do it. Talk to me.' About what? She is a stranger. Her life has not been happy. It is possible she is not clean, it is possible she walks the streets a lot and talks rubbish – any amount of it, of all different kinds. She is in a state of distress.

Still. She is standing on her chair, her face tilts up to look at the light fixture, wondering if the cord will hold. (There is the lampshade, back again, but this time at an angle, stuck out above her head, like a hat blowing off.) Nothing matters. The only thing that matters is that Rose should shout at this woman, to give her pause. After that, we'll see. And so she is wrestling with the window, which shoots open, and out fly her doubts followed by the only possible, the only human thing to say.

'NO!'

Maria puts the blood on the mirror because it is dripping on the floor. She can wipe the mirror later, although if she is dead then there will be no reason to wipe the mirror at all. She puts it there as a stop-gap, anyway.

She cannot make it home. She bought a plane ticket because if you fall apart in New York you die. But she is also dying. She is caught in a fold of time, like a fold of cloth. She is on the plane – slitting her wrists on the plane. She is at the baggage carousel, she slips into the toilets and takes some scissors out of her shoulder bag. No. She is still in New York, smashing her wrists against the side of the cutlery drawer. She is on her knees sorting through the knives that have spilt on the floor. She sticks a vegetable peeler into her wrist. She stands up and cracks a glass against the sink and pulls it back along her arm. She is in her bathroom looking for a razor. There is some blood but not enough. She puts it on the mirror. Just for now.

The pills are in her hand. She could not wait for them. She held them in her fist to keep her wrist taut as she dug through the skin to something white that flooded with red. When she opens her hand, it is yellow where she held the little bottle so tight. And the pills are in the bottle. The blood drips on the floor, so she puts the blood on the mirror, just for now.

She tries to open the bottle with her teeth.

'NO!' Rose shouts it. She shouts it clear into the street.

The woman does not hear. She is checking the floor, checking her feet on the chair. How will she jump and kick at the same time? She tries a little hop.

'NO!' The hop and jump seems to have jolted her. She has heard. She looks out the window.

Rose waves, ridiculous as it seems. Rose waves. And the woman sees. Her eyes dilate, even from here Rose can see them. And into the widening gap . . .

'NO!'

Already they have gone too far.

'I'm coming over,' shouts Rose. 'Hang on!'

What did she say? She said she would enter this woman's life. Then she told her to hang on. 'Hang on!' she said. The woman spreads her mouth in a smile.

It is a very slow smile, very contemptuous. It is intimate and distant at the same time. Rose is already in her life. It is not a nice life.

Hey. Nice knowing you!

She hops on her right foot, skips with her left, kicks with her right, like a Morris dancer. And then, like a Morris dancer, she shakes all her bells.

Duh-duh-duh-duh-duh-duh-deh-de-DEE-DEE. Duh-de-de-de-de-de-de-de-de-DEE-DEE. Duh. Duh. Duh.

'Fuck it,' said Rose.

There was no hanging woman. There was no shouted, awful pun. There was an arch and a lampshade, suspended on its core. Its *cord*. Cord.

Some time later, the phone down the hall starts to ring. Rose looks up. Across the road, the light is back on, the woman is rocking again.

She listens to the phone for a while and to the sounds of the street below. She reaches up to draw the curtains and the rocking woman looks at her. Rose, on the other side of the street, gives her a slight, tentative wave.

'Hello.'

The mirror is flat and cool against her skin. Maria can see the sheet of glass between the real blood and the reflected blood. It is very thick. It is very clean and calm. She is trying to open the bottle with her teeth. She looks into her own eyes.

'Hello.'

Wrist

Dublin, 1986

Maria felt like a fraud until the nurse asked for her date of birth and she could not get beyond the day and the month. Maybe it was the familiar Dublin accent, or the dampness in the air. Maybe it was because she was home, at last. She had made it. Or she had nearly made it. She was nearly there.

Because the bed was very close by then. Maria balanced herself with the flat of her hand on the blanket, and lifted her foot to take off her shoe. The nurse was still there and Maria felt she should undress in front of her. She knew that the nurse felt this was not necessary, but the bed confused her. It was too near. The nurse was sorry she had asked for the date of birth but Maria knew that once she was in the bed, then she would be in the bed and her date of birth would not matter.

'It doesn't matter,' said the nurse.

'The eleventh,' she said. The year was there all right. She just couldn't get to it.

She was worried that she might not get her clothes off in time, that she might be in the bed with her clothes on. She pulled her trousers halfway down and sat up on the bed. The nurse was ashamed at her legs, but that was what they were paid for. Maria pushed the trousers down the rest of the way, turned and plucked at the sheet. But she was sitting on it and it would not fold down.

Then the nurse stepped in and Maria let go.

She woke later and found her nightie folded on the coverlet

beside her: as if they knew she would not move in her sleep. How did they know that?

It was dark. She pulled her jumper over her head and unbuttoned her blouse, freeing her hands slowly from the sleeves. She tried to undo the hooks and eyes on her bra, but she could not. She ended up dragging the straps down her arms, so the cups were strung around her middle, inside out.

'So this is what it is like', she thought, 'to be alive,' as she saw her breasts bare in the hospital night. There was the sound of another woman crying softly down the hall, the sound of a nurse's shoes on the corridor.

She opened out her nightie half and half again, found the gap at the base and put it over her head. She lifted her face as the cloth fell past it, until it was out through the hole for her neck. Out into the same dark room. She felt for the sleeves, all the way down, until her hands came out the holes at the wrists. She had the nightie on then, but everything was rucked around her middle. She tried the hooks and eyes of her bra again. She pulled them round to the front, looked at them in the fold of her stomach, and tried to breathe. She would not get upset about it. She could sleep in her bra, if she had to. There was nothing wrong with that. Nothing much.

All the things she found difficult she did not have to do any more. She did not have to wash or speak or dress. She had to go to the toilet sometime, but perhaps not yet. The sunlight moved from one corner of the room to the other and broke her heart. She did not have to watch it. She could sleep instead, or just close her eyes and sleep. The nurse's smile was the right size as she handed her the tablets. There was nothing to it, the nurse held the cup. After, Maria slept a tablet sleep.

If she dreamt, she dreamt of sleep. If she dreamt it was of this room and this bed and her in it, sleeping. But she did not dream, did not cry in her sleep or even awake. Except for when she went down the corridor and found the toilet

160

and came back and got into the bed. She cried a bit then, but it did not matter.

After a few days, a nurse pulled the curtain back, by her bed, as if to say,

'Enough of that now.' She did it tactfully though. If they despised her they did not show it. If they pulled the curtain back, that meant it was time to pull the curtain back.

Maria felt her mind starting up again. She wanted to leave. Everything would be all right. The psychiatrist brought her down to the day room, full of butts, with a crucifix hanging on the wall. Maria was fine. She did not look at the crucifix or the ashtrays, she sat easily in one of the mismatched chairs, the green one with knobbly upholstery that people had been sitting on for years, some of them dressed and some of them, like her, in their night-clothes, so there was a feeling of other bottoms off it through the thin cotton; sad women's genitals, where the green was smooth and worn.

'So?' said the psychiatrist, who was sitting on the sofa. 'Better?'

'I'm not so drowsy. But the place is a little.' The psychiatrist moved from the sofa to another chair. Perhaps she didn't find it comfortable. She could sit where she liked, but there was no need to be so abrupt. As Maria talked, she found her eyes kept returning to the place where the woman should have been but was not. She talked about getting back into the swing of things, how she had decided that she might go back to college when this was passed. Or maybe not. She could just be bored for a while, if needs be, give herself time.

'Yes,' said the psychiatrist, from the wrong chair. 'Give yourself time.' And when Maria suggested that she might be able to leave soon, perhaps tomorrow, maybe the next day, she said again:

'Give yourself time.'

Back in bed Maria cried. She cried with her face but her brain was full of other things. Why did the woman move like that? She listened at an angle, letting Maria talk on, while she sat in the other chair. Then the angle lapsed. The decision was made. Maria talked on, but it did not matter. Talking wasn't the test, and she had already failed.

'Give yourself time.'

The woman had moved from the sofa to the chair to see if Maria could take it. And she couldn't. It confused her. She couldn't help talking to where the woman should have been. She was not 'better'.

Maria yanked the curtain closed down the length of the bed. There was no point leaving it open. She was not better. She couldn't be bothered.

She had made it here by herself. She had caught the plane. She had sat in her seat, except when she needed to go to the toilet. She had opened the plastic trays with the food on them. All this after putting her things in a suitcase and shutting the zip. And sitting in a cab. She sat in a cab all the way through the Queens mid-town tunnel. The one that had the sign 'No Explosives' at its mouth.

The man beside her took both arm-rests. She sat back in her seat, with her shoulders high and her damaged arm resting in her lap. After a while, she realised she could not let her shoulders down, because they were flying. She thought that it would never end. That she would be on this flight for the rest of her life.

She waited at the baggage carousel until everyone was gone. No one claimed her bag. She waited until another flight had gone through, but still no one took it away. She sat at the end of the baggage hall and watched it circling with her life inside, or the corpse of her life. And when the woman came over, she said her own name.

But if the plane had been delayed. If she had jumped out of the cab in the middle of the Queens mid-town tunnel. If she could not find the departure gate. Sitting in the toilets and killing herself, or walking out on to the tarmac and then killing herself as soon as she was able. She looked at her bag as it passed through the X-ray, like a cell on a microscope slide: the dark nucleus of her purse, the squiggle of her jewellery like strands of DNA. She would have to pick it up on the other side. She would have to get on the plane and keep her shoulders high, because this small thread of life took everything she had just to follow it, not to touch it and make it snap.

When the psychiatrist came back, she would be more flexible. Even if it was something uncontrollable like a woman coming in and asking did she want tea. She would be flexible. That's what being alive was.

They sat in the room in silence. Maria was relieved to know that it didn't matter what she said to this woman, how the words went, how her tone of voice lifted and played. A 'Here I am', in the way she rounded her sentence – then went back to gather the last little bit, 'There you are', a small irony, for them both. The psychiatrist moved from the sofa to the chair, day in, day out, for women, in cotton or rayon or silk, for women who showed their wrists as they smoked, while the skin across their chests withered and slackened in the hospital air. She moved for these people in all their dignity, while they explained to the chair she had left, as if it was stupid perhaps, that they had a life, A Life.

Or no life, some of them. 'I have no life.'

She moved from the sofa to the chair, like a bad morning – which has a different idea in the middle of it all, which shifts just when you have fixed it in your head. The next time, Maria would follow her with her eyes and look at her in her new chair and talk on, as if nothing strange had happened at all.

In the meantime, she lay there untangling herself, the monster and the ball of string. She waited for her life to unravel in the dark, so she could follow the string and slay the monster – which was nothing at all. The monster was this: lying in a bed, breathing up and down in the dark. The monster was breath.

'Better?' It was a word like a gift. These were the most important days.

'How's the constipation,' Evelyn said, while her father looked at something more interesting outside the window. 'Better?'

If she heard that word one more time, she would die.

Tissue

London, 1986

Rose sat in Melody's office, and thought about all the other people who had sat in this chair over the years, waiting for news, good or bad. It was a round-backed chair, covered in brown loose-weave fabric, with slim wooden arms. All the discarded children. They must have gripped the wood, as she did. They must have sweated from their palms some keen, musty essence of themselves. This is me. This is the smell of me, hoping.

She put her own palm to her nose. It smelt of iron.

'I'm sorry,' said Melody. 'I'm so sorry about this.' The woman was walking up and down the room. She was practically shouting.

The letter was handwritten, in dark blue ink. It was on a sheet of light blue Basildon Bond notepaper, you could see the watermark, and a scrap of glue where it was torn from the pad. It looked like a childhood thing. The writer had used a ruler, to keep a straight line, and the bottoms of the letters flattened out, curiously, as they told her that her father was 'unknown', and that her mother had died in childbirth, on 12 March 1965.

Please accept my deepest sympathy,
Yours sincerely,
Sr Agatha Simmonds.

Rose thought that it was all fine. She wanted to say this, but what she actually said was,

'Tissue.'

'Oh sorry,' said Melody, and snatched a Kleenex from the box she kept on the desk. But what Rose meant was tissue like the stuff they took out in a biopsy, like the cells they scraped off the inside of your cheek. What Rose meant was that it did not matter.

'What I am supposed to do', said Melody, 'is bring you in here and sit you down, and hand you that piece of paper and watch you cry.'

'It's fine,' said Rose.

'Those fucking nuns. They lied all the time, you know? It was just a thing they did. All the time.'

There was silence for a while, then Melody sat back behind the desk. She pulled the flesh of her face down with both palms and said,

'It's not over yet.'

'It's all right,' said Rose. 'I know she's dead.' And it was true. She did know. She started to cry.

'Oh, I am sorry,' said Melody.

London was so lovely in spring. Rose walked out into the clear air and sensed the shift in the weather – the first warm day. She started to wind through the streets for no reason at all. She started to wind through the streets, like a ball of string, trying to confuse herself with turns and changes of mind. She crossed from one side of the road to the other. She doubled back. She looked into people's faces as she went and decided that, yes, they were confused. Confused by her, confused by the weather.

Father unknown, mother dead.

She had been running on a long leash. All her life, she had been attached by an invisible rope and when, finally, she got around to tugging on it there was no one holding the other end.

Rose started to run. She ran all along Camden High Street to the canal, then tumbled down to the towpath and under bridges until she hit Regent's Park. She ran into the very middle of the grass, where she stopped and bent over to catch her breath, and sat down and lay down, feeling small and naked and pinned to the earth, here in the furthest place she could be from anywhere. She looked at the spring sky and listened to London in the distance, as it pushed its noise up into the air. Then she closed her eyes and felt the planet turn.

It was a Thursday. When she opened her door to her Thursday man, she told him that she could not possibly sleep with someone who wore a yellow V-necked jumper, that he would have to take it off immediately, along with those horrible cords. But when she came, it was high up and hard, as though something thumped her from inside.

'I think I'm pregnant,' she said, even though it was a lie. That got rid of him.

She showered and dressed and packed an overnight bag. When she turned up at her parents' door, she thought, impossibly, that they might not be in, after all.

In the hall she was startled by her own reflection in the coatstand mirror.

'Hello?'

She did not recognise any of the coats any more.

'Hello?'

She looked into the kitchen, where not even the cats were moving. The door to the downstairs bathroom was open, and a tap dripped its amber stain on to the enamel.

Rose wandered round the empty house, thinking that it was all true. She had died and woken up in the same place. She was dead and resurrected, and everything was exactly the same, and entirely changed.

She could do anything now.

In the front room, she sat down at the piano and played into the absolute silence. It was so simple. She sat down at the piano, with no music, and improvised.

Spring

Dublin, 1986

Maria wanted to find her watch, hefted herself around in the bed, reached for the locker and realised it was over.

The plane had landed.

It was nothing you could name. It was a change in the weather. It was a fly banging against the window that finds the gap between the sill and the sash and is gone. The silent woman in the next bed started to ooze tears like glycerine. No one here could bear change. The wind had shifted to warm and Maria picked up her watch. She wanted a packet of crisps. It was four o'clock. Fine.

There was a tune in her head and she hummed it as she swung her legs over the side of the bed, and felt her feet hit the warm floor.

She tried to figure out how long she had been there, and the fact that she couldn't remember made her despair, sweetly, made her feel important as she fastened the belt of her dressing gown.

'I had a nervous breakdown,' she said in her head, to a man who was wearing nothing but a sympathetic air.

She walked along the corridors, looking at all that misery.

'Goodbye,' she said. 'Goodbye,' but did not wave, in case they thought she was mad. When she packed her bag it was so small it made her weak. How long had she spent here? She pulled the zip up over the whole lot of it and walked out into the Dublin air.

5

Berts in Love

Spring, 1986

It was about this time that Berts embarrassed himself by
falling in love. It was a foolish thing to happen to a man of
his age. It was not something he either liked or could act
upon. Nor, in the final analysis, was it something he even
believed in.

The girl in question had come to his attention on the
night of the Christmas party. She had curled her hand
around his tie and pulled him over to the wall that she was
using for support. Berts was sober. He listened to her with a
smile on his face and stretched his arm across the wall
behind her. It seemed to him that she deserved what she was
asking for, more or less. And it did not take much, it took a
slight adjustment of his weight, before she was leaning, not
against the wall, but against the open doorway: it took a
mere shift in the balance between them before she was both
saving herself from falling, and pulling him after her, by
means of the tie she still held in her hand.

Once they were out of sight, he kissed her, in a way. It
happened awkwardly, as he handled her back up against the
banisters. She wriggled away from him and screamed and
gave him a puck in the stomach. Berts was angry and
confused, even before he kissed her. He had never kissed
the mouth of a woman who smoked, for example. It gave
him the uncomfortable feeling that he might be kissing a
man. He had never kissed a woman who could hardly stand
on her own two feet. He still found himself nuzzling into
Evelyn, now and then, but it wasn't a kissing sort of
marriage. Her mouth was not the sort of mouth this young

171

woman had, which made you want to squish it, and split it against her teeth.

Her body was all elbows and hinges, collapsing even as he tried to straighten her out. It was as he hoisted her up, and she grinned back at him, that their faces met. Another man would not have gone for the mouth. Another man would have simply dropped the hand. But the feeling he got, when she grinned at him like that, came, not even from his lips, but from the very root of his tongue. And so he had leaned towards her, not with his face, but with a sort of word that he wanted to say into her mouth.

So she wriggled away and screamed and pucked him in the stomach. But in the pause, in the first shock, her mouth opened under his, just a little.

'Happy Christmas,' said Berts, and stumbled, more than was necessary, back into the main room. That was all he did. He said 'Happy Christmas'. He should have given her a slap on the backside, just to show there were no hard feelings. But a lurching dread sent him back into the room.

Because her mouth had opened under his. Her large lips had tested the dry skin of his mouth, and when her teeth opened, just that fraction, Berts felt as though he were falling into it and would never hit bottom.

In the office the next morning he could not distinguish her moaning from the general shrieks and groans of the girls from the typing pool. Of course it wasn't the typing pool any more. He had to remind himself of that. Even so, she had behaved like a typist. And he, it had to be said, had been very foolish.

He did not see her that day. But a smart little one, who annoyed him for files, gave him a wink as she shut the door. And, as he walked the corridors on the way home, every person who bid him 'Happy Christmas' seemed to be in on some general, private, hilarity.

When Christmas Day actually came, Berts could not shift out of the bed. He felt the temperature of the house rising. Evelyn was up to high doh, Laura was Sulk-Almighty. Then

Cormac arrived and spent the entire dinner Having Opinions. Maria rang around six o'clock, already the worse for wear.

His sister Joan came out on Stephen's Day and Berts noticed that she too had been hitting the bottle. Where did they come from, these drinking women? They had crept up on him.

Twenty years ago it would have been a disgrace, but now a drinking woman was all the rage. All the rage, he said to himself, watching the slurry-load of his sister's life threaten to brim over and spill all over the house. She was thin. The clothes she wore were too bright. She had a blouse on like a TV screen that made her neck look, not so much old, as marked. She leant her elbow on the table and waved her forearm loosely at the room, while the husband, Maurice, just sat in the chair and worked his way, plumply, through a six-pack of stout.

On New Year's Eve, Berts went out into the front garden. He had decided to join the general slide and got through a fair amount of whiskey in the run-up to the midnight clock. Evelyn had made no remark. They sat and watched the television, Berts tippling through the Powers, which made it bearable, just about. Laura was off at a friend's house and Cormac, who said he had a party, was probably sitting watching the same rubbish they were. The drink had no effect that he could tell, and when the clock struck Evelyn looked over to him and he said, 'Well there we go.' He stood up and so did she and they met briefly in the middle of the room. She put her hand on his shoulder and he bent and pecked her hair, wanting suddenly to fold himself into her like a picnic table.

He kept himself upright instead and walked past her into the hall. She followed him into the front garden and called to the other few neighbours who opened their doors. Someone on Griffith Avenue let off a rocket. Berts watched it, and, after it was gone, found himself still looking at the stars.

It was a cold night. Evelyn checked him and moved back indoors, but Berts stayed where he was. He recalled a man he had worked under for years, who had retired and fallen apart. First one thing, then the other. He left the office, as he had come into it, a man with a future. He would be the type for a consultancy, for a seat on some board, but he had fallen apart, first the waterworks, then one thing after another, until Evelyn was driving him out one Saturday afternoon to Vincent's Hospital, saying, 'You always said he was good to you,' and they had walked the corridors while the wives sat, and poor old Dempsey in his dressing gown, until they reached, somehow, a mixed ward, and a woman who shouted, 'Tell us! Is that your handbag?' and Dempsey had laughed and tucked the colostomy bag in under the dressing gown and shuffled back to his own ward, talking about Planning Permission.

Berts found his eyes watering. He was drunk after all. But he wasn't trying to cry for Dempsey, who was so 'good' to him he had to hate him a little, had to gain some satisfaction from the knacker-woman shouting about the bag. He was trying to cry for the feeling he had had in his lips, the shaming weakness of his mouth when he had kissed the first strange mouth in twenty years. Even the word 'kissed' was an embarrassment to him. He went indoors.

During the months of January and February Berts kept himself to himself. He ate his sandwiches in the office and did not stray into the pub for lunch. Then Maria came home and put the whole house into a spin. Berts had to drive Evelyn out to the hospital night after night. After two weeks of it, he parked the car under a street lamp and took out the *Irish Times*.

The young woman in question did not intrude. She passed him in the corridor and smiled, tightly, as she always had. She put her head around the door and fed him some detail that might be useful for the matter in hand. The thought occurred to him that she might not even remember what had passed between them, but he could not believe that this was true. There was a resentment there. There were sudden changes of mood. One day she looked in for no other reason, it seemed, than to tell him a joke.

'What do you call a sheep with no legs?' she said.

'I don't know.'

'A cloud.' She pulled the door after her with a satisfied click and Berts sat there like an eejit, his heart pounding, wondering what the hell she meant.

Everyone knew, of course. It would be foolish to let it bother him, but he wished they would stop letting it slip every time they opened their gobs. The stupid bitch had fallen through a doorway, and he had fallen after her, that was all.

She was twenty-nine. She thought she was going places. And he had to admire her – the way she glossed things over, the way she segued on, as though she didn't know she was riding for a fall. Berts watched her, in the normal way of these things, but he could not enjoy it. He did not enjoy watching her lips move. He looked at her in meetings, talking on, and thought, deliberately, about that mouth around his private parts. But the flood of revenge he got was turned to weakness by a peculiar want. He wanted, for example, to tell her that she had biro marks on her blouse.

One day he saw her in the corridor, with a piece of tissue stuck to her shoe. He ducked in behind her, and stamped it to the floor. Then he walked on, leaving her standing there, with one arm as long as the other.

'Thanks,' she said.

That evening at home, Berts found himself in a mood of great hilarity. He rustled the paper from page to page, while Laura sat watching the television and picking her split ends. At least she had stopped eating it. She had always hated her lovely red hair.

'What do you call a sheep with no legs?' he said.

'Da-ad.'

'What? It's a joke.'

'I know it's a joke. I know that joke.'

'Well, so,' he said.

'An elephant's tampon.' After a moment she said, 'Well, don't blame me,' as he stood up and walked out of the room.

He could distinguish, or thought he could distinguish, her step; the click of her shoes on the corridor, the high hiss of nylon rubbing against nylon, between her legs.

She was all husband-no-children, she was three-bedroom-semi-detatched. Berts paused to think what it was that she might want and the thought that she might want him spread in a heat, from the back of his neck to his lips.

She had pulled him by the tie, she had wrapped the tie around her fist with a twirl of her hand and she had said,

'You know what your problem is?'

She was drunk. He had leaned his arm against the wall above her head and said,

'Sorry?'

'You know what your problem is?' she said again, as he shifted his weight on to the other foot, and she slid towards the door.

'What?' he said, after she had nearly hit the floor, after he had grabbed her under the armpits and was propping her up against the stairs.

'I forget,' she said.

It was then that he had felt the word at the root of his tongue, and all the rest of it happened, piece by piece.

March was a terror. The rain whipped through everything and the wind never let up. The garden was all light green buds in the occasional sunshine, and the branches wet and black. Laura was getting worse. She was coming home later and later. One morning Berts found the dried traces of his daughter's vomit when he lifted the lid on the toilet bowl.

The month rolled over into spring, and everyone felt the change in the air. That afternoon he walked, for the first time, into the small room she called her office. He did not knock. The room was empty and Berts looked around, amazed by her absence.

The place used to be a cloakroom, full of coats and hats, over-shoes and umbrellas. He looked at the row of hooks along a green plank on the wall and remembered the comfort of the place, the smell of wet wool, like school.

When she came in, Berts did not know where to look. As far as he could recall, her hair was brown, with a bit of a wave in it. As far as he could recall, she had a girl's hair. But the woman who came in the door had a cropped blond helmet on her head. She looked like a light bulb. Her eyes glittered at him from underneath it, as though he was supposed to notice, or pass some remark. He curled a finger around one of the hooks on the wall, and tucked the other hand into his pocket. He was not in the business of noticing people's hair.

She was putting a database together, which was all very modern and commendable. But it was messing with inter-departmental links; she was getting up everyone's nose, skipping protocol. He decided he would tell her as much.

'You might be hurt, that's all.'

'Hurt.' She seemed pleased by the word, she smiled around it.

'I mean,' and Berts lifted both hands as if to show that they were empty, 'it might be taken away from you. That's all.'

'They can't do that,' she said. 'It's my baby.'

Berts examined the hook. It was an old, graceful thing, curled like old handwriting, a scribble on the wall. What was there to say? That he loved her. That he wanted to stop her from making mistakes.

'These things are not as simple as they seem,' he said.

'They're not as difficult either.'

She was looking at him like he was the enemy.

'Well, I just thought I'd warn you,' he said, and turned to go. The door shut behind him and Berts found his handkerchief. He pushed it against his face, then he pinched the bridge of his nose.

'I have a daughter gone into hospital,' he said to her in his head, as he walked away from her room. 'Nerves,' he said.

'Oh dear,' she said, smiling. 'Oh dear.' As she brushed her lips across his forehead. 'Never mind. It's not your fault.'

'No, it's not my fault.'

So they gave the database thing to Carney, who would bury it decently and take his time. She arrived up to Berts, all agitated, and he tried to settle her down – these things were hard, after all. They talked for a while, but she did not move from the place she had chosen in the middle of the room. Berts spoke across to her, but she looked very small, and mistaken, and hard to reach.

At the door she stopped and faced him again, all drama. 'Don't let this happen.'

'And how,' said Berts. 'Could I stop it?'

'Of course you could.'

The door shut behind her. Perhaps it was true. The thought had not occurred to him. If it came to a question of him or Carney, he knew he could carry the day. Berts moved seldom, but he moved well.

'Of course you could.'

He threw it as a ball from hand to hand. He felt the texture of it, a dark sponge ball, such as dogs run after, full of their spit. He could take her side.

The next morning, her door was open, and she looked up at him as he passed. She was wearing a jacket with pads in the shoulders, and the pads were bigger than her breasts. Her small breasts. Her my-husband sort of breasts.

'My husband,' he heard her say once. 'My *husband*,' as though they were supposed to think the man marvellous just because she had married him. As though they had actually met the man and been fairly swamped by admiration.

Tell your husband *I know you.*

Still, by mid-afternoon, Berts had almost resolved to move. He went up to the top corridor and walked to the very end, passing the powers-that-be, door by door. He knew them intimately. He knew what they loved, by way of literature, or flattery, or policy. He knew them like he knew the inside of his own head. If he wanted to, he could move. He felt he might.

There was a window at the end of the corridor. Berts looked out over the dome of the Four Courts. He thought about the way she stood as if attached to a spot in the floor – if you pushed her over she would flip back up again, like a ballerina in a child's box. She was cheap music. She went on and on.

'Of course you could.'

She was full of 'could'. You could go to Spain on your holidays, or go to France, you 'could' go to bloody Malaysia. You could dye your hair so you looked like a light bulb, you could pull a man by the tie, for no reason at all.

The whole thing was a joke from start to finish. He paused for a leak on the way back to his own room. He glanced at his member, as he had done every day, several times a day, for the last fifty-eight years. He washed his hands, as he always washed his hands, and looked at his face in the mirror above the washbasin. And the whole thing of it, the whole miserable kit and caboodle, made him wince.

And when he went home that evening, he pointed his knife across the table and said to Laura that he would sit up, that night and every night, for as many nights as it took, and if he smelt drink off her, when she came in, he would pull her by that red mop of hers up to the Garda station where they would force out the name of the publican who was serving underage. He would pull her through the courts if necessary. He would pull her from here to Kingdom Come. He had the patience for it and he had the strength, she need not think otherwise, because he would not stand idly by while his own daughter fell into the gutter.

The Changing Room

Autumn, 1986

The man who loved his wife stood outside Maria's changing room and cleared his throat. Maria knew that he loved her because she was sentimental that day, but perhaps she wasn't wrong either. Today she fancied married men, with children on their shoulders and kind intelligent faces. This one did not have a child on his shoulders, but his wife was pregnant and that was just as good. Maria checked his shoes under the curtain as he waited on the other side. They were slip-ons, which was a mistake, but you couldn't be a snob in this job. People would wear anything. You'd go mad looking. Maria had been mad already and she wasn't going back now.

She arranged her numbers from one to four, and pushed the rejected clothes along their rail. She picked up her can of air freshener and put it down again, wanting things to be right for this pregnant woman; wondering what smell she might like, what smell she might leave.

Maria scanned the room from corner to corner, looking for who to protect and who to despise. It wasn't the baby, or even the woman whose husband loved her. It wasn't anyone, yet. Maria waited, though she did not know what she was waiting for. She knew this feeling and was not afraid of it. She was afraid of very little, here in her changing room, where people decided things if they could. She picked up her can of Autumn Essence and sprayed it into the air.

The new blouse was all wrong; big red poppies that would not match as the woman fastened them together from the neck down. The whole thing gaped to show her protruding belly button, like the nipple on a giant breast. Maria thought about the baby curled inside, charged and mute; the smell of Autumn Essence already translated in its tiny pink blood.

Maria started to cry. The woman in charge of the fitting room started to cry and wiped her eyes any-old-how on a pair of black trousers that someone might want to buy some day. She turned to her curtain to hide her tears, while the wrong blouse came off the pregnant woman. She was the one who should be crying, you might think, but the woman in charge of the fitting room did it for her, as she pulled the elastic of her trousers across her navel and then pushed it down again, because everything today was too tight.

Under the curtain, the man's feet flexed in his slip-on shoes. A gap opened between the leather and his sock, wide enough to slip a finger down. The pregnant woman put on her jacket and walked over to Maria.

'Any luck?'

'Not at all,' and the man could not take the thinness of the curtain a moment longer. He put his head into Maria's changing room.

'Do you mind?' said Maria. 'Do you mind?' as his eyes scanned the room.

'It's a bit sploshy,' said the pregnant woman, holding the blouse up for her husband to see.

'Excuse me,' said Maria, moving in front of his face.

'Sorry?' he said, as if she hadn't seen the way his eyes travelled all over the room; over women half-in and half-out of their clothes, women turning to the mirror, asking questions of their thighs. He took it all in with a jitter and sweep of his eyes, settled on the blouse, then switched to Maria, like she was in on the joke.

'Come on, you,' the pregnant woman said. His face disappeared from the curtain as she swivelled him back towards the shop. She handed back the blouse to Maria, gave her a filthy look, and followed him through.

Maria adjusted the curtain after they were gone.

Ordinary, ordinary, said Maria. You have to get used to the ordinary. This is what she had looked for; she had looked for what she could not bear. A man who cannot resist. A woman who will not let her legs show. And two women with a handicapped child who looks at herself in the mirror and laughs at her new clothes.

'I think she likes it,' says one.

'Oh *Like*,' says the mother.

And the child says, 'Like! Like!'

Some of the women took their skirts off first, and some their tops. Others stripped to their underwear and started over new. A few changed under their coats, just opened them like a flasher when they were done.

Nothing fitted. At least for a while. It always took a bit of smoothing or twirling before a new thing settled down. Maria ignored the clothes and looked for stories instead, a bad husband, a failed kidney – tremendous operations forcing the flesh into a badly stitched seam. She saw lots of appendix and, once, a catastrophic heart, a shiny zip turning the woman's torso into its own jacket. Mostly it was children: they came in sometimes, the little Caesars, all new beside the bellies that they had sloughed off. Might as well work in a morgue, she thought sometimes, wondering what the difference was in being alive. But,

'Suits you,' she said. 'No, really.' Making the leap for them, as they turned from side to side. And it was a gift: to be able to tell the difference like that, to turn the nearly right into the just perfect: to see the future and believe in it.

'That's a lovely colour on you,' she said. 'That's a lovely blue.'

The Interview Room

Autumn, 1986

Rose made her way up a set of concrete steps. Either the dogs were very big around here, or someone had been shitting on the stairs.

Rose hated the flats. She hated the smell of them. The balconies were stained with rain, and the central courtyard was deserted. A small boy, perhaps four years old, stood on the third-floor walkway, with his feet solidly apart. He lifted his face to her, full of things to say.

'Sorry?'

'You looking for Benny?'

Rose looked at him. Was Benny the drug, or was he the dealer?

'No,' she said. Then she said, 'No, sweetheart,' and the little boy ran away.

She found the right door, hefted her bag on her shoulder and slouched down. This was what the people in the office looked like when they went on a call. They looked sloppy, but their eyes were neat. Rose was jealous of them. They had a way of being angry, of dumping their big bags on their desks, of sprawling in their chairs and stubbing out their cigarettes with a twist. But their eyes were neat. Their eyes were able to judge and assess. She tried to imagine being one of them, every time.

The woman came to the door in her dressing gown, but it was only eleven o'clock, so that was fine. Rose walked through the rooms and judged as she went on the adequacy of things, looking for the signs of strain. In the kitchen she saw a snowdrop in a little liqueur glass by the sink. It excused everything, the stickiness of the carpet underfoot, the smell, the fact that the woman could not explain where her partner might be, or produce one of the kids. There was a snowdrop by the sink in a little liqueur glass, and, roughly translated, it said everything in this flat was just fine.

When she got the call the next day Rose decided, yet again, that she was in the wrong job. The missing child was in Casualty with four fingers that were not so much broken as *dislocated*. Of course the boyfriend was not to blame, the boyfriend was nowhere near him – but if this was true then why ring his probation officer? Unless it was to say, 'Take him away from me, now.'

Rose put down the phone and felt a rise of vomit in the back of her throat.

Because a small bit of her was pleased. A small bit of her – if she prodded it – was inflamed with a dislike of these people. Their endless mistakes, their fucking snowdrops.

That night she sat in and drank a bottle of white wine because there was no point in corking it, and woke up at four in the morning livid with hate. Welcome to the job.

Five weeks ago, her senior had rung in sick with flu. What he'd really meant to say was that he was having a nervous breakdown. Of course. Everything makes sense, but only if you translate it in time.

So now, she was making his home calls, looking at the stories people had, the photos tacked to the wall, the flamenco doll on the mantelpiece or the doll with helpless scribbles on the plastic crotch. She looked for things that could not lie: a scar, a tremor, dilated pupils or pupils like pins. She looked for burn marks on furniture or flesh, and always tried to listen to a room, convinced somehow that the angle of things, the way they faced each other or turned away, would tell her what she needed to know.

So the carpet was sticky underfoot, and there were no toys on the floor. The sofa was pushed against the wall and the two chairs were jammed up under the windowsill. But in the kitchen, on the draining board, in front of the window, there was a snowdrop in a little glass that said everything here is just fine.

When what it really meant to say, of course, was *Help!*

The woman who throws a chair across the room, the boy who spits on the floor, the man who looks at you and talks about your cunt.

Help!

And Rose did want to help people. She lay on her back in Regent's Park one spring day and realised she was a blank sheet. She had to be careful what she wrote on it. She would do good things.

But what if she didn't like people, after all? Maybe this was why she had ended up here, in the probation service, and not in Cerebral Palsy or Guide Dogs for the Blind – because she wanted to punish people, but slowly.

'No, not broken. *Dislocated.*'

She picked up a file and walked down to the interview room.

Attempted arson. Nineteen years old. Peroxide hair; his eyes very cool. He had strong white fingers, translucent to the bone. Rose looked at them and wondered where they had been.

'So you're clean?' she said.

'Yeah.'

'Are you?'

'I told you, I don't bother with shit.'

'So, Simon,' she leaned forward. He was laughing at her, the little shit. 'Tell me about where we left off.'

'Tell you what?'

Rose was still looking for the key. The tumblers would roll into place, and the damaged child spill out into the room.

'Whatever you like.'

She was hungry, still, for the stories people had. Rose wanted to bump into someone from college and tell them the remarkable place her own life had ended up. She had tried with William, rung him up to say 'Who are you, these days?' and when they met, he had pushed his hand down her knickers as she sat on the arm of a chair. Rose was astonished at his anger. She wondered, as she felt his blunt nail shove into her, how he could feel so connected as to want to hurt her in this way.

The little shit looked at the ceiling and Rose imagined the Styrofoam dripping on to them, in gouts of flame. This was a boy who liked to burn things down.

'Tell me about the fire.'

Rose sat and counted in her head from one to five hundred. She lost her place at two hundred and thirty with the sudden thought that if she loved him, then everything would be all right. She imagined kissing him and telling him it would be all right. She imagined pulling his hips towards her, with their large and beautiful bones.

'Just.'

She waited.

'I was fucked off.'

'Why?'

Veins

Autumn, 1986

A girl Maria knew from college walked into her changing room – didn't even see her, as she took the tag.

Tall, with long calves, very self-possessed. She wriggled into a cream skirt and went out in her broken-looking bare feet to show a friend outside.

'Brilliant,' said his voice and Maria tried not to smile. Tom. She wanted to put her head around the curtain and say, 'So what are you up to, these days?' She wanted to surprise him with where she had ended up – working for crap money and living in a Hatch Street bedsit.

Just for the laugh. You understand.

When they met, he was in first med, and she was in second engineering. It was the year before she went to New York. He hung around the student bar, chain-smoking and talking about dissections, about stealing some dead guy's dick and letting it hang down from the bottom of his trousers. Maria didn't believe a word of it, but she fell for him anyway. Mostly because of the way he never looked at her, but also because of the way he smoked, the hunger of it.

She got her friend Joanna to bring him on a double date to the Halloween Ball. He arrived pissed and sat at the table all night, picking the petals off the centrepiece. There was a bit of a lunge in the taxi home, a lot of tongue. Maria found it all a bit anatomical, but she spent the next three months chasing him. She went puce just thinking about it. About bumping into him 'casually' in Keoghs and letting him know, by the by, that she was on the pill.

Now she looked at his girlfriend – his real girlfriend. Valerie. In a short cream skirt with a gold chain belt. She had studied Pharmacy, which must be handy. A good body, apart from the feet. They probably had sex like normal people. They probably lay around afterwards talking about how they felt about things.

'I don't know, Tom.'

'Come on, Val, it's fine.'

She had slept with him, finally, in his family's summer house in Brittas Bay. The lino slithered with holiday sand. The bed was heavy and cold with damp, and you could smell the sea. He looked at her arm and told her she had an extra vein running down the inside of her left elbow. He traced it for her. We all have our mistakes, he said. Every corpse they cut into had something missing, or something added on.

Maria didn't tell him she was a virgin. She hoped he didn't go in for Gynaecology, and wasn't too surprised when he did not call.

The girlfriend dumped the white skirt on the floor, then picked it up like a rebellious child and hung it by the gold chain belt on a hook on the wall.

When she was gone, Maria checked the inside of her arm, quietly in the mirror. A flat hinge of bone. A faint map of veins. Flesh. Blood.

It was no use.

She had lost a secret. This, she decided, was her definition of a nervous breakdown: after a nervous breakdown, you were never sexy again. There was no mystery that could be broken with the grief of your name, whispered in the dark. *Maria.*

She walked home to Hatch Street, the fresh air crackling against her like cellophane. The streets were full of people like herself. She could see it in the way they crossed the road into the light or shade, shied away from shop windows. She could see it in the changing room, as they shifted their shoulders under new clothes. The way they said, 'I can't *take* black.' The way they said, 'It's too *busy*,' or, 'I need something more at the neck.'

Everyone had their rules. Maria just knew what hers were for. That was all.

She was going to keep herself alive. It was too simple. What man could understand it? That when she said no she meant no. That the morning was always like this, that some days were just no good. Some films were no good. Some food was altogether wrong. That Maria had her likes and dislikes like everyone else, but every choice she made led in a straight line to life or death.

'Suits you,' she said. 'No, really.' And hung up clothes and sprayed air freshener, and waited for the key to turn in the lock, whatever the lock might be.

Works on the Line

Spring, 1987

Rose rang her mother and said she would come out for the long weekend. There was a funeral she had to go to first, way out on the Thames Link. Afterwards, she would make her way back to Victoria and take the train back home.

Her mother just had to warn Rose about works on the line – always scrupulous about details and diversions: Rose, just as scrupulous, wrote it all down. Sometimes she had to shake herself to get her mother's habits out of her system. They were like a virus: the way she pulled her lips back when she put her lipstick on, the way she had to use three different chopping boards, and take her sunglasses off before she spoke. And now, a fading little series of farewells, like the phone was for whispering, and everyone you talked to on it was especially dear.

'Goodbye.'

'Goodbye, then.'

'Goodbye.'

'Bye.'

'Bye.'

Rose pressed the receiver back into its cradle. Her mother loved funerals. People died, and suddenly it was all worthwhile – all the stolen television sets and the syringes in the flowerbeds. If you had been kind to them, then their dying was a kind of success.

For Rose it was still a failure of the worst kind. She stacked her folders and clipped the tops back on to her biros and pens. She looked out over the sky of south London, and checked for planes.

A young man she barely knew was flying in from Amsterdam. He was flying in freight – in with the suitcases and boxes of tulips, his dead ears blocking and unblocking as they started to descend.

Rose had lost a client. She had temporarily mislaid a client and when she found him again, he was dead. She looked at his file. Attempted arson. Nineteen years old. On the bottom of the page she wrote 'Deceased'.

She should have known he was dealing.

For the funeral, she took out her interview suit, which was dove grey. She liked doing up the pearl buttons in the morning light. Here she was in her own flat – all her things: the CDs in a row, the colours tending to blue. The effect somewhat spoiled, of course, by William's last little visit. When they met, he kept telling her about his new BMW. She had smiled at the time, but perhaps growing up was all about rage.

Rose sat on the tube, and watched her shattered reflection in the opposite window, the two faces juddering apart. Poor William. Why didn't he die? She would have gone to that funeral in a minute. She would have gone wearing lipstick and her yellow chase-me-fuck-me shoes.

It was a fitful spring day, ragged with cloud. Rose found the church, a neo-gothic shed, and, feeling slightly ashamed, walked towards the door. In the porch, a young man in a good suit came over and shook her hand. She did not know if he was an undertaker or a priest. He gave her a long, loving look and she wanted to giggle. It was like taking a fancy to your dentist, licking his finger by accident as it entered your mouth.

'Hello,' she said.

'I'm Simon's brother Matt,' he said. 'Thanks for coming.'

'A friend,' she said, and ducked past him into the church.

How peculiar. She should not be here at all.

A cluster of people scattered slowly into their seats as Rose walked up the aisle. She wondered what was wrong, then step by step she began to miss the coffin. The body was not here. The boy had missed his own funeral. He was lost in transit – sitting on the tarmac in Caracas, or dumped in a hangar in Charles de Gaulle.

It was a memorial service, not a funeral, after all. Still Rose felt she had failed in some way, that she had forgotten the paperwork or mislaid the file. She was at some baggage carousel, the other passengers picking up their bags and leaving one by one, while the missing coffin circled, unnoticed and alone, at the other end of the hall.

The congregation stood and knelt and Rose stumbled after them as best she could. She felt she should go up to some counter, and point to the coffin shape on the plastic card, beside the picture of the backpack and the blue hold-all. These days, they probably just cremate you, bung you off DHL.

Matt turned to the woman beside him, lowering her gently on to the kneeler. His mother. She wore a black chiffon scarf over the bouffant of her hair, but Rose was ready to forgive her that, the Monaco feel she tried to bring to the death of her youngest boy. Everything matched, her ash-blond hair, the oatmeal-coloured trouser suit, the dull lustre of her cream slingback shoes. Her nose, as if to defy the soufflé she had made of herself, was hooked and strong. She hitched it up in front of her and followed it down the aisle, glancing at Rose as she passed. A flare of blood around her left iris made it leap into sudden violet, and Rose turned to follow her, as though she had planned it all along.

'You'll go with this lot,' said Matt, and she climbed into a car, where three strangers squashed over in the back seat to give her room. They were about to break the silence any moment when the boy on her right started to cry.

'A friend,' said Rose, when she got into the house, and they looked at her like she was the girlfriend they had never met. Such a lovely girl. Rose found herself beside a table of food and heaped a paper plate. She forked the stuff in: coronation chicken and chicken tikka, slices of roast beef and scrolls of cooked ham. It was a huge Irish funeral.

Cousins and sisters, in-laws, uncles, drink. Rose filled and refilled her glass with red wine and no one seemed to notice. She felt sober, but she wasn't in control. This was important. It was important to drink. To say the thing that was waiting to come out of her mouth – whatever it might be.

She heard the first laugh, cut short by the occasion, and after a moment, the room started to give. Rose picked up a plate of sandwiches and passed them around. She took up a tea-towel in the kitchen and started to dry the dishes, smiling at the people who passed. She was what they wanted her to be, the girlfriend that never was, the nearly sister-in-law, the woman who had no place, sad and important now that Simon had died. She started to cry.

The tears came from nowhere, blurring the sink and smearing his mother's face, which was smeared already with grief. She went into the living room and looked around, wanting obscenities to belly out of her, about these strangers who all knew each other, and bred with each other, and wore such terrible shoes.

'Your bladder's very near your eyes,' said a voice beside her. She had noticed him earlier, a middle-aged man watching her with the nearly sexual intent of new uncles, of borrowed family.

When she realised what he meant, all she could do was look at him. He started to laugh and she stared at the extraordinary droop of his jowls and chin, flying about.

Rose wondered how anyone's face could end up that shape. A sudden weight loss, perhaps – it had to be more than gravity. As if he knew what she was thinking, he pulled his hand in a broad stroke across his middle and said,

'I haven't been well,' the fingers digging a stave into the fat under his blue shirt. Rose realised that he was steaming drunk. She tried to move away, but there was something that she had to figure out about him first, a problem that held her. It was the kind of thing she would realise later, like a missing eyebrow, or two different-coloured eyes.

'Seriously.' His face fell – quite literally. The fat slumped down to his collar. The whole thing hung in front of her, a drop about to fall.

'That's my wife over there,' he said in a voice that did not mean anything. He gave a nod towards the other side of the room that forced him to take a drunken step backwards. Rose glanced around, despite herself.

It was a perfectly normal-looking woman. There was nothing to say.

'So what are you to the groom?' he said.

'I beg your pardon?'

'Simon.'

'I'm a friend.'

'I see. Sad business.'

'Actually, I was his probation officer.'

'A trying task,' he said.

'Sorry?'

'Probation.'

'Yes. Well, we do try our best.'

'Ah,' he said. 'Very good. Very sharp.'

Rose looked at the carpet, a swirl of green on brown. She felt that if she took one step away from him she would fall into its gaps and holes.

He took her by the arm to steer her around. There was a photograph of Simon on the sideboard and they looked at it together. The boy in the picture was dead. Rose felt the man's breath on her face and realised that he liked all this. He liked the realness of it, the access it gave him to people like her.

'Too young,' he said.

She felt the sexual cup of his hand under her elbow, the direct blue of his insincere eyes. And Rose was shocked by his air of complicity. He was waiting for her to betray something. And she did not know what it was.

'Anyway,' he said, 'pleased to meet you.' His wife had come up behind them. She gave Rose a difficult smile and turned him back to face the room.

194

Rose blundered around the house. Everywhere she turned there were people in groups, talking, touching, drinking. In a bedroom there was a young woman looking in a mirror and slowly brushing her hair. Rose sat on the edge of the bath, leaking tears. She stood by the wall of the living room, drinking red wine, her bones drying to splinters, her blood thickening to a viscous, wicked soup. She drank until she was the smallest thing in the room, every organ in her body small and hard and old. She drank until she was nothing. Sober and empty, no matter how much she tried to fill herself up with wine or gin. Old age was a bag with a hole in it, she decided, you can never get drunk again.

Rose smelt the cool sheets. Her bedroom was just the same, the same wallpaper, the same stones in a pattern along the windowsill. Her mother must have dusted over the years; even painted under them, and put them back, just so. The tree outside the window was pressed up against the glass now: Rose fell asleep afraid that it would crack through the pane and invade the room.

At six in the morning she woke, exactly conscious of where she was, her eyes seeking and finding the faces in the wallpaper – over by the mantelpiece, by the wardrobe, to the left of the light switch. She had been dreaming about a lost letter. She spotted it in a costume drama and rang the props department of the BBC to tell them it was addressed to her, but when it arrived, all scrawled and rubber-stamped, she saw that it was years old. It was from one of the boys, the one she had kissed, but he had nothing new to say to her. He had looked for her, and missed her, years before.

Sometime in the afternoon, Rose drifted painfully down to the kitchen. She had a violent need for fried eggs. Two frilly fried eggs, and toast, and a sliced tomato, and a basin full of tea. A bath full of tea.

The kitchen was deserted, apart from the cats. She ate and went upstairs again and slept like she was eating sleep.

At nine o'clock she woke and walked down the stairs in the dark. Her parents were home, she could hear their familiar silence, and see the yellow light pushing out through the gap in the door. All right, I was pissed, she said in her head. Yes everything is fine. No I am not in pain.

'All right, love?'

'All right,' said Rose. Her mother was thin. Her arms reminded Rose of eating chicken wings, the way the meat was attached to the bone.

Her father sat at the table, surrounded by bits of paper. He spent the days of his retirement writing urgent letters – health issues, committees, the local Labour party. All the lost causes, like he was running faster in fear of the wall.

He stood up and tested her forehead with the heel of his hand.

'You'll live.'

'Apparently.' He grazed her mother's cheek with his knuckle as he sat back down, and Rose was chastened. Who said there must be something missing in this passionate old house, where people believed small things – lived them exactly and to the brim.

'Anyone for tea?' she said.

Back in her own flat, the kitchen smelt of melon peel. Rose opened the window and tied up the rubbish. She put in a fresh bin bag, and the first thing she threw into it was the bag it came in. There was a certain satisfaction to it that made her smile.

Then she sorted through her head, shuffling her feelings and putting them back where they belonged. She would go to the gym, that was the first thing. She would buy a book on rape counselling and read it. She would find someone who could send a letter to her father. She would write and ask him where he was and where was her mother's grave. And when he wrote back to her, she would fly to Dublin and rent a car, and leave the car at a cemetery gate, and walk through the confused rows of the dead, until she found the right stone and the name it held.

Mother Alert

Dublin, 21 April 1987

Sinead, the manager, put her head round the curtain.

'Mother alert,' she said, and smiled.

Sometimes, when Evelyn came in, Maria took pity on her – this woman who looked around her room and held it all in contempt. Evelyn tried on the clothes like they would strangle her, or make her look working class. Deep down, she was just a snob. She had the snob's indignant little chin. It did Maria's heart good just to send her back out into the street, back to her hand-sewn tweeds and the faded velour of home.

But today, she was very wound up. Maria followed her out of the shop and wanted to explain things.

It was raining, and Jim on security cursed as he went back inside to switch off the alarm. Maria realised she had half a rail of wool-mix trousers slung over her arm.

She looked at Evelyn standing there and she didn't know what to say. She let her walk away, looked at her satisfied backside crossing the street and,

That's not it, she thought. *That's not it at all.*

A couple of months before she went to New York, Maria came home and found an envelope on the kitchen table. Her name was written on it, in Evelyn's handwriting, and inside, she found her blister pack of the pill. She'd only had sex once. In the circumstances, it looked sort of lonely.

Maria looked around the kitchen, which was immensely clean. She could imagine it all. Berts sitting at the table saying nothing, while Evelyn scrubbed the cooker. Berts giving a grunt or two, while Evelyn swiped the floor with a mop.

'She's your daughter,' she might say.

And Laura, smelling trouble, coming in to put on a couple of slices of toast.

For the rest of the week Maria came in late, and stayed in bed until after Berts had left for work. On Saturday, she heard the sound of the radio coming from his room, all morning. It was three o'clock before she braved the landing. The sound of her footsteps had Berts out of the bed on the instant, with her hair in his hand. She tried to get past him and through the bathroom door.

They did not speak. Evelyn was below in the hall, foreshortened by the stairs, a big anxious head and smug little feet. She headed for the kitchen.

Berts looked at the hank of hair in his hand, and let it go. She slammed the bathroom door on him and sat down to have a pee.

'Hurry up in there,' he said.

'Jesus,' said Maria.

'Hurry up,' said Berts. 'I have to go.'

When she heard him leave the landing, she ran across to her own room. He came out then to take his turn in the bathroom, and pissed for about half an hour.

He came into her room, dressed and shaved. He stood in silence beside the bed.

'When I met your mother,' he said, 'she was innocent. We both were. That was the way of it.'

They both heard his words, bare and helpless in the room. Maria hefted the duvet and turned her back on him. His lovely bride and their lovely love. It was bullshit. It was not her fault.

He sat on the end of the bed and said nothing. She started to cry.

'Oh Daddy,' she said. 'What will I do?' She was sobbing into the pillow. 'What will I do?' Berts sat there, patting her hip.

'Sure, he isn't worth it.' When she looked at him finally, he said,

'You know, you have your mother's eyes,' checking the door, as they both did, for the sound of Evelyn and where she might be.

Two months later, she was in New York, taking drugs, emptying the trashcans of the rich. Two months later, although she did not know it yet, she had left home, and college, and the lot. Everyone she met hated their parents. Maria listened to them and did not believe a word they said. She looked at them and thought, *But that's not it. That's not it at all.*

There was a confusion in her curtain. Maria checked round the side and saw a blind woman stirring the cloth with her cane. She was suddenly shy, just pulled the curtain back and stood aside.

The blind woman had a companion with her, who had a pile of jackets and coats over one arm. Maria checked through the hangers.

'Seven,' she said. It was way over the limit. Still, she said nothing, did not even reach for a tag.

The companion had the smallest eyes. She held each of the coats up behind the blind woman, professionally, taking her wrist and guiding it into the sleeve.

Maria found herself looking into the blind face, as though she hoped to be seen, or recognised. It was a west of Ireland face, good-looking with fine cheekbones and wavy black hair. She had irises of chilly blue that rolled and fixed. They made her look like she was trying, all the time.

The companion wrestled her into a tartan blanket coat, then turned her to face the mirror, checking her reflection there.

'Something longer. Then you're safe.'

The woman's eyes rolled at the glass.

'What's it like?' she said, her voice light and uncertain. Three more women had gathered to give advice.

'It's russet. It's quite nice,' said one of them.

'Sort of reds and browns.'

'It's like autumn,' said a young girl, trying to explain, and the blind woman lifted the lapel, weirdly, to smell it. She felt the stitching of the collar. She ran her hands over the fringes on the front, then over her breasts and down to her waist.

'Very neat,' said the companion, who rolled her own eyes at the group, in a secret sign. The woman reached her hand towards the mirror and,

'No,' said Maria. 'Blue. It should be blue for your eyes.'

She rustled along the rail for a cobalt cashmere mix, fitted and slightly flared with a black velvet collar.

She put it into the woman's arms. The woman felt the collar.

'How much is it?' she said. And Maria lied.

When everyone was gone, Maria wiped down the mirror and tried to forget what she was looking at. The whole place smelled of old sweat and perfume. She went around the changing room, dipping and lifting the ghosts of women who could not make up their minds. She hung them up on the rail: shirts, dresses and pants; discarded futures, other selves.

Someday she would bring a man in here and make love standing up. She would bring a man in after hours and smile at him until he backed her up against the mirror, lifting her skirt. They would undress each other, they would laugh and discard. Gravity would not work against them. Maria would check his eyes to see when they looked in the mirror and when he looked at her. And after they had finished, her backside would leave a damp mark on the glass, in the shape of a heart, or of a heart turned upside down.

She picked up a small black dress, and decided to try it on.

Maria let her skirt fall. Skirt first. She took off her blouse. She had two veins running down the inside of her arm

where one should have been. She had slept with a medical·
student once, who told her this. We all have our mistakes,
he said.

She ducked into the dress and as she straightened up,
Maria caught a glimpse of her own eyes.

All this happened slowly to Maria, her eyes snagging on
themselves and then sliding across the smooth surface of the
glass. It happened so slowly, Maria did not know if she was
in pain. She stood with one foot still in the crumpled circle
of the skirt and the other outside.

She was someone else again.

She was a woman in a little black dress.

She closed her eyes.

Maria stood in front of the mirror and closed her eyes.
Some days she was just nothing. Some days she was a
woman who was just waiting for herself to walk in the door.

Birth

Dear Miss Cotter,
   In sorting through the files of the Regina Coeli Adoption Agency, I came across your papers, which were unfortunately misfiled after a fire some years ago.
   Please find enclosed a copy of your birth cert, as requested by you in 1986. Tragically, your mother died in childbirth in 1965. I enclose her death cert, with my deepest sympathy. Your natural father is, as far as we know, still alive. Unfortunately I cannot give you any identifying information about him. I can tell you that he and your mother were married at the time of your birth, and that he was employed in an administrative capacity in Dublin. If you should wish to make contact with him, the Catholic Adoption Agency in London will be pleased to act as intermediary.
   Yours sincerely,
   Sr Maura Reynolds.

Rose looked at her birth cert. There was a U of rust in one corner; the paper was thick and light blue. All the headings on the form were printed twice, once in English and once in what Rose assumed to be Irish.

Father
Athar
Albert Delahunty
She traced the difficult letters in her head.
Ainm, Sloinne Cheile agus Sloinne Athar, na Mathar

203

Mother?
Anna Delahunty
Inion
formerly
Kennedy

6

Berts' Head

Summer, 1987

Evelyn found herself looking after Berts' head, as though it were the surprising child of their old age, a package someone had left on the doorstep wrapped in grey.

Even he was afraid of it. She could see by the careful way he carried it; by his puzzled look. They ate their dinner and turned on the telly and sat with it, Berts' head and what was poised inside his skull, like a yolk about to break. They both cradled it, Berts' poor head and the pain that would not go away.

'What's up?'

'Nothing.' So they sat in front of the television and kept very quiet, the two of them, because there was something wrong with this baby, it was deaf perhaps, you needed to sign to it that you were in the room, that you were about to approach, that it would be fed.

She might mention it to the doctor, get a prescription for anti-depressants. She could say they were vitamins, or mash them up and put them in his dinner.

'Where are you going?'

'Out.'

Evelyn started to spring-clean; did not know she was looking for something until the cupboards were sorted and the curtains washed and rehung. It was not possible that he was having an affair. Even the word made her laugh.

She had relined the drawers with new paper and was sorting through old cheque books and dead phone bills when she came across a letter with handwriting so like Maria's that she read it without thinking.

Then she finished cleaning the house.

A week later Evelyn cried into the washing-up and Berts watched her, or averted his eyes as she wiped her nose on her forearm.

This is where women cry, thought Evelyn. They cry into the sink. They cry into the dirty water and they keep crying as they rinse and stack. Where should she cry so that he would see her? She should climb up on top of the fridge and cry there. She should climb up on to the roof and roar.

'I don't know what you're crying for,' said Berts.

'For you,' said Evelyn. 'For the lump I married.'

She blew her nose with a bit of kitchen paper wet from her hands and followed him into the sitting room.

'Twins,' she said.

'Well, I couldn't take them both.'

She sat down then and they waited in their separate chairs, the fire rug between them and the television flashing in the corner they faced, each from their own angle. There was a film on, a man searching through a house in the dark, and the light from the screen opened and shut into the room, while they watched without seeing and thought about the two babies asleep in their glass box.

'Did you answer it?'

'I did not.'

'Marie.'

He did not move in the chair.

'Who called her Marie?' she said. 'Did you call her that?'

'I called her nothing.'

'Well, someone had a good laugh.'

She looked at Berts, who looked at the television. She got up to dry the dishes and left him there, in his own mess. Cleaning up. All her life she had been cleaning up. And Berts had watched and never told her what thing it was that had been spilt.

Evelyn lay in the dark. She could hardly believe that Berts was not down on his knees, or prostrate on some bar floor, but flat on his back as he always was flat on his back, with Evelyn beside him as she always was, waiting for the first high, flabby snore.

They had gone through the ritual of the evening, and with it, all the other evenings of their marriage: the clocks wound and the bottles left on the doorstep, though the clocks worked on batteries these days, and the milkman did not call. They walked through the ghosts of old routines as they performed the new ones, switching on timers, setting alarms.

Evelyn slipped in under the blankets. She watched Berts as he came in and took off his watch and his wedding ring, and put them on the locker. She looked at him as he let his trousers fall. She saw him step out from one leg, then lift the other foot. She saw him dip down to take the hem and pull. She looked at his body, the pockets of grey, the loops and lozenges of yellow from the light on the landing. She saw his nipples, the fat around them gone for years. She saw the flesh that flowed down from his ribs to a belt around his waist. Every inch of him was a mystery to her. Every soft noise he made was a pang to her, as he sat into the bed, as he rolled into his dent in the mattress, as she kept her eyes open and listened in the dark for the exact and astonishing moment that Berts would fall asleep.

Twenty-four years ago, she went into Clery's for the January sale and bumped into Joan. It was in the lingerie department and the place was stuffed with nuns, she remembered, in for the annual corset – and, it had to be said for them, never much more than a glance at the lacy stuff, never so much as a smile or a look of regret. They had a fierce grip on themselves.

Evelyn, on the other hand, lacked grip. She had the best of Berlei, she had silk and artificial silk. She had plenty of time for regret, because modestly, sinfully, underneath, Evelyn was all style.

She was all style that day, as she saw Joan slowly touch a

sateen nightie, and pull her hand away. Then Joan spotted her too and pulled a big smirk.

'Would you look at you?'

Look at her indeed. Sometimes Evelyn took comfort in these girls from school, all married and fat, and sometimes they made her feel like crying. But Joan did neither. Joan said she had three of them, and it was murder. And her mother had some disease, which as far as Joan was concerned was called sitting on your fat backside.

'And yourself?'

There was little enough to say. Her parents still ambled along and Evelyn still ambled home to them, to a father who still called her his lamb and smoothed the back of her hair, to a mother who spent her days in prayer. Evelyn's father was given to sudden disappearances, and to sudden charm. He was also subject to humiliations of dress, to occasional incontinences. Apart from that, he was the sweetest drunk you could wish to find. By mid-afternoon he was silent. Things started to break under his gentle touch and his glasses missed his nose. There was a trail of snot, perhaps, on his lapel. Evelyn always knocked before entering the toilet, but sometimes she might find him there, slouched over, or leaning back with his flies open, oblivious. In any state you like. It was all politely, delicately done. As though his body were too good a friend – he would not presume to prevent it from doing what it pleased.

He reared a daughter who went to meetings of the Legion of Mary and the Dublin Film Society, who had fluent Irish, who could swim in the coldest weather, in Killiney or in Dublin Bay. He reared a daughter who fled from men – was bitter when she should flatter them, and silent when they wanted her to speak. That was the thing about family secrets – they made you awkward in company. Her father had reared a daughter who was so lonely she could die. There was also a son on the missions, and a younger daughter who was as gentle and sweet as he was, a novice with the Poor Clares in Leeds, with a doubt over her final vows on account of her fits.

But that day in Clery's, Joan took one look at her and said, 'You must come out, sometime. Come out for tea.' It was the kindness you afford to spinsters, but Evelyn took her up on it, and sat playing with the children on a Sunday afternoon, until the ring came on the door that brought Berts.

Berts. A man in a brown suit, even on the weekend. A man with a child in his arms, who talked little, and did not touch a drop.

Evelyn knew her weaknesses. She fell in love with Jimmy Stewart in *Harvey*, with Cary Grant in *Philadelphia Story*, all those easy, dangerous drunks. She knew that when the film ended, the real story was just begun.

But Berts began and ended where he was. He stood in the doorway and did not know how to shake her hand, or where to put down the child. Evelyn saw there was no smoothness in him. He did not find things easy. This was a man who had to organise his life, before he could live it. A good man.

He started to snore. Evelyn heard it and was astonished. It was for this she married him, for his ability to sleep. He would not leave his flies open, or bring men home who would eye her up and start reciting 'My Dark Rosaleen'.

She had chosen Berts, so she did not have to love him. Perhaps that was her sin. Perhaps that was the reason she was to blame. But she had loved him with her life, had she not? She had loved him with her days.

Evelyn lay in the dark doing her accounts, over and over, trying to make them tally. At three in the morning she finally reached out and clamped Berts' sweating nose in two fingers. There was a surprised silence, then his body bucked in the bed and his mouth opened and he turned away from her.

Peace. She wiped the ends of her fingers on the pillow slip.

After a while, he turned towards her again and she felt his face on the top of her back. She could not tell if he was awake. For a while she thought he was and her heart pounded. Then he said,

'Absolutely.'

He was asleep, and the touch of his face was terrible to her. She wondered could she leave him, at the nonsensical age of fifty-four. Evelyn lay with Berts' cheek clamped to her back, the rest of him stretched away towards the far corner of the bed. She could feel the distance between every inch of him and every inch of her. His face pushed deeper, and she sensed something pass through his body. A sigh, a tremor. Then a terrible wetness. It was hot – as hot as his body was, inside. It spread over her skin, then cooled and itched on the nape of her neck.

Berts was crying in his sleep. Or Berts had woken up and started to cry. After twenty-three years of marriage, she could not, for the life of her, whisper his name in order to find out.

The Keepers of the Gate

Rose cleaned the flat before she left, thinking that there were few pleasures to compare with leaving a place clean, if you never knew when you would return. She relished the silence in the kitchen after the fridge was switched off, then the slow drip of the ice melting; the first tray full of water, so wide and shallow, you always spilt some on the floor.

At three in the morning the silence woke her. She got out of bed, stood in the kitchen in her bare feet and punched at the ice with the breadknife, white slabs breaking wetly as they hit the tiles. The ice creaked and broke as she levered open the freezer compartment that had been frozen shut for months. She threw out the packet of spinach she found there, then worked the ice with her bare hands. She wanted to get it out clean, she wanted to hold a box in her hands that she could leave in the sink, melting like a treasure.

In the morning she picked up her suitcase and went home.

The first twenty minutes after she walked in the door her parents talked about how she had got there, the trains and buses, the minicabs and the weather. Rose used to think they did this in order to keep her from going anywhere, but now she knew it was simply true. There was never a clear way to get to the house she grew up in. Step out the door, and London was not on your side.

Her mother lost her temper with a hot baking tray. She grabbed it with a tea-towel and rattled it on the cooker top. Rose thought about the long days they spent in each other's company, now that her father had retired. They rubbed against each other until they had rubbed themselves away.

Things could get at them. They were permeable to the world.

After dinner, they each sat as they used to; her father reading in a loud wicker chair; her mother grazing around the kitchen, shifting objects from one place to another, and not making the slightest difference. An old transistor radio talked to itself on a shelf, a survivor of the foster boy wars. Rose rubbed the dial round until she found Radio 3. The oven needed doing, but that would need a symphony. This sounded like a Britten piece for oboe and piano, so she dumped small things into the sink and picked up an old toothbrush and started to clean.

After they drifted off to bed, she made her way upstairs and ran a bath. Last bath here. Last bath before she knew who she was.

When she was eleven she had fitted this tub perfectly. She looked up at the light, the damp spreading its dark mould around the ceiling rose. She looked at the shower rose. She looked at the roses on the dressing gown that her mother gave her when she was sixteen. She looked at her body and was surprised by how huge it had grown. The sigh and slap of water as she lifted a leg and put it back down, the broken ball of her belly, as it dipped below the water line.

Rose.

She hated flying.

'You have everything?' said her father at the airport, his eyes fixed on the top of the escalator, which sank, step over step, as they were pushed to the top.

'Not really.'

'Give them our best,' he said, as if he were reporting what someone else had said.

'If I find them.'

'Yes. Well, hopefully.' He was sad and uncomfortable, not sure if he was at fault, somehow. She kissed him.

'Oh pooey,' she said. They walked up to the check-in

and his whole body was a nuisance to her, the length of his arm beside her, the fact that he was old. He had pretended to be her father, so that he could love her. What sort of a man did a thing like that?

He put her suitcase on the weighing machine and stood back. She walked past him and laid her ticket on the high desk.

Rose was on her way. She was on her way to people who were as vicious as blood, who were as real.

She had imagined it so many times. Over and over she walked up the path to the door. She ran a gauntlet of flowers: dahlias, or gladioli, or nothing perhaps, a balding lawn, a stretch of gravel, a line of rusting tin cans and spare parts for cars. She walked past all these things up to a door which, for some reason, was always the same – a ray of wooden slats fanning out from the bottom left-hand corner, over a field of frosted glass.

She knocked on the door.

'Did you pack your bags yourself?' The ground hostess pulled the tip of her pen down a list of questions. As Rose walked up a boreen and passed a dog tied with twine, as she checked the sky for rain in a suburban estate, as she squared her shoulders and lifted her fist, and knocked.

Her father leaned into her suitcase to tighten the front buckle one more notch.

'Do you want me to wait?' he said as Rose took the boarding pass. She looked at him.

There was a blinding white light when he opened the door.

'No, Daddy. I'm fine.'

He stood there. Her father. A second wife behind him in the hall. An aunt, perhaps. She would sit with them and drink tea. He would wear certain things, he would have a certain personality. There would be a particular cup in her hand, of china, or ceramic. She would look at the furniture, the piano in the corner perhaps, upright and out of tune.

'Good luck, then.' Her father's cheek was rasping and dry.

'Thanks.'

She would sit and sip and see him as he was, this stranger who had an accent, a way of standing, a way of talking. She would not blame him. She would gather all her adult powers, all the stories that she knew, and force humanity to triumph over blood. She would sit there and smile. Or she would sit there and cry. She would ask him about her mother's grave. She would give in, like a child, to the blindness of the light.

'Bye, then.'

She watched her father's back, as he walked away from her, and she lost him to the crowd.

The flight was delayed.

Rose felt a strange wrench as she took the exit from Terminal 1. She tramped along a metal walkway, past arbitrary rooms, a conference centre, a series of offices, the staff shop. She was off the beaten track, she was in a whole other place, an ordinary place where people never went, but was full of people all the same. The keepers of the gate.

When she came out suddenly in Terminal 2 she felt excited by the foreign smell of cigarettes, as though they were already in Warsaw or Dar es Salaam. Downstairs, there was a low hangar full of check-in desks that made everyone look like a drug smuggler, or a refugee. Rose pushed against the flow, and felt like she was going to a place that no one had ever heard of.

Outside, there was a multi-storey car park and no path. Rose crossed a tangle of roads and found herself beside a sign that said 'Emergency Point' – a set of concrete steps spiralling down to a basement, each marked with a yellow strip of paint, as though they were afraid someone might park on them.

The Heathrow Chapel was a bunker. It reminded her of

216

a nightclub she had gone into one morning to look for a lost bag. There was a main altar, made of steel, and side altars set in concrete bays around the wall. An airline worker in orange overalls leant on the back of a chair, a set of industrial ear muffs dangling from one hand. He was praying.

The blue altar cloth had little embroidered airplanes flying across it. Midnight flights, edged in gold.

Rose walked around like a tourist in a cathedral, looking at the art that was not on the walls. The Catholic altar had a 3-D picture of Christ that shifted, as you moved past, to an image of the Turin Shroud – like one of those tacky postcards. Rose swayed across and back, watching the dead sockets switch to living eyes, then empty again.

She realised that she was looking for the boy who had died – as if his coffin would be lying there in the centre aisle. Because if a body went astray in an airport, then this church was the Lost and Found.

But there was no body. There was a 3-D picture of Christ and a man in orange overalls, leaning on the back of a chair.

She sat behind him, and watched his shoulders as he prayed. He held his forehead and rubbed his finger over and back along the hair of one eyebrow. He sighed, and Rose felt that he could tell her something that had nothing to do with God. He could tell her something about traffic. About the pauses that come, now and then, into which the better thoughts can fall. It would be something to do with his grey hair and the middle-aged, stockbroker's face he carried, above the worker's overalls.

Simon Clark died outside a bar in Amsterdam. He wasn't stabbed. He did not die in the toilets, with a needle sticking out of his arm. Rose thought of all the boys who had bled over her parents' carpets, or shot up in the coal-house, or disappeared. All of them lost, as Simon was lost. As she herself was. Lost or thrown away.

217

Simon was hit by a car. That was all. There was no talk of blame. There was no talk of what was in his bloodstream, or if anyone held his hand as he died. Though no one held bloody hands these days, no one would dare. All she knew was that he had 'multiple fractures' in his head. She could feel his skull in her hands, through the living skin and the hair. It was so hard and heavy and full of him. It was so intimate. She turned her hands up, and believed in nothing, and felt the bone bowl of his head pressing into her palms.

The airline worker got to his feet and made his embarrassed way down the central aisle. The door shut behind him, then opened again to let in a man in a Salvation Army uniform. Rose got up. In a moment someone would come over, and touch her, and smile.

There was another man in the porch, in a priest's leather blouson jacket, his face polite and public even before he knew she was there. The place was stuffed with them, waiting for the call to the tragedy just in from Morocco, the heart attack in the Duty Free; men in black, who knew a short cut around the control tower and a quick way under the car park at Terminal 3.

Out in the light she looked up at the sky and the thick, secular grey of the clouds. She watched a plane lift heavily into the middle distance and hang solid in the mist. It was very loud. It hesitated for the longest time, then disappeared.

It was time to go. She made her way back to Terminal 1 and joined the queue for security. Glancing at her bag as it crossed the X-ray screen, she saw a cell under a microscope, the dark sac of her make-up bag, the biological bullet of her lipstick, various zips, like worms of DNA, all of it floating in the translucent fluid between her keys and an organic growth of coins.

She picked it up on the other side, and walked on.

Wallpaper

Of course she would not leave him. It would be too silly at her age. But Evelyn started to redecorate, without so much as discussing it. She decided to start plain, because that was the easiest way when you were replacing one thing at a time.

Besides, she thought of the child, knocking on their front door, walking into their hall, taking one look, and thinking, *Well, I'm glad I didn't grow up here.*

She went into Arnott's and got curtains in a sort of brown, she bought five litres of magnolia matt emulsion, she came home and started to rip the carpet up, all by herself.

She loosened all the sides first, then she winkled out a corner and pulled. She did not know how she managed it, the edges and cut-out angles leaving the skirting board with a tear and pop of staples. The lint and the dust flying, until her chest was full of it. The lifting carpet was growing in front of her, pushing her back as she pulled it more, until it felt like the room was on top of her.

'Well,' she said, her heart clattering in her chest, 'if I don't go now then there'll be no killing me ahead of my time,' as it curved up like a wall into the room, a wave sweeping her out the door.

Then she got sense and dropped it. She made herself a cup of tea and looked at the thing. Then she rolled it with a great humping across the diagonal, with the furled triangle of the corner pointing out the door.

When Berts came in from work he stood at the threshold and looked.

'Don't ask me how,' she said. 'But I'm going to sort this mess out. Once and for all.'

He leant his shoulder against the frame of the door.
She didn't bother with his tea, let him fend for himself,
and started stripping the wallpaper off the walls.

Voice

Rose booked into an hotel that seemed to be in the centre of things. And then she didn't know what to do. She looked at the wallpaper and realised that she had made no plans, except to find a man called Albert Delahunty, who had not answered her letter, and a whole family called Kennedy who might not know that she existed. As far as they were concerned, her life had never happened. Rose tried to tell them they were wrong.

'I have always done the right thing,' she said to them. Or, 'I have always tried to do the right thing.'

She gathered her loves and losses in her head, sorting through her memories for something that would prove that she had lived, that her life was worth it. There wasn't much.

There was a hotel bedroom with a Bible in the drawer and a little leaflet to tell you how to work the phone. There were flowers on the wall in peach and pink with faded green leaves.

Ordinary. Ordinary. She said to herself. There is nothing wrong with the ordinary.

But it made her rise and walk out into the street. She browsed for a while outside a bookshop that had paperbacks set out under an awning. Then she walked up past a building that looked like an old academy or hospital, but which turned out to be the Irish Parliament. Beyond it was a museum and she ventured inside. The the place was full of stuffed animals in glass cases: flying foxes, the skeleton of an elk, monkey foetuses in jars. The whole bloody museum should have been in a museum.

She came out, upset, and tried to concentrate on nothing at all. Her breath. The feel of the pavement beneath the soles of her feet, the trees and parked cars on the other side of the road.

She reached the hotel and took the key and made it back to her room. Registry of Births and Deaths. A solicitor. A title search, a company search. Or if he had gone to America a list of visa applications. Or if he had gone to England, then what?

In the morning, she asked at reception where she could find a post office that had all the phone books. The woman reached under the desk and put two in front of her.

'That's them,' she said.

'No,' Rose said. 'No.'

'No, really. That's the lot.'

Then she would not let Rose take them up to her room.

So Rose stood in front of her, a woman in a Kelly green suit, and opened the phone book and turned to A for Adoption services, and R for Registry of Births, Marriages and Deaths, and D, for curiosity, where she saw her father's name sitting on the page. The address was the same. It was the same address as the one written in blue ink on her birth certificate twenty-five years ago.

Delahunty, Berts. An address. A phone number. Her father. He had never moved house. He hadn't even bothered.

She asked for a pen, but found that she could not write the number. She put the pen down on the desk and picked it back up again. The woman in the green suit was talking into the phone, she was saying, 'Not at all. No problem. Not at all.'

And Rose was violently insulted, by the awful suit and the easy tone, by this incredible country – where people could be found in the phone book, just like that. Where people did the most appalling things, and shut their mouths, and stayed put.

She made her way up to her room, lay on the bed and woke up six hours later, shivering and fully clothed.

At four in the morning she woke again with the thought

Registry of Births and Deaths. A solicitor. A title search. Then she remembered. She let her eyes settle on the bedside table. The number was still there, beside the hotel phone.

The next day she could not find the courage to go out on to the street. She looked at the floral wallpaper in the hotel room and traced the faces she found there. She listened to the sounds outside the window. She watched the BBC. She imagined another life.

At seven in the evening she dialled the number, trying to picture the house at the end of the line. The phone rang four times. She felt the silence after the click of connection, as the receiver travelled through the air.

'Hello?' it was a girl's voice. 'Hello?' and all Rose could say was,

'It's me. Marie.'

'Hello, stranger,' said the girl, and then shouted off the line. 'Mom!'

The phone went down with a clatter. Rose could hear a distant radio playing. A sister. She had a sister, who knew all about her. Her whole story was being stolen and spoiled.

She held the handset over the receiver, but could not put it down. A woman's voice.

'Maria? Maria? Is that you? Hello?'

Rose put the phone back to her ear. There was nothing to say. She held her breath for as long as she could, because this silence was all she had to give.

Lungs

'She rang. I think she rang.'

'Who?'

'Who do you think?'

That night Evelyn got up to go to the toilet and when she got back to bed, saw that Berts was not there. She decided not to let it bother her, but the thought of him keeled over and dead somewhere in the house would not let her sleep.

She got up again and put on her dressing gown. The lights were all out. He was in the sitting room, gutted as it was. He was sitting on the sofa in a little nest of newspaper that fanned out around his bottom like a butcher's display.

'Come to bed,' she said.

'I've been thinking.'

'It's all right.'

'I've been thinking about my wife.'

'I'm your wife,' she said.

But he told her anyway.

'Right,' she said. 'Right.' She put her hands on her knees and pushed herself up off the chair.

'Right,' she said again. Evelyn put her hand to her head. The bone of her skull was singing.

'I'm your wife,' she said.

After she left, Berts looked at the room, and hissed.

'Hssssss.'

There was a bit of tobacco stuck to his lip, and it pulled a piece of skin with it when he scraped it into his mouth. He chewed it even after it was gone, rolling it with his tongue even after he had swallowed it. He pulled his mouth down at both corners, and blew the smoke out with a disgusted lift of his face. This was what happened after Evelyn went to bed. Berts lifted his face to the ceiling, and fitted the cigarette to his face, and swallowed the smoke into his lungs like water to a drowning man.

'Hssssss.'

He stubbed the cigarette out on the bare boards, then stood up and walked across to the window. He looked out into the darkness at the tree his wife had not seen for twenty-five years. It was nearly as tall as the lamp-post now. It waved across the streetlight in the wind; all black, with a shifting mess of green.

Berts lit another cigarette and leaned his head against the window.

They had wanted to give the child oxygen, they said, but there was something about it that would damage the mother. He could not understand. Either the child would drown inside her, or she would drown in the pure air.

So they had given the child oxygen and his wife had died.

He had gone in to see her, but he was not sure she was dead. She looked very quiet, but he wasn't sure she looked dead. They told him she was dead and he had to believe them, but he still felt he should talk to her, give her some noise. The air was pushed into her by a bellows and there was a machine bubbling on the floor.

They checked the baby by the hour. The room was full of students, and a man came down, all the way from Belfast. He said,

'This child is a miracle,' and he lifted his stethoscope from her stomach. Berts thought he could have warmed it first.

Joan came in with some clean clothes for him. She took one look at Anna on the bed and left the room.

Then the cleaner. The cleaner came in and banged her bucket and hit her mop against the bed and didn't even apologise. After the cleaner, he knew she was dead.

His wife was lying in the bed. Her chest was pushed out

with air, like a fist, the tubes up her nose were choking her, the wires to the heart monitor were shocking her into a pulse. There was another tube in her hand and a nurse came in to coax it every now and then, ran the pad of her thumb up and down a little disc at the side and tut-tutted, something to do with pressure, he assumed, the pressure inside her body and the pressure of the fluid in the tube. The nurses brought him cups of tea. He wanted tea all the time, was mad for tea. This was one of the best hospitals anywhere, they said, for the infant survival rate, better than America, better than Germany.

'The best for tea anyhow,' he said.

His wife did not move. He thought of the baby drifting inside her, floating, wired. Its pulse was confused, but real. While hers was not real, they said, because she was dead. Berts found he avoided looking at her stomach. He sat staring at the light shifting across the floor. It was afternoon light, very open and uncertain: it moved like it didn't want you to know it was moving at all. But Berts was patient. It is hard to fool a patient man.

He saw a kick in the corner of his eye, the slightest thud hitting the underside of the counterpane, and now he found he could not take his eyes away from her bump. He leant forward so her face was hidden by the curve, as he waited for the next shiver in the cloth. He did not want to see her wince: there might be a spasm, something that looked just like she did, when she was surprised inside. Berts watched for a long time: waited for the baby to kick her alive. He looked away. He watched again. The light turned. He started to hate this thing, who knew he was watching and hid from him, who played him at this waiting game.

You killed her, he thought. *You killed her.*

Skin

Rose got into a taxi and showed the driver the address.

'How much to go there?' she said.

'About six quid.'

'That's fine. Thank you.'

But when the taxi stopped at a set of lights, she found herself wrestling with the door. She threw what was probably a five-pound note on to the front seat, and fell out on to the road. Then she picked herself up and started to run. She ran down the street, wanting to bump into people as she passed, to bang into them and make their shopping spill on to the ground.

She was finally halted by the smell of roasting coffee and went into the café to calm down. When she heard her English voice, the girl behind the counter looked at her as though she did not exist.

Rose sat at a table and looked around for something she could steal. A bowl full of sugar. A small jug of milk. She could just drink it and slip it into her bag. She could just drink it straight from the jug and then tuck it into her bag.

No one in this city cared.

'I am looking for my father,' she wanted to say. 'Isn't that a laugh?'

She was going to see a man who did not want her. She should drop him a line, tell him not to worry – she did not want anything from him, not even love. What she was actually looking for was something of her mother: a photograph, or some piece of her, a film she liked, or a book she had read. She just needed to know if she had smelt of lavender, or rosewater, or Wright's coal tar soap. And whether she could sing. And where her grave was.

Rose finished her coffee and looked at herself. She was wearing jeans. She should wear a suit, something frightening. She would wear a soft dress, in jersey or in wool. She should wear something rich and plain, something that said, 'It's me.' She should walk into her father's house naked, as he had left her, twenty-five years before.

Rose went into a shop across the street, and checked the colours on the rails. There were no plain dresses. There was a black suit that looked promising, in linen that would crease. She took it off the rail and slung the hanger on her index finger and walked into the changing room.

'One,' she said, holding it up for the shop assistant to see.

'One,' said the shop assistant, and looked at her.

7

ANNA

Lists

I was born in the middle of the Emergency in the townland of Dunskeen, which falls west from the Letterkenny road to the sea. As a child I thought the Emergency was the place that all babies came from. I thought that babies were like oranges – you couldn't even imagine what they were like, until you got one yourself. When I was told that the Emergency was the whole Second World War, I didn't know what to think. It was a big place to come from – and not even our own. But the idea persisted as a family joke and so I remember it when other things are forgotten.

It is hard, then, to describe my early life, without other jokes to remember it by. My name was the same any way you looked at it, AnnA AnnA, and sometimes I said it backwards to myself, all day long. Once my father said he was going to Killapig and when I asked him where it was he said, 'A mile west of Gweedore,' which was a town on the coast. The pig made a terrible noise when it died, but even as we were eating it I was thinking of the map on the wall at school, with blue sea stretching west of Gweedore – as if 'Kilapig' could be drowned somewhere under the waves, or hidden under the block of blue that said 'sea'.

I don't think I was a peculiar child. But I did not see my life in any way you could write down – 'the grass is green, the sky is blue'. When I was a child the sky was either raining or not, and grass was just what it was. The only list I could make is of the things I did not notice. I could list the things I did not notice and I would remember them only as the words I use to describe them by: the rain, the grass, the milk in a bucket, the blood in a bowl, the dress I had of

scalloped crochet, which I grew old enough to hand down
to my doll.

My mother was a great maker of lists. She had the
mother's feeling that she had forgotten something, that
there was one thing that had slipped her mind, but she
never wrote things down, perhaps because paper was
something then. My mother's lists were things that she
shifted around the kitchen; the tea cosy placed on the table
for more tea, the lid of the bread bin propped open for
flour, the cat's saucer upside down beside the door when we
needed polish for our Sunday shoes. The whole room was a
reminder to her. There was no telling, when you touched
something, what it might mean. 'Who moved the sweeping
brush?' she would say. 'When we haven't a sausage in the
house?'

And so her exits were full of things to trip her up, a stick
across the threshold, a prayer turned to the wall. I worried
about her in the shop, looking at the shelves, with the
kitchen shifting and dancing in her mind's eye. When I was
old enough I wanted to do the messages for her and she
might let me. She would sit at the table and check the room
and I would hold the list of things translated in my head as I
ran down the road – which was a long road – repeating
them over and over: a twist of baking soda, sugar, a wick,
two wicks, a bar of soap cut down the middle so it leaves
itself on the knife.

Now, if I were to list the things in my life, that is the way
I would like to do it; moving things from place to place and
knowing what they meant, not just a string of words – the
shopping list bouncing in my head, my own breath cutting
it short at every step. You move the tea cosy from the pot to
the table, you move it to the side of the range, you turn the
cosy inside out. I am stricken, here in my grave, by what the
smallest things meant.

When I was dying, I thought I should write things down,
but the words made no sense. I thought that if I could write
I would not die, but that made no sense either. There is no

story to living and then dying. There is no story to living, and having a child, and dying. Not for me. No matter what order I put them in. So I put vegetables in the wardrobe and buried my clothes. I turned the hoover on itself, all the way up the flex. I rolled along the wallpaper, like Cleopatra coming out of a carpet, and I wrote lists on the floor. Don't get me wrong. I was not reared for display, of any kind. I was reared to be proud, but not proud of myself. I am terrified, here in my grave, by words and what they might want.

Mother. Father. Brother. Sister. Home.

My parents had two families one after the other, because the first lot went wrong and had to be replaced. I was second in a family of three, that was followed years later by three more. Valty, my older brother, was dark and big-boned. He ran away from home and it broke my mother's heart. Brendan, the brother who came after me, was never right and died when he was four. Although I have no memory of his death, I do remember my brother Valty at that time. It is an embarrassing memory but I can't help that.

I would like to have a picture of my small brother alive or dead, the shape of his face or the colour of his hair. But I do not even know what killed him or if I tended him, as my mother said that I did. There must have been a wake, with neighbours and food. They must have laid him out, very small, on the table; the adults drinking, the children escaping to play outside. I can make up the picture of this from other wakes, but maybe Brendan was too small for all that fuss.

Because when I think of that day, all I can remember is the front field, and Valty handing me a packet wrapped up in a dock leaf that was warm and heavy. Valty was very wayward, but I loved him in a way that could not tell between us – until then, I suppose. I suppose feeling the heat of the thing, and catching the smell of cack, I realised he was not part of me at all.

I think it was Brendan's death that turned my brother astray. So when I try to find reasons for all the troubles that came after, my dead mind sticks there in the front field, with the feel of a leaf in my hand and the curious warmth. And when I try to find Brendan, his little death, or his face, I feel that Valty stole him from me then, just as he stole the years that followed, with all the trouble he made.

He was meant for big things – university maybe, and a job in Dublin – and Brendan was meant for the farm. When Brendan died they had to start over again, I suppose, though who is to say what brought them together or split them apart in the night. The new children started to arrive when I was eight, one after the other: Ambrose, my best darling; Katie, who left; and John, my best darling as well.

We ignored Valty, and avoided the strap. We were brothers and sisters, which is to say, we drew our heights on the jamb of the door and spent the years trying to catch each other up. We compared the colour of our arms, the colour of the inside of our wrists, the bruises we got and the books we took to school. We were jealous of everything: a ruler, a rubber, a broken bone. We were Kennedys. Katie, who was dark like Valty and full of badness; Ambrose, who had red hair but was steady even so; John, who was just lovely. Which one of us was clever? Valty was clever, Katie was too clever by half, and I was clever in my own way. Who did we take after? Valty got his mother's fine eyes. Ambrose got his red hair from a passing tinker, and Katie looked like her grand-aunt Maggie, who was so big when she died, they had to pull the house down around her, just to get her out of it.

I met Katie in the station in Dublin when she was leaving for England. She was arriving in Kingsbridge, and had to get across town to catch the boat train at Amiens Street. I brought some sandwiches for her journey and hoped that they would choke her. I was going to bring a miraculous medal so she could pin it to her vest, but just the word 'vest' made her seem dirty to me. There might have been boys involved, but that was not the point. In her letter she had written, 'I have to get away from that woman, and everything to do with her.' I did not understand. I loved my mother, as only the eldest girl can. She was a friend to me. All through my life, from a small child, she had shown to me a proper pity.

I saw Katie on the platform, her face stuck behind strangers' faces, and was surprised to see how young she was. As she walked towards me I noticed all the things she had done to make herself look ridiculous: a new ribbon tied under an old collar, fresh lipstick on a face still dirty from the journey. I wanted to shake her. I wanted to tell her how she was wrecking her chances – that too many men is no man at all, and no money, ever. I remember her as she walked towards me, not smart as Katie Kennedy was smart, not clever either, her fine ankles only ankles, her good blue coat only a blue coat, her family just people, her father no one at all. I remember her walking towards me because I did not have a good word to say to her then, or afterwards.

She wrote to tell me she had met a man in England and married him. And all I could say to Berts was that Englishmen would take anything. I did not like him when he laughed, but the fault was mine, so it was no use complaining.

Because she made Berts look like something else to me, not the man I had danced with and would stay dancing with, because he had asked. She turned him into one man among many and I wished her to hell as the train pulled away.

Katie had it easy. She was all daughter and daughter again, because she had our own mother and she had a little mother in me. I had none of that. I remember the day when my childhood ended. I came into the kitchen and told my mother I was dying.

'Look around you, child,' she said. 'It's everywhere.'

She sat down a second and wiped her eyes, then she stood up and shook me by the shoulder, warning me off men from one end of the room to the other – not hard, but fierce enough and even.

'Blood is nothing,' she said. 'Remember that.' But for tea she made me a special little cake and when the others started to whine she said, 'That's our secret, that's between ourselves,' handing it to me with a new kindness, because we were in this together now.

So Katie had it easy. I think it must have been hard for her to grow up, finally, when she was too old and too far away. Still, as we walked towards the boat-train that day, I could not open my mouth to her and let her carry her suitcase by herself. She said that she wanted a drink and we went into a pub. I am glad I did that at least, though I did not know where to sit or what to ask for. We made our way through the men, who seemed sober enough, and sat in the snug, and Katie seemed pleased with all she knew – how to sip a drink and flick her eyelashes up at you, when the glass met her mouth. Looking at her then, in her old blue coat with a new ribbon at her throat, I wished that I believed in God, so that he would look after her.

No, that is not true. Of course I believed in God. I just didn't believe he would look after her.

But if I move Him from one place to the other in my mind, what difference does that make?

Oh, I still remember that cake – the taste of it. It was a cup-cake with a glacé cherry on top, and blackberry jam to spread on each half. The paper casing was brittle from the oven and it clicked off like a spreading fan, sticky with crumbs that you could suck off later. The pain in my stomach was so warm as I ate it. I could feel blood falling in slow clots out of me, like cream, and the secret lump of cloth I was sitting on changed the whole room.

The first time I had lemonade was in a hotel in Enniskillen. It was after the war, when the Americans had gone home and there was talk of the flying boats they had sunk in Lough Erne, Thunderheads and Catalinas, a whole fleet of them under water, with fish nosing the controls. We must have been visiting my uncle, who was rich. I don't know why I wasn't left at home to mind the other children, so the lemonade had a guilty sort of taste, of freedom, or of luck. Surrounded by the noise of the town that I was too stunned to hear, the bubbles were so quiet and slow, you might even count them.

I was a lucky child. I found money on the ground and sent off coupons. I entered a Campbell's Tea competition and we got a map of the world in the post, rolled up in a long, cardboard tube. There is no understanding luck. Berts brought me to the races on the Easter Monday of the spring we met and it was the first time I saw him annoyed with me – all my horses coming home, except one. I could not help it, though. Even the worst things came out right for me.

The day that Valty ran away from home we found an empty noose hanging in the barn and we stood under it, amazed, looking at his invisible body swinging there. It was a filthy thing to leave behind. Ambrose was too small to climb up along the beam to take it down and my father could not be asked to touch it. Nor could we send for a neighbour, in case people found out. It was my mother's brother who finally shinnied along the beam and unknotted it, a day later, the bullocks in the haggard frantic for hay.

I often think of that noose, hanging there as the dusk fell – the sky inside its hoop a shade lighter than the sky outside. The noise of the bullocks went through the night and I could hear John whimpering in his sleep next door because there was too much room in the bed. I listened to the wind and thought of it swaying and waiting, a tear that could not fall. Whose neck was it for?

Valentine. First born. The first are the quietest, they say, but something went wrong. My father had to strap him three times a week. He fired the stubble one night when he was eight and the flames could have leapt the ditch and on to the house. I saw him once, sitting in the trench where the cows pissed. Just sitting. Another time he put his bare foot into a bucket of milk and we had to drink it and say nothing, because of the trouble it would cause. I know he was just a child; but I saw him that night the stubble went up, with his shirt open and his little white chest rosy in the heat. He was stamping from foot to foot in the middle of the smoke and he was not laughing.

It was my Uncle Fintan who took the noose down. He was my mother's brother and this made sense, because Valty was my mother's child, not my father's, now that he was gone. I am just saying that there is a rightness to these things, even if it is slight. Had there been nobody, the calves would have been fed, life would have gone on until the rope rotted off the beam. Or my father would have got tired of it and taken it down some quiet morning by himself. But one thing is sure. Even if the noose had hung there for ever, no woman would touch it, or walk under it. She would not have wanted to.

When Valty left, I got his schooling. They put me on the train with a case full of clothes, my name written on each collar, Anna Kennedy. Anna Kennedy. Anna Kennedy. Even the worst things worked out well for me. I was twelve and in the wide world. I was the luckiest, I was the best girl in the class.

I fell in love with Berts on Easter Monday. We had met when the frost was on the ground and walked out in the long, slow months before spring. But I did not know, until the world finally started to turn, what it was to love him. The thing I liked about him first was the back of his neck, which was so long on its way up under his hat. A year later it repulsed me, this foolish stretch, the barber never finding the end of it so he could start on the longer hair. I saw him by accident, one afternoon, turning into a doorway, the back of his neck like an apology to the street, and I thought, 'I cannot love this man.' But that was because by then it was too late – I did love him, neck or no neck, and there was nothing I could do about it.

From the front, Berts' face looked sort of stuck on – long and bony and flat. His hands were slim and easy and somehow not Irish at all – dark like his face and too fine. His teeth were small, they made him look hungry. And he would have been dangerous altogether, loping and foreign, if it weren't for his eyes.

Oh, give me breath enough to describe Berts' eyes. They were like a place to me. So warm, you would think they were brown, but there was green in them, especially when we were married. After we made love, I would turn on the lamp to go to the bathroom and Berts would lift his head, still asleep, his eyes pure green and the pupils like pins. 'It's you all right,' he'd say, like he was dreaming of me. Another man might be startled and try to flush me out, but I knew by that blind green that I was in the very centre of Berts. It was in that confirmation, rising out of sleep, or falling into it, that I felt most loved by him.

Brown was the social colour of his eyes, intelligent and light, sharp and mild. That is enough now. Berts' eyes were, somehow, not like him at all. I felt that, as he aged, the back of his neck would say it all for him and the green of his eyes would speckle and fade. I saw it in the street that day, as he ducked through a door away from me – a future full of evasions. But when I was young, when he turned towards me, I lived in Berts' eyes.

He came into the office to check things, when someone tripped on a path or hit their head against a bit of scaffolding. I would sit there with my notes while old Mr Blood–Burke strolled up and down.

'Did she fall off the bus, or on to the path? That's the question. Did she have one leg on the bus when she fell, or both feet on terra firma? Could you check the leg situation there, Miss Kennedy, like a decent woman. A simple preposition might be all we need.'

While Berts sat opposite me, leaning back, one leg stretched out and the coat he would not take off draped from the chair to the floor. He gave nothing away, except the smallest wink to me when the old man's back was turned. Berts was quiet, like a country man, which is what I liked about him. Some of those Dublin men – they would tell you anything at all.

I fell in love with Berts at the races on Easter Monday when I won too much and he was annoyed. We had walked out for months and he had been kind, and careful of me. But the horses slipping away around the track, the silence of them far away and the yelling when they came close, brought something out in him that he could not help. A sort of sneering when I won (though it was the horse that won, I was only lucky) that seemed to me like family.

The races were very glam. People wore new hats for spring and knew who each other were, while the rolls of money came out of pockets or were stuffed back in, dirty and exciting. You could see how rich people had bastards and did not care, or took to the drink for a joke. This was the place where men went to the bad – and I realised that I had been searching for my brother all afternoon in the crowd.

'Number nine, Berts. Sky blue with purple dots.' Everything I said came out in a high voice, as if people were looking at us.

'Look at the form,' said Berts. 'Look at the form.'

'But I love blue, Berts.' I had to wheedle him into putting on every bet for me, and I won four times out of five.

We got the bus home in silence and he walked me up my street. It was Easter Monday and the whole city felt new, and lonely.

'I had a brother who left,' I said.

'Really?' said Berts.

'Years ago. You know. I don't think he was right in the head.'

I had said what had never been said, either in the family or out of it. Now anyone could look at a Kennedy walking down the street and have themselves a good laugh.

'I think maybe he was gone in the head. Maybe he was too young to tell.'

I said it to show myself weak for him. But the world had turned and I was lucky. Berts kissed me more fully than he had ever done before. He kissed me even though his serious horses fell and my foolish ones did not. He kissed me even though I was the wrong girl. Because you looked to people's breed, you looked for pioneer pins, a bit of height – you did not look for the County Home. I ran up the steps and put my key in the door and knew he would ask me to marry him, before the summer was out.

Those horses, they moved so slowly and so far away. You could not hear them, or believe them fast, until they bundled past the post, all legs.

Berts was an only son, which is what made him so indifferent and ready to be loved. But the sisters surprised me. Joan, the second, hissing 'He got the best of everything', making me feel like I was second best. He betrayed them by marrying me – his mother first and the rest in a line. And Dada. Dada was a little humpy man with a child's smile, who caused a stir and a clearing of the best chair any time he walked into a room, and then was ignored by the lot of them. I liked Dada best of all.

They were city people. The house we grew up in was just a gateway to the farm beyond, but Berts' house was like walking into the neck of a sack. His mother was always in the good room pouring tea that had to be brought in specially and it was the sisters that did the running. I could never bear a sickly woman. Berts' mother seemed withered and soft, in the middle of all her things. She hated me on sight and, when we were married, she did not come to call.

I stood by the window and watched them finishing the houses on the other side of the street.

I was not pregnant – not when the slates spread up the roof, nor when the guttering was fixed in its iron brackets. I was not pregnant when they cleared the drive or sprayed the garden wall with pebble-dash, the stones thundering out of the machine. I thought I was pregnant, all the time, but I was not.

So I stood by the window and watched the other people moving in. There was something about the bareness with which they arrived that made us friends. You would see them being driven into the street, bumping along in the mud, the way the driver stood back – a brother or a friend – and let the couple walk up the path by themselves. Then later the van would come with a few things: sheets to tack over the windows, a chest of drawers that would double as a baby's cot. There was something about Mrs Brophy coming back from the shop with a bale of briquettes in an empty pram, with her big stomach pressing against the bar and 'Look at me!' she said. 'Putting in the practice. You think I could have used the bike.'

We had chop wars. 'A chop for his tea.' 'Oh, a chop for his tea.' 'I thought I'd just get a nice lamb chop, for his tea.' Mrs Brophy talking about sausages with a laugh. We never called when the men were home. If your mother was from Dublin she would come during the day, on the bus, and you would clean the place together if she was that kind of mother, or she would sit and watch you clean. Mrs Hegarty standing on the windowsill at eight and a half months, with a wad of newspaper soaked in vinegar, and the other hand gripping the iron window frame, swinging her clear. The grass was seeded and the trees planted, and the front doors were always open, when the babies came.

They came one by one in taxis, or new cars. They came wrapped in woollen shawls that were yellow, or white. I wanted to know what it felt like, but all they said was: 'Fourteen hours and a caesarean,' or, 'They let her go twenty-three – can you imagine it.' Or nothing was said at all, because we were shy about these things. We were shy about our husbands, apart from their lamb chops, and we were shy of the lives we had left behind. Mrs Lovett, Mrs Hegarty, Mrs McCarthy, Mrs Barr, Mrs Delahunty, all new names, even to ourselves. We were there for a new life, and it might well be a long one. We expected, somewhere unsaid, that one day we would see each other die.

Berts came home on the bicycle and kissed me. I listened to the radio. I spent too much time at the window, and went too often to the shops. Once I caught myself walking up and down the hall, talking about chops like I was Mr Blood-Burke. I read a lot – rubbish mostly. The house was still a shell and the dust was fierce. I got polish for the furniture we did not yet have, I got sodium bicarbonate in the raw and steel wool for the pans. I was getting it ready, getting it ready, laying down carpet, putting paper on the walls – building up a debt to the bank that only a baby could pay.

Not that I wanted one all that badly. I wanted one so badly it hurt, but I wasn't sure if the hurt was real.

But if I move the hurt around, from one place to another in my mind, what difference does that make? There was nothing else for me to do.

I was bothered by memories: the smell of hay rotting, the class we had at school where a woman in a white turban explained the right way to sit into a car, the way my father killed the dog, by tying a stone to its legs and hanging it from the cowshed roof.

I remembered one day at school, I passed Sr Maolíosa, who was standing by a flowerbed on the curving front drive. She said a line to me in German, without glancing up.

'Translate, Anna.'

'Sorry, Sister?'

She was fingering a peony rose, deep red. She said the line again for me and I tried,

'Neither childhood nor the future will get smaller, Sister.'

'Will diminish, Anna, will diminish.'

It seemed to me odd that I knew what the words meant in German, but did not have the English for them, as if the world was peeling away in different layers. The peony dipped in front of her, a vegetable rose, and she stroked the bursting head, her hand translucent to the veins.

I was sixteen. I thought, 'None of this will diminish, will ever diminish.'

Now, I planted things in the garden and watched for them to grow. Words started to follow me about, and I

245

scribbled some of them down on scraps of paper, but they were just themselves and did not join with anything else.

I was always pregnant. I was never pregnant. I walked from room to room, ambushed by all these things. The past and the future were as big as they ever were, with nothing in the middle, except this empty, waiting house, my blank body in the centre of it, like a gap in the middle of a hole. I was bothered by memories, I was bothered by things that had not happened yet. I was squashed between two unshiftable things and I started to rearrange the house, moving the furniture from room to room.

One day a Corporation lorry pulled up and two men walked up the path carrying a mirror between them that reflected the other houses as they walked. I never thought Berts was the kind to steal, if that was what you call it. The mirror was from a demolition in the city centre, eighteenth century maybe, cracked along the corner, and with one side of the frame completely gone. I liked it, secretly. They left it in the hall.

It leant there all day, the gilt extravagant against the wallpaper, the glass rolling down in folds. I felt sorry for the left-hand side that was missing its rim, and I wondered what the mirror had seen over the years, who had looked in it, and were they ever pleased.

When Berts came home he said he knew a man that could cut it down and sell it on and I did not know what to say. So I said nothing and the mirror stayed in the hall. I passed it back and forwards all day, and took out a cloth to give it a clean. I felt how the glass was too heavy for itself, had sagged over the years, so that it was thicker now at the base. I waited for Berts to get rid of it, wondering what would happen next, and did I know my husband at all.

One afternoon, I took off my clothes and stood in front of it. It was a silly thing to do. I looked at myself in the liver-spotted silver, the glass flowing over it, buckling like water, and I did not know what to think. I don't know if I had seen my body before, full length. At school we washed under a shift, and when I was in digs, the long mirror was in the hall. But I am not a complete fool. I had seen all kinds of things before. None of it helped. I looked at the body in the mirror with no baby inside or with a baby inside. I looked at Anna Kennedy starkers in the middle of the afternoon, with her dress around her ankles, and I could not find the words for it. Pink. White. Hill. Cunt. Move. You move the tea cosy from the pot to the table, you move it to the side of the range, you turn the cosy inside out.

Move

I wrote words down and I buried them in the garden, the names of flowers: wallflower, phlox, peony rose, dog rose, tea rose. A twist of baking soda, sugar, a wick, two wicks, a bar of soap cut down the middle so it leaves itself on the knife.

I knew I was pregnant now. I knew the words would never grow. There was something wrong with me, but I could not stop myself. I wrote words down and I ate them, but I knew they would not keep me alive. I did this, I did that. Berts brought me to the doctor. I looked at AnnA, who was the same, any way you looked at her. And when I died the mirror went blank.

Nothing hurts the dead, they say, they say. Nothing hurts the dead, they say. Except maybe the life they had to live. But I could not say it was a bad life.

When I died Katie came into my room; she said, 'Come stay with me. I have a split-level condo in Maine.' When I died Valty came into my room and said, 'Shit Bitch.' When I died my mother ran all the way to the shops, crying.

I am in hell. This is what I see, this is what I see, I see the turd, I see the rope, I see my own private parts that I never saw and Berts' private parts that I never saw, I see them clearly. I shift them around the room. I give my husband breasts. I am not ashamed. I shit through the noose and I cry through my backside. I am in hell. I rearrange my life in hell. Berts' member that is bigger than my own body that surrounds it, I let it creep up the back of his long neck and tip off his hat.

I have all the words I want, but they are in the wrong part of the room. I have a new ribbon under my collar, I have a suitcase with a rope to tie it by. I am in hell now and it is full of words. You write the people and the peonies are penises and everything is like, like and everything is because.

I live in Katie's house. I live on my own. I run down to the shops and I keep running until I hit the sea and I keep running until I am in the middle of the sea and I keep running until I am on dry land again and I keep running until I hit the sea.

I live in Berts' eyes.

I see my children that I cannot see. I see my mother clutching her old bones that hurt her and taking them apart and putting them back on the other way around. I am in hell. My mother is swinging by Valty's rope, he is making nooses in Dagenham, Leeds, London Town. He is swinging and leaving, swinging and leaving, Valty is in a madhouse in London Town, in a white jacket, first born, the bullocks not fed, the dirty things he says. I live in his house. He has a wife. His children talk like this – Nyar nar nar nar darn'tya nyar. Valty is clever, I am clever in my own way, he is an orthopaedic surgeon. He breaks bones, for a living. He stitches them up.

Here is Berts. Hello, Berts. Berts has a zip in his skin from his belly-button down. He pisses little babies out of his tip. He unpeels his banana right back and there is a child asleep – oh – do not wake the child, curled up in Berts, curled up in Berts' penis, the white child so soft and waxy, curved in sleep.

I am not dead. I am in hell. And I blame the feet that walk over me.

Mama Dada Valty Ambrose Katie Brendan John Berts Berts Berts

I blame the feet that walk over me.

248

8

The Gap

Berts spent the day by the window.

Evelyn brought some clothes in for him, and he put them on over his pyjamas. Laura came back from the shops with cigarettes, without being asked. The pile of butts grew on the floorboards, and from time to time there was tea.

At three o'clock, the taxi pulled up and he saw his daughter getting out, twice. He saw his daughter pay the driver while his daughter put her hand to her throat and looked at the house. He saw his daughter walk up the path while his daughter shut the gate. He saw his daughter smile at his daughter, who was also smiling. He saw his daughter look his way, while his daughter looked his way, and he saw one of them nod hello.

And the place he had put his wife disappeared. The place where she had stayed for twenty-five years, speaking to him sometimes, or sometimes smiling, sometimes looking at him with a malice that would never end – a sexual malice that he turned to in his sleep – that place just vanished. She was dead. For years he had swindled himself with memories and with forgetting. For years he had allowed a gap in his head where she could live undisturbed, and now it was not even she who was disturbed, but nothing at all. It was not even she who fled, as the gap closed, but no one at all.

He turned to the room; the wallpaper hanging off in strips, the carpet gone.

The day the diagnosis came through, she took out the hoover and did the whole house. He could see her, over by the mantelpiece. She was wearing a blue blouse, with a collar that collapsed in gentle folds from her neck. And there was something about the lightness of the cloth, the gentleness with which it fell, that made him imagine her sweating, just there, between her collar-bone and her breasts, as she worked from room to room. The hoover was reluctant, the furniture confused it. And it broke Berts' heart to see the way she wrestled with it – all that suction. And the bag – full of dirt. Pulling it all in, sucking the carpet into place, stroking the floor; hoovering between life and death, between the sofa and the wall.

How long had he lived here, in the dead self of his wife?

I have been living in a grave, he thought, *I have been living nowhere at all*.

The doorbell rang. And the hoover of his wife turned around and sucked itself up. The house of his wife turned itself inside out for him. The house of his wife flipped over in space; with the wallpaper showing on the outside and the furniture drifting into the garden, and the lampshades floating off the roof; vomiting Berts out on to the road.

Like, Like

'One,' said Rose, and held it up for the shop assistant to see.

'One,' said the shop assistant, and looked at her.

The thing that amazed them both afterwards was the time it all took. They saw each other and then they turned away.

Rose started trying on the suit, and thought about the woman in the corner, who looked just like her. The Irish version. It was true, she thought, she did not exist. She was just a slip of the pen that had gone on to live an entire life. Rose Cotter, Marie Delahunty. Everything she had done – the hard choices, the willed compassion, her difficult, educated heart – all a joke. No wonder they had given her away. They had another one, just the same.

Maria looked at the woman who was trying on the black linen suit (it would crease, but perhaps she could make it crease with style) and thought – it is the girl in the photograph. Or rather, the girl in her mind. It is the girl in the white jeans, the girl in the little black dress. It is the one who does not have to care.

Anything was possible, even then. But when Rose took off her sweater, Maria saw two veins running down the inside of her elbow, where one should have been.

Rose put on the jacket.

'That really suits you.'

'Do you think?'

They each took two steps. Who was it raised her hand first? Perhaps it was Rose. Who was it laughed? When they turned to the mirror there were four of them. Which was when Sinead, the manager, came in and said,

'Tracey! Mairead! Come here! Jesus Christ.'

Berts turned from the window to face his two daughters, worried for his heart. He did not want to be forgiven.

But they sat on the sofa and seemed to ignore him. An equal flush of red spread from under their collars, blotching each neck.

The girl on the left looked over at him as a stranger might, slyly out of the corner of her eye. Berts felt the unfairness of it and shifted in his chair. He did not know this person. He might know her, but he did not know the *person* she was. He said,

'So, "Rose", is it?' and the two girls looked towards him, as one.

And so they sat in the ripped-out sitting room. Evelyn tried to make tea, but kept forgetting when the kettle was boiled. She could not stop looking. She could not even hear what they were saying. She dabbed her eyes with a tissue and Berts was astonished, again, by women. How they have no choice.

They finally got their tea, and drank it from china cups with a pattern of irises on the side. Berts sat in one armchair, Evelyn sat in the other. Laura sat on the edge of the fireplace and hugged her knees. The twins sat on the sofa, turning into each other, now and then, and then back out to the room. The fact that there were two of them made it somehow easy. They could be happy and sad at the same time. When one smiled the other let her eyes drift around the room.

Rose spoke carefully, telling them about her life. She was shy as she sipped her tea, but every time she looked at Maria, she shook her head and laughed. Or they grazed one another by accident and looked, shocked, at their hands.

Even their voices were the same pitch. You would think Maria's was lower, you would think that Rose was lighter and more crisp, but no, they hit the same note precisely when Evelyn said, 'This is amazing,' and they both chimed,
'Isn't it?'

Everyone paused.

Evelyn gathered herself together then and spoke for Berts. She apologised for him, and he did not like her tone. She told the story of their mother's death, while he sat with his pyjamas sticking out of the ends of his trousers, saying,

'Right,' from time to time. 'Right.'

'I'd like to visit her grave,' said Rose. It was a very blunt thing to say. It made her look English again, and strange. Berts was conscious of what he had lost. He would have to earn her back if he could, but he didn't know how. He turned to the window and said,

'Your mother. Your mother loved that tree.'

'Did she plant it?'

'No, but she always liked it.'

There was nothing about the tree to remark upon, but they looked out at it anyway.

Evelyn said quietly, 'We should tell the others.'

'What others?'

'Your sisters. Joan.'

'Joan knows,' he said.

Maria looked at him then. 'Auntie Joan?'

'What about the rest of them?' said Evelyn, and Berts said, 'Ah, for God's sake, there's no need to tell the whole world.'

'Right,' said Maria. 'Terrific, Da. Thanks.' Soon after that, the twins left.

These are the things they discovered about themselves.

They both had a best friend at school called Emily.

They both hated potatoes and, no matter how little they were given, always pushed their portion to the side of the plate.

They both liked Euthymol toothpaste, Mozart, the colour blue.

They wre both afraid of falling.

They liked patterns, but only on other people, and neither of them could wear a skirt above the knee.
They both had two veins on the inside of their left elbow, where one should have been.
They had both, in their different ways, been kissed by the same boy.

There were also the things that they did not discover.

They both enjoyed putting in the bin bag the bag it came in.
They both held their shoulders high when they were in an airplane, as if this might help keep it off the ground.
Neither of them liked taking photographs.
They both liked the smell of a man as much as the look of him.
They dreamt the same dream of being lost in a crowd.

Some of these became apparent to them over the years. Some did not. They also discovered some intriguing differences.

Maria had better ankles, but Rose was slightly longer in the thigh.
Rose had the poorer eyesight. Maria slept around.
Rose had a dodgy elbow, Maria's wrist was not to be discussed.
Maria looked older. Though as the years went by, she seemed to halt a little, as though she were waiting for Rose to catch up.

And they were the astonishment of everyone who met them. Rose brought Maria to Leatherhead. Her mother looked almost cheated, for a moment, and then she smiled. Her father looked from one face to the other, he looked back again. His hand dabbed back from his side. He said the most unexpected thing. He said,

'Well, my dears, God is good.'

Which made Maria uncomfortable. She did not know this man. She discovered a strange loyalty to Berts as he went on to say,

'I can die happy, now.'

'Oh, don't be silly, Daddy,' said Rose. And Maria said,

'I'm sure you would have died happy anyway, Dr Cotter.'

He smiled at them both, but particularly at Rose. He looked at one girl who was not his daughter, and at another girl who was not his daughter, and thought that life was a cruel bonus. He had no difficulty in telling between them, alike as they were. And he was interested to discover that he loved them both equally, though he preferred his own.

Acknowledgements

Many people showed me kindness and hospitality during the writing of this book. Thanks to Colm Tóibín, to Michael Loughlin and Veronica Rapalino in Barcelona; Mary and Bernard Loughlin at the Tyrone Guthrie Centre, Annaghmakerrig; Dr Edward King and the committee of the Heinrich Böll House, Achill; Anaig Renault of the Institut Culturelle de Bretagne, Erwan, and all at the Film Festival in Douarnenez.